U Can't B Serious

By Rocko Bess
Published by BSG Media

To book Rocko to speak at your next event, visit us at www.theBSGgroup.com!

U Can't B Serious

By Rocko Bess
Published by BSG Media

U CAN'T B SERIOUS

ISBN: 9781077681859

BSG MEDIA
A DIVISION OF THE BSG GROUP
NEW YORK CITY, NEW YORK
www.theBSGgroup.com

Printed in the United States of America
FIRST EDITION

To my Dad, a man of wisdom, strength and integrity. The face I see whenever I look into the mirror. Your sun never sets: it continues to shine its light through me.

- RIP Albert "Bubbie" Livingston

To all the men and women who are in the struggle inhabiting places where only the mind travels freely. I also dedicate this to you, a little bit of laughter for your soul.

- Rocko Bess

Table of Contents

1. The Present 1
2. Just Want to Be Left Alone - Doug 25
3. I Know I Got You Open - World 38
4. Live and Learn - Dooky 54
5. The Things We Do 80
6. It Gets Greater Later 107
7. Don't Hate The Playa 136
8. If It Ain't Rough… 173
9. It's A Crazy "World" Out There! 193
10. Strictly Business 210
11. Just Say No! 228
12. Critical Thoughts 244
13. You Can't Spell Game Without M.E. 325
ACKNOWLEDGEMENTS 366

Chapter One

The Present

"Ayo, what time is it?" World asked from the passenger's seat of the Reliant K automobile. His eyes were fiery red and his bushy unibrow was formed into an angry frown. He was still high from the weed and drunk from the alcohol they had been partying with earlier, but the high was coming down and he was tired and ready to go home.

"It's still early kid, its only 4:15," his partner Dooky responded from the drivers seat, his eyes were darting from left to right trying not to miss anything while he sipped on a warm 40 oz. of Old English, as they cruised through 48th street in mid-town Manhattan soliciting the prostitutes that loitered the streets late-nights. So far this summer, this had been their routine on the weekends after they left the last of the many nightclubs they frequented every Friday.

"4:15?... 4:15?... Yo kid, it's 5 o'clock in the fucking morning! I'm tired, I'm fucking hungry, and I'm ready to go home nigga! Take... me... home!" World yelled, saliva forming in the corners of his mouth.

Dooky was ignoring his homeboy because he had his eyes focused on a redbone ho that was walking down 47th street. Her ass was so big and jiggly that it looked like it could've been filled with water. World was still yelling and cursing at him because he was ready to leave, and Dooky was about to say fuck it and head for the highway until he spotted what he believed to be the perfect ho standing on the corner of 48th street. She had a big ass and tits with a pair of lips that looked like a catcher's mitt. "That's what I'm talking about nigga! Look at that bitch over there in those florescent green shorts! You see that shit? That bitch got an ass like a horse son! You see it... Look! I'm getting that bitch... she BADD!" Dooky said, tapping World with the excitement of a six-year-old. However, World was not impressed, he barely even looked up. He wanted to go home, and he felt like punching his childhood friend in the face.

Dooky reached over into the glove compartment to find one of the fake twenties he kept just for occasions like this. Before he got fired from his job at the United Postal Service for receiving the highest score they ever recorded from an employee, after testing positive for cannabis in a random drug urinalysis, each Friday after he cashed his paycheck he would carefully cut the two-zero off of a different corner of four twenty dollar bills. He would then take the corners and carefully glue them onto a one-dollar bill giving it the appearance of a twenty. At first glance – and if passed the right way, even in dim light, it was good as gold. Dooky thought he had one of the ready-made twenties in the glove compartment and after removing all of its contents and throwing them on the floor by World's feet, he came up empty. He was determined to end his night 'freakin' off' with a ho, so he drove to the corner and stopped at the bodega. He pulled out the $23.00 he had in his pocket, opened the car door and was about to run in the store when he decided to remove the car keys just in case World got one of his crazy ideas.

"I'll be right out," Dooky said over his shoulder. As he entered the store, he turned around to see World in the middle of a temper tantrum, banging on the dashboard with both fists looking like a big kid.

World watched as Dooky came out of the store and got into the car with the brown paper bag. Once he saw the Elmer's Glue, box of razor blades and the $20.00 bill he knew exactly what his boy was up to and he was furious. "That's all you wanna do is fuck with these ho's nigga! I told yo dumb ass I was ready to go mafucker! But nooo, I gotta wait for you to finish acting like a fake ass trick daddy with your fake ass one dollar twenties!"

Dooky didn't pay any attention to his partner's insults. As far as he was concerned World could either wait, walk or take the subway back to Mount Vernon. And he knew his friend would much rather wait.

Dooky only had one twenty-dollar bill. He already knew that World was not about to let him cut any of his money - not that it wouldn't be spendable, but because he was throwing a fit about going home, so he was going to try and pull it off by using only one corner. If he folded the dollar just right, it would work anyway. Once the ho saw the two-zero she would snatch and stash then get to work. Dooky put it together and admired his work as World watched him with an attitude. He folded it just right and set it in his pocket so he could pull it out when she asked. The blood was already rushing to his dick as he thought about those catcher's mitts. He had to hurry up because he wasted a lot of time and pretty soon the sun would reveal the light of day.

Fuckin' with a ho without the cover of darkness just didn't feel right – especially outdoors. He put the key in the ignition and turned it, but nothing happened. No lights, no radio, no engine, no nothing. The car was dead.

"I told your dumb ass!" World screamed right before he punched Dooky in the face, and the two of them started fighting in the car.

Back In The Day

Ten-year-old Dookiah Douglas was walking home from school. He was only a block away from his house, but his stomach was growling for something sweet to eat. He reached into his pocket and pulled out all of the money he had - two dimes and a nickel, which was hardly enough to buy jack shit. He paused before entering the store on the corner of his block and prayed that Lucy was working and not Sal, who was the owner of the store. When he stepped inside and saw Lucy he smiled to himself.

"Hi Lucy."

"Hey Dooky," she responded with her ear to the telephone.

Young Dooky looked around at all the varieties of cakes, candies and chips that were all situated in the front of the store. He knew that this would be easy because old lady Lucy never paid any attention to anyone who entered the store. She was an elderly, badly wrinkled white woman with long gray hair. And Dooky figured that she was either from the old school where they trusted all of their customers or she just didn't give a shit. He was more inclined to believe the latter because all she did was talk on the telephone all fuckin' day, and today was no different.

Dooky quickly went over to the candy rack and picked up two Snicker bars. As a precaution, he glanced over at Lucy to see if she was looking. She wasn't even facing in his direction; so he slipped both candy bars up his sleeve with the flick of the wrist. On his way to the back of the store where the soda cooler was located, Dooky picked up a Suzy-Q and a vanilla cupcake and tossed them down the sleeve of his jacket. When he reached the cooler, he looked at Lucy through the mirrors positioned above the aisles, which were used to watch the customers, and saw her yapping away and fuckin' with her fingernails. He grabbed a bottle of Mellow Yellow - his favorite soda and slid it down the other sleeve of his jacket. Then he reached for a 25-cent juice and headed for the counter. The forearms of his jacket looked like Popeye's arms, but Lucy didn't even look up when he threw the two dimes and the nickel on the counter and walked out the door.

When Dooky walked into the house his great grandmother "Nana" was there to greet him.

"Hi Nana."

"Hey baby, gimmie some sugar."

Nana always wanted a kiss from Dooky - "some sugar" she would call it. And he didn't have a problem with that because he loved the shit out of Nana. Besides Nana's kiss was just a peck, unlike some of his aunts who would wet half of his face.

The house was neat and comfortable, everything was clean and it looked lived in. No antique couches covered in plastic or glass tables that you couldn't rest your cup on without a coaster. Everything was earthly colored and warm. The smell of chicken or lamb chops coming from the kitchen made his mouth water, and he rushed to the stove to remove the lid on one of the pots to see what it was. Before he could lift it, Nana smacked his wrist and sent him to wash his hands. Dooky left the kitchen without bicker and headed for his room to unwind. When he got to his room, he saw a note taped to his door. The note was from his father and all it said was "*stay your ass in the house until I get home*". Underneath the note from his father were three absence notes that Dooky had World write for him, and a note from his teacher Ms. Powell snitching on him about his conduct in class. Dooky started to get nervous and he let out a fart. He had gotten notes sent home from his teachers before in the past, he wasn't worried about that, what had him shook was the note from his father. His father rarely got mad. It was his mother that gave him every ass whoopin' he could remember. So to think that this one was coming from his pops was enough to make him cry.

Nana was standing behind Dooky the whole time watching his reaction. She almost laughed when he farted then started crying. But the smell of his gas was so noxious that she almost choked. Instead of hugging her baby boy, she escaped to her room.

It took a minute for Dooky to glue himself together. He couldn't think of a lie to tell to get him out of the trouble he was in, so there was only one thing left to do. He called his homeboy World. World was three years older than Dooky and only lived a few houses away with his mom. At thirteen years old he stood about 5 foot 10 inches with a full mustache and beard. When Dooky's family moved on the block, World was happy as a dog with a bone. Even though Dooky was only 8 years old at the time, he was black and that's pretty much all that mattered since all the other kids on the block were white and had way too many "nigger" jokes. World had fought every last one of the white kids on the block on a different occasion. Even some of the girls – it didn't matter. Win, lose or draw, once they used the "N" word it was on! Dooky and World clicked automatically, as well as their families. They were inseparable and not just on the strength of color.

World's phone started ringing...

"Hello," World answered.

"Wassup my nigga?"

"What up Dook? You comin' out?"

"Yeah kid, that's what I was calling you about. I was thinking about running away and I wanted to know if you wanna be out with me?"

"Where you wanna go?" World asked curiously.

Dooky was standing in the kitchen and whatever Nana had on the stove smelled so good that he almost aborted the plan. Then he thought about receiving an ass whoopin' from his dad and lost his appetite.

"Where you wanna go yo?" World asked again, bringing him back to his problem.

“I don’t know. Where do they film Soul Train?”

“I think down south yo,” World answered.

“Nah, I don’t wanna go down there, my aunt Kathy live down there... her kisses is too wet. Plus she smell like nail polish remover yo.”

They both laughed then Dooky said seriously, “Yo, where do they film Good Times at?”

They both started singing... “Temporary layoffs - good times - easy credit rip offs - good times.”

“I don’t even know,” World said. “But Thelma is my chick”.

“Watch yo mouth! That’s my future wife you talkin’ about”.

For a minute Dooky forgot about all of the trouble he was in with his father until he looked down and saw the note in his hand. He let out another nervous fart before he got back on track.

“So yo World, are you gonna runaway with me or what?”

“Fuck it! I’m wit dat,” World said enthused.

"Yo World, don't front on me kid, as a matter of fact, if you serious break that big ass mirror in your mother's room and meet me at the store in two minutes".

"Yeah alright my nigga. I'll meet you in two."

Dooky felt better now that his best friend agreed to runaway with him. And he was happy to be escaping what he imagined would be the worst ass whoopin' in the world since it would be delivered by his dad. Dooky's dad had never ever issued him an ass whoopin' except for the one time he gave Dooky a punch to the chest after realizing that the arcade sized pinball machine that Dooky begged for before Christmas was broken - the day after Christmas. Dooky had somehow managed to insert marbles and little green army action figures into the machine until the machine was no longer operable, and when his father went to play a game and pulled the puncher, it released into his hand, detached from the machine. There wasn't even a pinball in the machine anymore. The machine went out in the trash the next day, and for that $200 wasted, Dooky got punched in the chest. The punch didn't hurt him, it was the respect he had for his dad that made him cry hard and loud when he got hit.

Nana was still in her room when Dooky went into his parent's bedroom and opened his mother's top dresser drawer. In the back, behind the clothing was an Optimo cigar box. Inside the Optimo cigar box was the money his parents kept for the bills. Dooky put the five one hundred dollar bills into his pocket and crept out of the house while Nana was in her room. World was already on the corner when he got there. Dooky greeted him.

"What up kid?"

"Dook Dook what up?"

"Did you break ya moms mirror?"

"You know I did. Now I got seven years bad luck."

They both laughed.

"Yo..." Dooky said seriously. "Let's be out b'fore Nana come out here".

"Ahiight, we out".

They walked around Mount Vernon for over four hours, never actually descending a three block radius from their homes. It was somewhere around

8pm because the street lights were on and they were both tired when World said, "Yo Dook, what you gonna do? It's getting dark and I have to go home and eat dinner. After that I'll ask my moms if I can come back out."

Dooky felt like he was about to cry.

"What the fuck you mean 'dinner' nigga? We s'posed to be running away! Plus, your mother gonna whoop dat ass cause you broke that big ass mirror."

World just looked at Dooky like he was stupid. "What you gonna do Dook? Cause I gotta go home."

It was then that Dooky realized that his friend had played him and he started crying. World looked at his man and said "you a crazy nigga Dook. Why you don't wanna go home? Matter of fact, check it, if you really don't wanna go to your crib you can stay in my garage tonight ahiight?"

"Ahiight." Dooky nodded and they headed for World's house.

They cut through backyards until they got to World's house. Dooky looked down the block to his own house and saw his parent's car parked out front and started farting. "What the fuck is that smell?" World asked, covering his nose. "It smells like shit!" Dooky shrugged his shoulders unaffected by the smell while he cautiously stared at his house for any sight of his parents.

"Damn!" World shouted as they reached his garage. "That fucking smell is following us!
What the fuck is that. A shit ghost?"

He checked the bottoms of his sneakers then asked Dooky if he had stepped in shit. World instructed him to wipe his feet off before he entered the garage. Dooky stepped in and looked around before he got settled, and World left after promising to come back in a little while. Dooky sat down next to some old tires, the garage was dark and had an empty abandoned building kind of smell. Momentarily feeling safe, he reached inside his sleeves and pulled out the Mellow Yellow and the Suzy Q he had stolen earlier and started munching. He was just about to start on the vanilla cupcake when he heard footsteps. He quickly hid under the tires right before the door opened. He peaked up and saw World and his mother.

Dooky are you in here?" It was the voice of World's mother. She had a flashlight in her hand and was shining the light all over the garage. She turned to World, "Worldin Jr., I thought you said he was in the garage."

"He was ma, I'm not lying."

"Then where is he?" she said moving closer to where Dooky was hiding.

"He was in here ma, I swear. I don't know where he went." The light from the flashlight passed right over Dooky causing him to get nervous.

"Jesus Christ!" World's mother exclaimed, covering her nose. "It stinks like shit in here!

Remind me to spray this place on Saturday." She said before she left the garage.

Dooky stayed in his hiding place behind the tires too scared to move. He heard footsteps again followed by the familiar boom, boom, tap, tap, boom, tap" knock on the door which is the way he and World knocked on each other's doors. He peaked up and saw World standing outside the door alone. Dooky was happy to see his boy but at the same time he was mad at World for telling his mother where he was hiding. He came all the way out from behind the tires and did a jumping jack so World could see him.

World shouted, "There he is! There he is! I told you he was in there ma! I told you...
there he is." The door opened and Dooky's mother, father, sister, Nana, World's mother and World all came into the garage. They all got a whiff of the smell but only Dooky and Nana knew what it was.

Back to the Present

World and Dooky were inside the car locked up like two pit bulls. World was bigger and stronger than Dooky and he had Dooky in a headlock trying to apply enough pressure to pop his head like a pimple. Dooky could not pry World's hands from his head so he bit World hard on the fatty part of his stomach. They were both growling in pain until World let him go. Dooky held his bite a little longer for emphasis, then he backed away and looked at his partner venomously.

"Okay Nigga, you wanna fight! You wanna scrap? We can do this! Get out the car you silly ass nigga! Get out the car!" Dooky yelled.

"You ain't sayin' nothin' Dook!" World said returning his stare. "You know you don't want it nigga! You wanna do this? I will fuck yo ass up? Let's go!"

World got out of the car and he looked back just in time to see Dooky pick up one of the razors he had just bought to cut the corner off of the twenty dollar bill. He knew that Dooky got real crazy when he was mad and didn't hesitate to use anything with bad intentions. World was nobody's fool. He was searching the ground for something - anything he could use against the razor, but Dooky was too fast. Dooky rushed him slashing at his face with the blade in his hand and World backed away just in time to save himself from getting cut.

"Yo Dook, chill wit dat razor man, you buggin'."

"Now *I'm* buggin right nigga? Just a minute ago you was trying to squeeze my fuckin head off!"

World was still backing up when Dooky rushed him again missing his face by inches. "Okay, you got it nigga! You got it. Chill wit dat razor b'fore you cut me man."

Dooky wasn't actually trying to cut his partner, but he would've if World hadn't moved. At the same time, he wasn't going to tolerate anybody punching him in the face like that.

"Yeah okay nigga, but I'm saying, if you ever punch me in my face like that again..."

Dooky opened the trunk and took out a pair of jumper cables. Then he popped open the hood of his car and waited. Shortly after, a car pulled up to the bodega and offered him a jump.

The ride home was quiet and uneventful. Neither of them had much to say to one another. When they arrived in Mount Vernon and reached World's crib they didn't exchange goodbyes or give each other a pound like they usually do. They both just mumbled a barely audible "peace out".

After dropping World off, Dooky drove a few blocks back to the 24 hour store to pick up a few loose cigarettes. The block was quiet and empty as Dooky stepped out of the car and approached the bulletproof window that the store owner operated behind after hours. He purchased his loose cigarettes and when he turned around, this crack head chick was standing behind him and asked if he had any spare change. Dooky eyed her suspiciously, he was trying to figure out where the bitch came from. He had only been at the window for less than a minute and nobody was behind him. This chick came out of thin air. Dooky took a closer took at the crack head lady now standing in front of him. He could tell that she must have just started smokin' because her clothes were clean and her hair was done nicely. She had to be what they called a 'functional crack head', cause even her shoes were clean. Besides all of that, Dooky noticed that the broad was kind of cute and she had a fat ass with some big ol' trumpet blowing lips that he pictured would fit nice around his dick. Dooky said fuck it and he tried the lady.

“Listen, I don’t have any change, all I have is a twenty”.

“We can get change right here,” she said wiping her palms on her pant legs.

“I’m saying...,” Dooky said looking at her slyly, “ I thought you might wanna earn this whole thing.”

“I don’t really get down like that, but um... okay.”

“Yeah whatever bitch,” Dooky mumbled, “my car is right here, get in.”

Dooky made sure nobody else was around before he got into the car and pulled off. He drove a few blocks before parking on a secluded block by Mount Saint Michaels Catholic School near the Bronx - Mount Vernon borderline.

“Okay girl, let’s see how good you are.”

“Where’s the money?” she asked, looking at him strangely.

“I got the money...” Dooky answered removing his already hard cock from his pants. “Now do your thing.”

“Uh, uh money first nigga, you know how it go.”

"I thought your lying, silly ass said you don't get down like that?"

"Nigga you wasting time and the sun about to come up."

With that said, Dooky reached into his pocket and passed her the wrong twenty. He gave her the real one. Only reason he knew this was because the broad examined the bill and complained about it being ripped before she put it in her pocket. Dooky was upset with himself for making such a careless mistake, but he had to admit that the bitch gave head like a professional. She made him cum in less than two minutes. He felt like he just got cheated.

"Let's go another round," Dooky said.

"Let's go, I can get you back up, but first gimmie the money."

Dooky pulled the fake twenty from his pocket and tried to 'flash and pass', but the chick was too swift for that. She opened the bill and saw that it was a phony.

"What's this bullshit? Nah I'm good, you trying to play me now," she said rolling her eyes and passing him his fake twenty back.

Dooky was tight. He was more angry with himself for giving her his last twenty dollars than he was for getting busted. His mind was turning trying to figure a way to get his money back.

"Ahiight ma chill, my bad. Don't get all bent outta shape. You can't fault a nigga for trying; especially with that unbelievable head job you just gave me. I was tryna get a double-dose dat all. Take it as a compliment. We cool right? Where do you want me to drop you off at?" Dooky charmed, he was trying to laugh it off but he was still a little upset.

"That shit is far from funny nigga, and it ain't no compliment either. If I wouldn't have checked I would've sucked your dick for a dollar! Would it be funny to you if I got my cousin Unique to fuck yo ass up? No, right? Drop me off back at the store."

Dooky couldn't believe how she just spazzed on him. Who the fuck did this bitch think she was? She didn't scare him with that "cousin Unique" threat - *was she serious?*

"Yeah okay ma, you got it."

The night was turning to day as Dooky stopped for a red light about two blocks away from the store. The crack head broad was sitting there bouncing her legs up and down while rubbing her palms against her pant legs. Once the light changed to green Dooky reached and grabbed the back of her neck.

"Gimmie my fuckin money back bitch!"

"Ah man, don't do that to me," she said.

"Fuck that! Gimmie my money back lady!"

She opened her car door but Dooky grabbed the back of her shirt so she couldn't get out. He stepped on the gas with her car door still open and her shoe scraping the concrete. He was losing his grip on her shirt so he accelerated up to 40 MPH hoping she would be too afraid to jump out. Before he could make another demand for his money shorty broke free and jumped out of the car. Through the rearview mirror Dooky watched as her body did three cartwheels and rolled for at least 20 ft. Then she just got up and ran like it was nothing.

"Wow! In-fuckin-credible! A Bionic crack head!" Dooky said aloud.

He couldn't wait to tell Loafer about this one, he thought as he sparked up his Newport and drove home.

Chapter Two

Just Want to Be Left Alone - Doug

Whether the victim, or the aggressor, Douglas Campbell was always in some kind of mischief. He was one of those kids that had everyone fooled by the way he spoke, dressed and carried himself. At first glance, a person would perceive him to be a "preppy boy" or even a homosexual. His low Caesar haircut and the fact that he frequently got his nails and eyebrows done after his weekly haircut gave him that appearance. Doug had always been stylish but homosexual he was not. For the most part his style was all his own. When all the kids were hustling or working to get the latest Air Jordan kicks, Doug was saving to buy penny loafers. He would always say, "Yeah nigga, you ain't up on these!" He even had the nerve to put nickels in them instead of pennies. He was always trying to start a new trend. But nobody picked up on Doug's style of fashion. In fact, the way he dressed caused him to be the punch line of many jokes, which in most cases resulted in fist fights.

Back in the days while Doug was trying to impress this young lady, this older cat that they called Big Tree asked Doug for some change to make a phone call. Doug was visibly shaken by the presence of Big Tree and the possibility of being embarrassed in front of the cute young red bone in the cheerleading uniform that he had been shooting low-budget game to for the past 20 minutes. So Doug ignored Big Tree's question in hopes that he would see Doug spittin' game and just go away. Doug wiped a bead of sweat that formed on his forehead and proceeded to sweet talk the young cheerleader, but before he could get a sentence out Big Tree slapped the shit out of the back of his head and neck. The sound of the impact was sizzling. "I said, do you have some change you lil bitch?" The cheerleader immediately did her disappear cheer and dashed around the corner leaving Doug standing there alone with Big Tree. Doug was somewhat relieved that she ran because now he could really beg for mercy. "I'm sorry, I said that I didn't have any money Big Tree," Doug lied. Big Tree smacked Doug again for lying, this time in his face. Then he snatched Doug into a headlock, spun him into a 'Full Nelson', then flipped him into the 'chicken wing'. "You a lying piece of shit and I'm gonna crush you like a paper cup!"

Doug yelled in pain as Big Tree twisted his body through the different wrestling positions. He was close to tears when Big Tree bent and twisted his legs into the figure four leg lock. Doug screamed, "Oh God please!" The cry for help only made Big Tree squeeze him harder. "My LOOORRRDDD!"

Doug cried in pain. As if on cue, Big Tree's attention turned to the nickels in Doug's penny loafers and he snatched Doug's shoes off of his feet. He removed both nickels, tossed the shoes into the street and kicked Doug in the hip as he laughed and walked away. Doug laid still, he was in a lot of pain physically and mentally. He looked down at his feet and noticed a hole in one of his silk socks. He scanned the street for his shoes and as he spotted one and attempted to retrieve it, the excruciating pain shot up his back to his shoulders. Despite the pain he went and picked up his shoe and saw the other shoe further up the block, badly scuffed from the traffic. Just as he brushed himself off the cheerleader came back from around the corner.

"What happened Doug? Are you okay?"

"Ain't nothing baby girl, I just had to handle that and I ended up having to put my foot in that motherfucker's ass. Look at my shoe," Doug said with a smile and a wink.

The cheerleader laughed and Doug chuckled along with her. Although he was still in a whole lot of pain he was willing to put up with a little extra pain for some pussy. Doug noticed that the cheerleader was still laughing.

Damn, he thought, *it was funny but it wasn't that mafuckin funny!* Doug sensed that somehow the joke was on him. "What the fuck is sooooo mafuckin funny?"

Noticing the change of his tone, the cheerleader regained her composure before asking her question. "Did you fall in water while you were beating up Big Tree? I'm just asking because your pants are all wet," the cheerleader giggled.

Doug took a deep breath because he felt like he was about to explode. Worried about what he might see, he slowly looked down at his pants, then coming to terms with the fact that they were soaking wet. Seeing that he wet his pants burned his insides. Doug felt the fire rise within himself. He hadn't even noticed that he had pissed his pants and the fact that this girl had thought that this was hilarious enraged him. Doug reached down and snatched off the badly scuffed loafer and used it to beat this girl that he had just met. He took out all of his frustrations and used all of the energy that he did not use in the fight against Big Tree to hurt her. He did not know how long he had been hitting the girl, but he did remember how hard he cried when the cops handcuffed him and put him in the back seat of the patrol car due to the minor injuries that the cheerleader suffered. Doug was 16 years old and had never been arrested. He plead guilty and because it was his first time ever in trouble with the law, the court gave him 5 years probation.

Months after the incident Doug had been keeping a low profile. He tried to go back to school to earn his high school diploma, but he just didn't fit in with the high school setting. The way he dressed attracted some of the cutest girls, but it also got him beat up and robbed by most of the tougher kids in the school. So he decided to enroll in night school and focus on getting his GED instead. The night school vibe was more to his liking because most of the girls there were young single mothers and the guys didn't pay to much attention to him. Everyone was more or less just trying to earn their GED and go on about their business.

On the first day, Doug's teacher had him introduce himself to the class, gave him a few books and assigned him a seat in the back. Doug was a little nervous going to his seat because he could tell from the looks of this guy he was about to sit next to that he was no different from all the other niggas that gave him problems. Doug sat in his seat and tried not to look at anyone. He heard a voice say, "Yo, what up?" Doug tried to act as if he was so interested in what the teacher was saying that he did not hear the voice.

“Yo! Penny loafers... I said what up!”

Doug turned to the voice and said, “Oh, what’s up? I didn’t know you were talking to me.”

“Fuck you think I was talkin to silly nigga!”

“My bad,” Doug said.

Doug turned to face the voice that had addressed him. His oval face and clean, almost bald head made him look somewhat friendly. But Doug noticed something about the stranger’s eyes, it was either his eyes or the way that his eyebrows arched when he spoke. He couldn’t quite figure it out, but there was something in his features that warned Doug to be cautious.

“I don’t want any problems, please. I don’t have no money and I don’t want to fight you. I wasn’t trying to be disrespectful, I swear to God I didn’t know you were talking to me.”

Dooky was shocked. In all of his 17 years he had never met anyone who was this pussy. This nigga copped a plea before any threat was even displayed. Dooky immediately felt bad for making this new kid expose how weak he was to anyone who was within the sound of his voice. He spoke softly when he said, "I don't have any problems with you penny loafer and I don't want your money either. I was just saying what up - that all." Dooky stuck out his hand and Doug feeling embarrassed shook it.

"What's good Loafers? They call me Dooky."

"What's up man? They call me Doug."

Dooky said, "Okay Loafers nice to meet you."

As the months went by Dooky and Doug became more acquainted. They were almost extreme opposites, but they clicked and sometimes they hung outside of school.

Doug lived with his elderly grandmother and tended to her needs during most of the morning. He had lived with her since he was a young child. His grandmoms was a nice old lady when she was sober, but as soon as that "yak" entered her system she was the wicked witch of the west. The first time that Doug introduced Dooky to his grandmoms she was so drunk that she cussed Dooky out. Dooky thought that this was the funniest thing he had ever heard in his life.

Doug on the other hand did not like his grandmom's drunken behaviors. At times she would go overboard and become violent. Now that Doug was older, bigger and stronger it had been easier for him to block or subdue her outbursts of violence. But he can remember and show scars from the countless times as a youngster when he was not so lucky. But Doug loved her dearly and he had always been there for her. And every morning he was up bright and early preparing breakfast and taking care of his chores and her little errands. He made sure that his grandmother was taken care of until the home attendant arrived. Then he would just go where the wind blew. Usually he could be found loitering in front of some store or mall trying to find a chick to play "hide the hotdog" with. And sometimes you never knew.

A few months prior to his arrest, him and Dooky was riding around Hunt's Point Market in the Bronx one late night fuckin with prostitutes when Doug got out of the car to talk to this rather cute Betty Boopish looking redbone ho that was sitting alone in a park. Ten minutes later the broad was in the car with them heading to Mount Vernon. Neither Doug nor Dooky had any money and Dooky got a little worried - wondering what Doug had in mind, because he was not about to take no pussy. Dooky let out a small fart that killed the inside of the car.

"Got damn!!" Doug said, "Open the window."

"Damn!" Dooky said frontin', "This bitch stink Doug."

"I know you don't think I did that shit," the ho said. "Matter of fact, let me out! I'll find a ride back to the point."

"Naw chill baby - you wit me," Doug said. "My homie is just frontin'. He know he pushed that thing out his funky ass. Matter of fact, let me come back there and holla at you."

Doug climbed in the back seat and whispered a few words then he pulled his dick out and the ho started giving him head. Dooky was a little tight. Ordinarily he would've roughed him up for talking shit but that would be done later, in private. Doug was his man and he did not want to embarrass him in front of the ho. Hearing her giving Doug head filled Dooky with anticipation because he knew he was next. But when they got in front of Doug's grandmother's house Doug grabbed the ho by the hand and said, "I'll call you tomorrow Dook." Doug could tell from the look on Dooky's face that he was furious but he didn't care. He would take whatever Dooky had in store for him tomorrow, but tonight he would be in some pussy.

That next morning Doug and the ho walked down to Dooky's house. When Dooky opened the door the first thing he noticed was the ho's neck. She had hickeys everywhere. When he looked at Doug he had hickeys all over his neck too. *You a nasty nigga*, Dook thought, as he looked at the two of them distastefully. As the days turned to weeks, Doug eventually fell in love with the ho but he couldn't stop her from working the streets. One night she just disappeared never to return. Doug was heartbroken and Dooky clowned him every chance he could. He realized that his friend was crazy and when it came to women he could not be trusted. I guess he never heard the saying, "You cant turn a ho into a housewife!"

Despite the physical and verbal assaults, Doug enjoyed Dooky's company. Dooky introduced Doug to World and together they were like Earth, Wind and Fire.

Doug was in the kitchen preparing breakfast for his grandmother when the phone interrupted him.

"Yo, fuck is up Loafer?"

"Listen, I keep telling you to kill that Loafer shit!" Doug said with very little hostility.

"That's what I be trying to tell you silly nigga!" Dooky responded. "If you haven't noticed - soft, silly nigga, it's 1988 and mafuckers ain't rockin' penny loafers! Matter of fact nigga, tell me when or what year was niggas rockin penny loafers?"

"It doesn't matter when or what year peo—."

"That's what I thought!" Dooky cut right in. "Anyway silly nigga, I was callin' to tell you about last night."

Dooky went over last night's details as Doug listened. Doug and Dooky had been on numerous "Fake $20 bill missions," so Doug laughed as Dooky took him through the event.

Doug then asked, "Serious though, did you speak to World yet?"

"Nah not yet," Dook said. "But I'm gonna call him later though."

"Yeah," said Doug. "Because y'all need to squash that dumb shit."

"Ah, I ain't sweatin' that! That nigga was so drunk he probably don't even remember." They both laughed.

“So what up for tonight?” Doug asked.

“I don’t know. I’ll let you know later.”

“Okay, so call later on.”

“Ahiight Loafer,” Dook said.

“Yo, I told you to stop that bullshit!” Doug said to the dial tone.

Doug’s grandmoms came into the kitchen ranting and raving and smelling like alcohol.

“You always on my fuckin phone you no good nigger! Gimmie my got damn phone you no good son of a bitch!”

Doug said, “Grandma, the person called me.”

“I don’t give a fuck you lying piece of dog shit! Gimmie my got damn phone!”

“Take your phone grandma and here take your breakfast!” Doug said as he gave her a plate of scrambled eggs, bacon and toast.

His grandmoms took the plate and the phone and continued yelling and cursing until she got back into her room and closed the door. Doug fought the feelin' of putting one of his loafers in her ass and silently prayed that things would get greater later because God knows that shit has been worse first.

Chapter Three

I Know I Got You Open - World

World woke up in his bed with a serious headache. The left side of his head felt like it had been used in a game of kickball. He tried to pull himself together but the odor in his room was making him nauseous. “What the fuck is that?” he said to no one in particular. The stench smelled as if it were coming from every direction in his room. He looked over the side of his bed and found the source of the smell. It was vomit. He didn’t remember chucking up his guts on the floor so it had to happen while he was sleep. It wasn’t unusual for him to get drunk and not remember his actions. But he usually pretended to remember just so it wouldn’t seem as if the effects of consuming so much alcohol was taking a toll on him.

The smell of the vomit was getting to him. His mouth was beginning to fill with saliva, and he knew from experience that this was a sign that he would soon vomit again. Before he could get out of bed, he felt it coming, so he reached for the trash can but it was too far away and the impurities inside of his body were already rushing up his throat. He grabbed the first thing he could reach and vomited. “UUUHHHGGGAAAKKK”... food, liquor and some indescribable contents spilled into his Calvin Klein jeans. He let out two more chucks and the fluids were leaking out of the bottom of the pant leg. "Oh God please!!! Please!!!" is what World said as the last few remaining empty chucks pulled from his stomach. "I promise!! UUHH!!"

World's mother had been in the kitchen when she heard her son's cries. She rushed into his room and the smell caught her off guard.

"World Jr.!! In heaven's name what are you doing to yourself?"

World could not even comprehend the question not to mention answer. His mom looked at the vomit on the side of his bed and then looked at the vomit coming out of the bottom of the pants her son was holding to his mouth and she felt as if she was about to get sick. She had to cover her nose and mouth and back away. This was not the first time she witnessed the aftermath of her son's involvement with too much alcohol. How could she ever forget the night she went into the bathroom and found him unconscious, half on and half off of the toilet with his pants down. He had taken a shit but most of it was on the toilet seat and his head was rested on the rim of the tub, which he had vomited in. Now that she stood outside of his room witnessing yet another episode, it filled her eyes with tears.

"World Jr. please stop drinking that poison!" She must have said these words to her son a thousand times.

Feeling a little better now. World said, "I know Ma, I will stop, I promise."

After hearing her son's promise for the third time was when she knew that his words were empty. She knew that if she did not get him some help he may eventually die an alcohol related death.

"AH DAMN!" World said as he looked at his new pants. "Shit, why the fuck did I have to grab these?" World went to toss the pants in the trash can and splashed bits of vomit on his bed, dresser and pillow. "FUUUCKK!"

It took World a few hours to clean his room, wash and put something solid in his stomach. His head was still throbbing and he didn't have anything to take that pain away. He knew that if he had a beer that the headache would disappear. But just the thought of alcohol made him nauseous. He found two Tylenol's in the medicine cabinet, popped the pills and stretched out on the couch.

As the Tylenol reduced his pain, World's thoughts drifted towards Dooky's sister - Tammy. She was the perfect picture of what he desired to have as his woman. She was 5'5" and had the clearest honey brown caramel complexion. Her eyes were dark and penetrating and often hidden behind her long curly eyelashes. She had full lips that were constantly red and moist as if her tongue were made of tropical punch. She had a habit of biting her bottom lip so seductively that it drove World crazy. World thought that Tammy was the woman of his dreams and that she would intentionally look extra sexy and bite her bottom lip because she knew it would get his dick as hard as prison bars. As he laid back on the living room couch, he pictured Tammy in his bed - naked, on her knees, face down, back arched in the 'doggie' position, reaching backwards with both hands as she spread her ass cheeks giving World a beautiful view of the brown ring which circled the opening of her anus, and the meaty crevices on her mound of pussy. She bit her bottom lip and turned her head to look at World. Then she put her middle finger in her mouth and sucked on it like it was made of candy then stuck it deep inside of her anus, pumping it in and out slowly. She watched World watch her finger fuck her asshole until it got her pussy dripping with juice. She pulled her finger out of her ass and it made a light popping sound. Like a bubble from a piece of Trident gum. With the same finger she motioned for World to come closer.....

World was in a zone lying on the couch. Thinking of Tammy was his past time hobby. He looked down and saw that his dick had made a tent out of his sweatpants. Unconsciously, World began rubbing on his dick. Slowly at first, then he began to rub it fast and steady right before his mother entered with the telephone in her hand.

“Get your nasty, funky ass off my couch and out of my living room, NOW!! You have some nerve!”

World’s mother put the phone on the table so that he would have to get up off of the couch to retrieve it.

“I didn’t even hear the phone ring Ma,” World said reaching for the phone and hiding his hard on.

“It’s obvious that you didn’t hear me calling you either.”

“My mind was somewhere else Ma,” he said feeling embarrassed and hoping that his mother didn’t want to discuss it any further.

“I don’t even want to know about where your mind was!” she said as she spun on her heel. “Just keep it out of my living room!" her voice boomed as she returned into her bedroom.

World shrugged it off and picked up the phone. "What up?!"

"Damn son, why you sound like your goldfish just died?"

"Cut the bullshit Dooky! I'm telling you right now Yo, I love you like a brother but! If you would've cut me with that razor... I would've killed you son!"

Dooky moved the receiver away from his mouth so World wouldn't hear him laughing. "Hold up World, I'm saying - you punched me first my nigga. Just because yo moms be making you do the dishes, doesn't mean that your hands are Palmolive soft. Besides, you're my son and I wouldn't..."

"I'm just saying nigga, if you would've!!!"

"Ah World stop the bullshit! Coulda, woulda, shoulda shit! I didn't! If you want an apology then, I apologize to your silly ass. But don't put your hands on me again. You know there's two of you. There's the World I'm talkin to right now, and then there's the drunk, crazy World that I was beefing with last night. Both of y'all better keep your hands off of me from now on!"

World still wasn't ready to let it go. He was trying hard to remember what it was that made him punch Dooky in the face in the first place. But Dooky had already decided that it was over and had already moved on.

"Ayo, come to my crib. I got a 'forty' of Old Gold and two yellow bags of
dat shit!"

Just the mention of the liquor made World's mouth fill with saliva. Right now he didn't want any parts of the beer but he could use a blunt. It would get him charged up and ready for whatever.

"Where's ya moms?" World asked.

"I don't know, they were gone when I woke up this morning. Just me, Tammy and Nana here. Ayo, you coming or what?"

"Where Tammy at Yo?" World asked curiously.

"She right here, she just woke up a while ago and her breath smells like baby shit!"

World heard Tammy in the background asking her brother who he was talking to on the phone. He heard Dooky say his name and wondered what was going through her mind now that she knew it was him on the phone. The tent started reconstructing itself in his sweatpants.

"Yo, lemme speak to Tammy right quick."

"Yo son, I just told you that her breath smell like shit. If I give her the phone then the phone is gonna smell like shit."

World heard Tammy tell Dooky that she didn't want to speak to him. Then she said something about Dooky having doo-doo stains in his undershirt.

"Damn my nigga... I think somebody took a shit in my sister's mouth f'real son."

World didn't laugh at Dooky's joke, he felt some kind of way about Tammy not wanting to speak to him.

"Yo, why you always dissin' your sister like that?"

"Ah nigga please! You've been sweatin my sista for how many years now? What? You on some "Fatal Attraction" shit huh? I ain't worried about it though, Tammy can handle herself. She's worse than a fire-breathing dragon so you betta be careful nigga!! Damn, you just made me forget what I was about to say."

"You buggin out son, I ain't sweatin Tammy," World lied, "I just be..."

"Yeah, Yeah, later for that shit you talkin," Dooky interrupted. You comin through or what?"

"Yeah I'll be over yo, gimmie like 20 minutes," Dooky was about to hang up the phone but then he remembered... "Oh, that's what I was about to ask you, what was your moms beefing about before she gave you the phone? I heard her calling you sick and nasty. You got a cold or something? Cause if you sick you can stay yo ass home, f'real."

"Nah nigga I ain't sick, I just had my feet on the couch that all."

"Oh, ya moms is trippin' over that? Damn! S'pose I come over there and put my foot in her ass? I'm just fuckin wit you my nigga," Dooky said laughing at his own joke. "20 minutes right? Ahiight I was about to take a quick shit but Tammy just jumped in the shower and I'm telling you kid, she needs one. It smell like she has a midget in her mouth...," he chuckled then continued "...with shit on his boots," he added laughing harder.

World wasn't paying Dooky any attention. His mind was now on Tammy being in the shower and trying to come up with a plan to get a peak of her sexy body. Dooky had already given him the blueprint on how that could be accomplished but it had been years since he had traveled down that road and although it was tempting, he just couldn't see himself taking that route again.

But he remembered it like it was yesterday...

When World and Dooky were younger, Evyln, one of Tammy's close friends at that time had spent the weekend with Tammy at their house. Dooky had a crush on Evyln and he would always annoy her whenever she came around. Once he found out that she was spending the weekend at his house he started scheming. His idea was to wait for her to take a shower then run to the back of the house and look through the bathroom window like a 'peepshow' and he invited World to join him. Although World thought that it was a sick idea and drugging her with Spanish fly would work better, he decided to tag along and get a peak at those chocolate titties. Dooky had set the stage by parting the window and shower curtains so nothing was blocking their view.

The first night of the sleepover they both impatiently waited by the bathroom window for hours to see her shower or use the bathroom. Dooky became so frustrated that he went back into the house and started clowning her about how ashy and funky she looked and smelled. And when that didn't work, he tried to slip her a laxative.

Dooky was persistent but nothing he tried was working. He figured that she either knew he was scheming or thought that there were sharks in the shower water. But that didn't deter Dooky from trying while World waited outside in the dark by the window. That's when the unforgettable moment occurred. Tammy walked in and closed the door. She washed her hands then looked in the mirror. After checking her teeth, she stuck her tongue out as if she were teasing herself. The next two things that she did will forever remain In World's database of 'special moments'. Tammy lifted up her shirt removing her bra exposing her firm, round, mouthful of honey brown titties. She examined them in the mirror as if she was trying to decipher which one was the prettiest. World was in a zone. He had always pictured her breast to look exactly how they were and here he was secretly watching her play with them. His dick grew hard in his pants and he started to rub on it. He was so close to the window that he was fogging it's pane.

Tammy put her pretty perky titties away and reached down and pulled what looked to be a stepping stool closer to her. She stood on it so that she would be able to see the lower part of her body in the mirror. She unfastened her pants and slid them down to her ankles, exposing the red cotton panties she wore which highlighted her curves and her thick almond thighs. Her ass was shaped like an onion and her legs were shaped like the females that run track. She pulled her panties down next and turned sideways to check her profile while giving him an unforgettable view of her ass as she tapped it to check its jiggle. Then she checked her profile from the opposite angle, allowing World to look at a perfectly trim mound of triangle hair.

World was so excited that the front of his pants was wet with pre-ejaculation. He put his hands in his pants and played pocket pool while he watched her examining her body. She must have seen some hidden flaw on one of her thighs because she frowned and bit her bottom lip, which was the face she made that World loved, and it was enough to make him cum in his pants. And just then, as if she knew her show had come to its climax. Tammy began to dress. World tiptoed away from the window and was about to head out the back when Dooky came rushing through trying to get to the window.

"C'mon World, I think the laxative is working... she about to go in." World had already seen all he

needed to see. He didn't give a fuck about Evyln's titties anymore and he damn sure wasn't trying to watch her take a shit.

"Nah... I'm good Dook... I don't wanna see shorty takin' a shit!"

Dooky was disappointed but only momentarily. "She about to pull that fat ass out son, you better come see this shit."

World wasn't with it. If what had just happened didn't happen, he would've been right there foggin' up the window. But he was done. He shot his load already.

"Knock yourself out Dook. I'll see you tomorrow". World said walking back into the house.

"Whatever!" Dooky said looking at him strangely and quietly walking out of the back door. "You be acting gay!"

Dooky's comment did not stop World from leaving like it was intended to.
"If only you knew World mumbled," with a smirk, "I'll see ya tomorrow."

On his way out of the house World saw Tammy standing in the kitchen holding the refrigerator door open. He stopped to say hello.

"What up Tam?"

Tammy gave World a "where the fuck did you just come from look," then mumbled a barely audible "Hi," as she continued to look in the refrigerator. In World's mind, the two of them had just made love. He couldn't believe how sexy she was with her clothes on or off. Tammy was staring at World like he had eighteen heads because for the last 10 seconds he had just stood there like he was lost in hyperspace. She knew World liked her, she didn't think he was ugly or nothing like that, she just wasn't interested in any of her brother's friends. She cleared her throat extra loud and snapped him out of his daydream. World had been stuck thinking about how It would feel to really make love to his goddess. And if opposites really attract, then he was in luck because Tammy was thinking that she had better stay on point around World because he acted like a creepish stalker. She walked past him and went to her room and she heard World whisper "See you later beautiful" and thought "Yeah, I really gotta watch this nigga!"

Since the day he peeped Tammy through the window World had been secretly creeping into

Dooky's backyard at night, quietly hanging out by the bathroom window hoping to see Tammy again - but it never happened. After the night he saw Nana, Dooky's grandmother naked from the waist up, gravity having the last say-so on her once firm breast that were now pulled down so far that she looked like she had four arms, was the night he declared that his 'Peeping Tom' days were over. Besides, he was confident in his ability to sweet talk the ladies out of their panties. And if he drank a few 40 ounces first... forget it... he was Don Juan. Only Tammy was able to deflect his advances and make him feel unwanted. She was his Superwoman and World was determined to find her kryptonite.

Before World stepped out of his house, he checked his appearance in the mirror. He admired his tall 6ft frame and chocolate brown complexion. His black hair was shiny and made it look like he had Armor All on his 360 waves. He would always lie to the ladies by telling them that his father was Indian, but his father was Haitian and lived somewhere in Detroit. World had warm, non-threatening brown eyes but his bushy uni-brow kind of gave him a thuggish appeal. He tapped his belly as if he were proud of the weight he gained from all of the Malt Liquor, wiped a speck off of his crispy black and white Addidas, then smiled. Somewhere in his funny shaped head he heard music and starting doing the robot. He broke into a Michael Jackson 'Billy Jean' kick before he headed out the door. "I'll be back Ma, I'm going to Dooky's."

Chapter Four

Live and Learn - Dooky

After hanging up with World and finishing the sip of orange juice someone left in the refrigerator Dooky went into his room and fell backwards on the bed. He felt cluttered and he lifted his head and looked around the untidiness of his bedroom. Clothing and sneakers were scattered all over the room and floor. Dresser drawers were open with socks and T-shirts hanging out of them. His closet door wouldn't close because of all the jackets he had on top of each other, hooked over the corner of the door. Inside the closet, he had piles of sneakers on top of sneakers and so many jeans and shirts that some of them weren't even on hangers, they were just packed in so tight that they stayed in place. Phone numbers, colognes, loose change, cups, plates, old amusement park photos, broken watches, a half-eaten candy bar along with a photo of him and his parents covered the top of his dresser. He once had a nice full-sized bed, a gift from his parents that was now just a mattress on top of a box spring - with no sheets. The room had a thick scent of funky and cigarettes, and still he didn't have a problem entertaining company here. The only thing in his room that was organized was his collection of pornos. And he had plenty - he didn't discriminate. They were all his bitches. At least once a day, he would show them some love regardless of the broads he sexed, beating off was a part of his day that he hardly ever missed. He called it his 'me time'.

Dooky looked at his room and thought, "I gotta clean this shit." He got out of bed to make an effort to organize his room but instead of really cleaning, he just picked everything up off of the floor and attempted to hide it in his closet. It wasn't actually clean but, "*Fuck it*," he thought, "*At least there's more space*," and he felt better.

Just was he was about to lay back down the doorbell rang.

"Damn!" Dooky said aloud, "What the fuck he do... run to my crib?!" He went to the door and let World in.

"What up nigga - how you?"

"Ain't shit," World replied. "Lemme get something to drink."
"Nigga, why the fuck you ain't drink something at your own house?"

World sucked his teeth, "Son, this is my house."

"Yeah? Well, since it's your house silly nigga then you already know that there ain't nothing to drink in this motherfucker!" They both laughed.

"Nah, f'real...". World said kind of seriously "Lemme just get some water Yo."

"Like you said, this is yo house so go get it yourself."

"Yeah ahiight." World said anxiously as he went into the kitchen.

When Dooky went into his room World doubled back and knocked on the bathroom door. Tammy yelled from behind the door, "I'll be out in a minute!" World's dick began to get hard knowing that the woman of his dreams was on the other side of this door - naked with her long hair wet and wavy and water dripping from her sexy body like a beautiful mermaid. He listened to the shower water run for a moment then he touched the door gently before he turned and went back into Dooky's room. Dooky was dumping the Tobacco out of a cigar when he turned and saw his partner re-enter his room.

"Where's your water you silly ass thirsty nigga? What did you do, drink it straight outta the . . . Ayo what the fuck!" Dooky stopped dumping the tobacco and the expression on his face read, "Warning! Danger!"

World followed Dooky's eyes to his crotch area and saw that his dick was pointing straight at Dooky and there was a little premature ejaculation stain on the front of his sweatpants.

Insulted, angered and confused Dooky screamed "Fuck is up wit you nigga!? You a fuckin homo or something? Get the fuck outtta here pointing your dick at me mafucka!!!"

The telephone rang and interrupted them. It was Doug calling to ask if he could bring some chick over. Dooky told him to bring her and hung up, never taking his eyes off of World. World went to sit on the bed next to Dooky and Dooky jumped up.

"Yo Dook, stop playing with me nigga."

"Motherfucker? You just walked in my room with yo fuckin dick pointing at me through your sweatpants nigga! What type of trench coat shit is that?"

"You fuckin stupid Dook... you know that? Just shut the fuck up and roll the blunt."

"That's what I was trying to do you silly ass nigga, but now you got me scared to lick the motherfucker," Dooky responded lightheartedly.

World laughed, "Fuck you nigga."

"Yeah I know," Dooky chuckled "I also know that you need to go wash your hands."

World laughed hard, "You stupid son."

"Nah son, I'm serious. Go wash your fuckin hands, man! Or you ain't touchin' this blunt. On some real shit!"

World was laughing real hard and was on his way to the kitchen when Tammy came out of the bathroom wrapped in a towel. He almost walked right into her. The smell of her shampoo mixed with the fragrance of her body wash had him stuck. He looked down at the bare skin of her thick legs that wasn't completely covered by the towel. They were still a little wet and he followed a thin line of water that rolled down to her ankle. Her bare feet were cute and unpolished, and he noticed that she had tiny fine hairs on her toes. Her scent was so intoxicating that he tried to breathe all of her in.

Tammy watched World as he looked her up and down, and for some strange reason she didn't feel uncomfortable. In fact, although she didn't want to admit it, she was excited. She felt a tingling sensation between her legs and her nipples began to harden causing her to bite down on her bottom lip - a habit she had whenever she thought about sex. She felt playful so she decided to tease World a little by readjusting her towel and giving him a quick flash of her nakedness. After she did it she noticed that perspiration had spread all over Worlds nose and she looked down and saw the tent that had formed in his sweatpants right before she made her exit into her room.

World was stuck. His eyes followed her, glued to her ass and the back of her bare legs until she disappeared into her room and closed her door. World's features were zombie-like as he went back into Dooky's room. World entered Dooky's room in a daze. The snapshot photo of Tammy's nakedness was displayed in his mind on a giant super high definition screen. Dooky was sitting on a footstool with his back turned when World walked in. He had just finished emptying a $10 bag of weed into the cigar paper. He turned to face World's dick pointing at him, eye level with his face. World had a stupid looking expression on his face and had an even bigger wet spot in the center of his hard on. It almost looked as if he came in his pants. Dooky was heated.

"You think this shit is funny you fuckin homo! What kinda faggot ass games you playin' wit me nigga! You think I won't cut yo gay ass?!"

Dooky jumped out of his seat and rushed to his dresser drawer to retrieve his 'Rambo' knife. World ran out of the room heading for the front door. He pulled the door open just as Doug was about to ring the doorbell.

Doug was standing there with a cute light skinned female. She was a little on the heavy side but she wasn't sloppy. Her body was shaped nicely like a light skin version of Janet Jackson.

Dooky caught up to World but seeing Doug with the girl paused his intentions and caused him to disregard World for the moment. Doug didn't wait to be invited inside and Dooky could tell by Doug's air that he was acting out some movie script that his deceitful mind concocted. Doug walked in and looked at World and Dooky professionally as he escorted shorty into Dooky's room.

"Peace Gods, what's today's mathematics?"

They both looked at him strangely, but Doug gave them a look that urged them to play along as him and the female awaited their response.

"Today's mathematics is sunshine," Dooky answered.

"All that being born to sunlight." World added.

"That's definitely a peace almighty," Doug said. "This is Lashonda, she wants to be the queen and y'all know and understand before she can be the queen of the equator we have to all agree and honeymoon to build the energy in the universal planets."

Lashonda was amazed. She hung onto Doug's every word. World and Dooky didn't know what the fuck he was talking about but they knew it involved sex so they nodded their heads in agreement and kept saying "Peace God."

The four of them smoked, drank and listened to Doug kick some more of his scientific bullshit before the three of them took turns sexing her. But before they did anything, Dooky pulled out his stash of condoms and put two sheets on his mattress. After the shit World did a little while ago, he just didn't feel comfortable pulling his pants down while he was in the room.

About an hour and a few strokes later, Doug told Lashonda that her new name was Queen La, just like the rapper. And that he would make sure all the gods knew that her word was bond. Her and Doug exchanged numbers and she was all smiles as she was leaving to get in her cab. Before she left she shouted "peace gods" and they all responded "peace queen" and started laughing.

The three of them were in Dooky's room chillin' - World and Doug were sitting on the bed and Dooky sat on the footstool.

"Ayo Doug, where the fuck you find that bitch at?" Dooky asked curiously.

"I met her a little while ago yo, right down the block. I was gonna take her to my crib but my grandmoms was acting crazy so I called you."

"Where she from?" World asked.

"I don't even know, but she said she was out here visiting a relative," Doug answered.

"Ayo Loafer, you the illest son" World agreed.

"Ayo Loafer, check what this halfway gay nigga World did earlier..."

As Dooky told the story about World and his hard-ons Doug couldn't stop laughin'.

"I'm sayin' Loafer, the shit ain't even funny son, this nigga World is bugged *the* fuck out!"

World couldn't find the right words to explain the situation so he just kept quiet. Dooky and Doug started to clown him, but he ignored them. Even after just getting some pussy, he still couldn't stop thinking of Tammy. *"Did she know that I just saw her naked body? Was that a mistake? Nah, she had to know ain't no way she could've made a mistake like that. Plus, the way she looked at me... that was attraction. I saw it in her eyes... I saw it! I know I ain't buggin. I know my mind ain't playin tricks on me."*

World felt the blood rushing to his dick again and decided it was time to leave before him and Dooky had to really fight for real. He already knew that his partner was a little crazy and he couldn't front, he would feel the same way if a nigga kept getting hard-ons around him.

"Ayo, if yall niggas gonna get into something later, give me a call at my crib." World said as he got up to leave.

"You out? Ahiight, I'll get up with you later. Peace god," Doug said with a chuckle.

"Yeah... peace queen," Dooky said, looking at World suspiciously. "Make sure you slam the door."

World paid no attention to Dooky's wise-crack as he headed out of the room. On his way out he stopped by Tammy's door but it was closed, He was tempted to knock, but his gut told him not to press her. Not yet. So he just left.

Dooky and Doug were still chillin exchanging stories about the different broads they slept with. Dooky rolled and sparked another blunt and the potency of the reefer had them both spaced out.

"Yo what was in that weed yo?"

"Fuck you mean you silly ass nigga? That wasn't no weed, that was dust."

"Dust? Ah man yo. I don't fuck wit no dust, Dook."

"I'm just fuckin wit you Loafer, wasn't nothing in it but I hear you, I'm fucked up too son. Word!"

A moment passed where neither of them spoke because they were both stuck. Dooky snapped out of it first.

"Yo Doug, you ever heard about that cat they called, Get Mines to Me?"

"Nah," Doug said, his voice sounded like it was about to crack into ten pieces.

"Word to mother Loafer, you never heard about Get Mines to Me? Wow son, a yo, he was the illest cat in the world yo f'real!"

"Nah, I never heard of him," Doug said with very little enthusiasm, and he really didn't care. All he wanted was to be left alone so he could sit and enjoy his own thoughts.

"You really is a silly ass nigga Loafer, you know that? How could you not have heard about Get Mines to Me. He's a legend!"

"I guess you're going to tell me who he is," Doug said rearranging his boxer shorts and sounding irritated.

"Don't get smart, silly nigga! This cat is a part of history and if you don't know your black history at least know your hood history."

“Yeah? I’m listening,” Doug said as he took a deep toke on the blunt.

“Yo, Get Mines to Me was probably the most feared gangster in N.Y. If he said he was gonna kill you, then son, go kiss the kids and say your prayers because your ass is as good as dead already. The nigga was ruthless. He ain’t give a fuck. He would kill anything and anybody. Remember the Martin family that used to live on Fulton?”

“Nah,” Doug said weakly.

“That’s because he killed them - all of them - even their relatives down south,” Dooky whispered.

“I ain’t never heard about no nigga killing a whole family and not...”

‘That’s because you don’t keep your ear to the street,” Dooky continued, “I remember the day that he caught up to this hustler they called Big G. Big G owed Get Mines like $20,000 from a dice game and he had been ducking and avoiding Get Mines for months, until the day came when he caught up to Big G at Ed’s Barbershop. He pressed Big G about his money and of course nobody walks around with 20 G’s on them, so you know he didn’t have it. But Get Mines wasn’t trying to hear it; he was like "*if you don't get mines to me right now, you dead!*" Ayo son, the whole barbershop cleared out except for a few of us. Everybody knew what was about to go down and they was trying to put much space in between them and the action. Not me though, I stayed right there."

"You was there?" Doug asked curiously, suddenly interested in the story.

"Of course I was there, silly nigga! How the fuck you think I know all of this?" Dook lied. "Now don't interrupt me anymore... And pass me my fuckin blunt back!"

Doug took another toke and then passed him the blunt. Dooky took a long pull, inhaled then blew smoke towards the ceiling.

"Now what was I saying?"

Doug answered, "People started getting up outta there because..."

"Oh yeah, because mafuckers knew what was about to go down. Big G knew it too, and he was trying to cop a plea," he said. "*Don't worry Get Mine, I will have your money tonight,*" Big G pleaded. "*I'll bring it wherever you want and blah, blah, blah.*" Get Mines had already warned him about what was gonna happen before, so Big G had his chance. Big G was getting all wet under his armpits while he was talkin, he lied and said that he had half of the money on him and would bring the other half tonight. He went in his sock like he was about to pull out the money and pulled out a .38 snub instead."

"Word?" Doug said excitedly, "He shot Get Mines?"

"Did I say he shot him? You silly ass nigga! If you keep interrupting me I ain't gonna finish the story." Dooky took another long pull of the blunt before he clipped it. He picked up a can of Lemon-scented Pledge off of his dresser and sprayed it around the room.

"Ayo, that shit is for polishing wood," Doug said fanning the mist from his face.

"I know what it's for, silly ass nigga! But, fuck what it's for, what do it smell like? It smells like lemons right you fuckin lemon! Listen, you want me to finish the story or not?"

"Go ahead wit the story yo," Doug said, still fanning the air in front of his face.

"Ahiight so, the nigga Big G got the .38 pointing at Get Mines face, and he was so scared that the gun was shaking in his hand. Me, I'm sitting there saying to myself, "*G ain't gonna pull that trigger.*" If it was me yo, Blam! Blam! Blam! And the problem is solved. But that's me; I'm cut from a different cloth. But back to the story, so Big G is standing there with the gun pointed, shaking like a rattlesnake. Get Mines laughed at him then frowned." He said, "*You gonna pull a gun out on me punk?!*" He reached in his waist and pulled out some big, black, Clint Eastwood lookin' shit, and that's when everybody ran outta the shop. The only people that stayed was Get Mines, Big G and me."

"Why you stay? You crazy yo! I would've been out," Doug voiced.

"Why not? Son, I ain't scared of no gunplay. Plus, I wanted to see what was gonna happen. Anyway," Dooky continued, "Get Mines pulled out this big ass cannon and points it at Big G's head. Both of these niggas got their guns pointed at each other's face like a movie yo. But G is shakin' like a car with bad tires. Instead of him just shootin' Get Mines when he had the chance, this nigga G turns the gun on himself, puts it to his head and pulls the trigga... BOOM!"

"Get the fuck outta here yo! Why the fuck he do that?" Doug asked, disappointed.

"Yo, the silly nigga was scared son. I mean, I could only guess that's why he went out like that, but no one knows."

"That's crazy!" Doug said, feeling bad for Big G. "I would've just closed my eyes and shot Get Mines to Me, dat all."

"I'm saying Loafer, it ain't over. There's more to the story."

"What you mean it ain't over?" Doug asked confused. "I thought you just said the dude Big G killed himself."

"I did say that!" Dooky said getting agitated. "I also told you that Get Mines is a legend, and if you can just shut the fuck up for two more minutes. I'll finish telling you what happens next." Dook re-lit the remainder of the blunt, took two pulls then passed it to Doug. "Listen, yeah. Big G killed himself. The bullet blew his brains all over the barbershop mirrors and some of that shit even got on my jacket. I was kind of tight cause it was my yellow Lakers jacket... But yo, Big G's body was on the floor and he was still twitchin'-n-shit like that and Get Mines started buggin out. He was talkin aloud and pacing back and forth with the gun still pointed at G's body. I thought he was in shock or something, until I heard what he was saying."

"What was he saying? I don't understand?" Doug asked confused.

"He was yelling at Big G for killing himself. He was saying, "*You think yo punk ass is gonna get away from me like that? Ha, ha, you ain't getting away that easy nigga fuck that! You can't run from me nigga! Get mines to me nigga*!!" Get Mines put that big cannon in his own mouth and 'boom'... he blew his own brains out. He fell right beside Big G."

"Get the fuck outta here!" Doug yelled, "I know he ain't do no dumb shit like that!"

"Yep, he did it. He chased Big G into the grave."

"Ah man yo, he's a stupid ass nigga f'real yo."

"How is that stupid?" Dooky questioned, "He said that he was gonna kill Big G and that's what he did."

"How do you know? How do you know that's what happened?"

"Cause I told your silly ass that I was right there."

"No...," Doug said "I'm sayin yo, how do you know if he ever saw him in the grave?"

Frustrated, Dooky answered, "I don't know."

"And that's what I'm sayin," Doug said making his point. "He could've killed himself for nothing. So he's a fuckin jackass! He ain't no legend!"

"Now you see...," Dooky began, beginning to get upset at his partner for not embracing the story like he did. "That's why I shouldn't have told you the story. You're just a silly ass nigga that don't have the balls to do no gangster shit like that! If a mafucker owed me 20 G's and did some sucka shit like Big G, I'm gonna do the same thing! I'm goin' to get mines!"

"Yeah?" Doug said laughin, "And how you gonna spend your 20 G's yo? Matter of fact, don't worry I'll spend it for you. I'll open up my fish and chip restaurant... just send the money back to me through Jesus."

"Listen you stupid ass, punk silly motherfucka, it ain't about the money or spending the money! It's about the principle!"

"Yeah whatever Dook," Doug said nonchalantly. "That shit sound crazy to me and I ain't doing no dumb ass shit like that stupid, ass nigga did for no principles or any amount of money... fuck dat!"

"So...," Dooky said in a menacing tone, "... you sayin I'm stupid?" Dooky was visibly angry and insulted because he didn't like the way Doug was disrespecting someone that he considered one of the most legendary, historical hood gangsters of all time.
Doug picked up onto the vibe quickly and answered "See Dook, now you trying to switch my words around. What I said was, if you think that what you just told me made sense or was the most logical solution to the problem that Big G and Get Mines to Me had, then all I'm sayin is that your judgment might be a little off balance... Dat all. I never said you was stupid."

Dooky rushed Doug quickly putting him into a headlock. He managed to get his forearm around Doug's neck and almost put him to sleep. Doug gasped and sounded like he was about to vomit. Dooky let him go and swiftly maneuvered Doug's body into a wrestling submission called the backbreaker. He bounced Doug up and down on his shoulder then spun him around in the air three times before slamming him down on the mattress. Doug bounced off of the mattress and onto the floor landing hard on his tailbone.

"Now who's stupid, silly nigga?"

Doug was rubbing his tailbone and looking up at Dooky who was standing over him.

“I said that I wasn’t calling you stupid, I said that Get Mines to Me was stupid... not you.”

Doug pleaded, not realizing that this was the reason why he was being attacked. Dooky jumped right back on him, this time grabbing his legs and twisting them into the figure four leg lock.

“No!” Doug screamed, trying hard to resist, “Not the figure four! Please! Stop Dook, I have water in my knees!”

Dooky ignored Doug’s pleas and applied the lock and the pressure. Doug screamed in pain, “AAAAHHHHGGGEEEAH!” Dooky kept the pressure steady bringing Doug to the paramount of pain and his cries for help were now religious.

“Jesus please God, Moses... Oh Lord make him stop!”

Nana and Tammy came rushing into Dooky’s room and Dooky let Doug go.

“Stop this nonsense... now! Dookiah what are you in here doing?” Nana voiced.

"We just playin around Nana," Dooky lied.
Nana looked at Doug who was on the floor rubbing his legs.

"Are you okay Doug?" Nana asked.

"Yes Nana, I'm okay. Dooky just gets carried away sometimes."

Doug had enough. He was tired of getting abused every time him and Dooky disagreed. This was going to stop. He was tired of it. Tammy was standing in the doorway behind Nana. She looked at Doug and felt sorry for him. She knew her brother always picked on Doug and she didn't like it. Besides, she thought Doug was nice, not to mention the fact that she had heard rumors that his dick hung to the floor, made her like him even more.

"Dooky you a punk!" Tammy voiced over Nana's shoulder, "You always pickin' on Doug! But when that little Spanish boy who used to live across the street used to whoop on you until you farted, you wouldn't even fight him back! You had to go get World. And if it wasn't for World, that boy would probably still be whooping your ass! Now you wanna bully on Doug, you a punk!"
"That's enough!" Nana yelled "And Tammy, watch your mouth! Yall are gonna stop this nonsense...

now! I mean it! I will not tolerate anymore of it. You hear me!? Do you hear me!" Nana exclaimed and they all nodded their heads in agreement.

Even though most of what Tammy said was true, Nana did not want to hear it. Plus Tammy was yelling over her shoulder and the bad smell that was coming from her mouth was making Nana dizzy. She made a mental note to discuss the importance of dental floss to her granddaughter. She was too pretty for her breath to be that funky. Her breath smelled like the old billy goat from Nana's relatives down south.

"Yeah," Dooky added, "Put a lid on that trashcan!"

"What did I just say Dookiah?" Nana said sternly.

"Sorry Nana but—"

"No buts! I don't wanna hear it. Now stop the nonsense!"

In his heart, Dooky felt the sting of his sister's words. It had been a long time since he had been reminded about Tito. But those days had been over. He would whoop Tito's ass now. But it still kind of hurt his ego.

Nana and Tammy left, and Nana purposely left Dooky's bedroom door open so she could hear what was going on. Doug sat up on the floor embarrassed. He silently wished for the courage to stand up for himself. He thought that maybe he should start working-out, something... he had to do something, because he was tired of being picked on.

Dooky was sitting on his mattress feeling ashamed for getting carried away. Doug was one of his closest friends, more like his brother but sometimes Doug got on his nerves and said things that made him flip. As if nothing happened Dooky asked,

"So what up for t'night?"

Doug, still rubbing his leg said, "I think I might stay home tonight."

"C'mon son, don't act like that. It's Saturday, and I'm gonna ask my pops to let me hold the car again."

"I don't know, I might just chill," Doug answered. He really didn't feel like being around Dooky.

"Alright Loafers...," Dooky said layin' down on the floor "Go ahead and get me back. Put me in the figure four and apply as much pressure as you want. Just don't break my leg."

Doug looked at Dooky like he was crazy. He was tempted to take him up on his offer but he knew that Dooky would end up getting him back.

"Nah that's ahiight. I'm good. I don't want to put you in the figure four."

"What you wanna do? Punch me in my face? Go ahead," Dooky said bringing his face closer to Doug's hands.

Doug definitely wanted to punch him in the face but instead he just said, "I'm good yo, I don't wanna get you back." Dooky grabbed Doug's hands and forced contact with his face with a few slaps.

"Chill Dook, I'm good yo. I'm about to go to my crib. Holla at me later on yo." Doug got up to leave and Dooky said "Yo, I apologize Loafer for getting carried away. You know you my nigga son."

"No doubt, it's ahiight yo." Doug responded.

Dooky slapped Doug five and gave him a hug.

"Ahiight silly nigga, I'll call you later on and see if we can get into something. Maybe we can find a party or something."

"Ahiight call me." Doug said as he limped towards the door. "I'll be at my crib."

"Ahiight Loafer, be easy son."

Chapter Five

The Things We Do

Dooky laid back on his mattress with his arms folded behind his head. He couldn't stop thinking of Tito and his sister's interpretation of that whole chapter of his life. His mind started replaying those yesteryears when Tito and his family lived across the street.

The house across the street was a long, but narrow, lime green woodened framed one family home. It looked like a small barn with the width of a one-car garage. Most of the time the house was vacant, and Dooky and World, and probably many others, had once claimed it as their clubhouse.

Standing inside the front door, you were able to look straight through the house to its back door. There were only four rooms in the house, not including the bathroom and the kitchen. And none of these rooms had doors, which made Dooky wonder how anybody could have any privacy.

When Tito's family moved into the house, Dooky was about 10 yrs. old and he was in front of his house being nosey, acting like he was entertaining himself by throwing an old basketball in the air and catching it. He was really just trying to see who was moving in. He was trying to tally the number of people that were carrying things inside the house and lost his count at 14. He thought that there was no way that fourteen people can live in that house with no doors on their rooms, and he was right. Five of Tito's relatives were just helping them move in, eleven of them were actually going to live there.

Tito was the only member of his family that was close to Dooky's age. He was twelve years old at the time, but he was a big twelve yr. old. He was only a year younger than World, but he was a little taller and wider. Tito had big hands and feet, and his left eye always seemed to drift towards his nose. He wore his hair in a short ponytail and tried to act like he was a young Steven Siegal.

The first time him and Tito actually spoke was on a Saturday afternoon when Dooky was on his way to World's house.

"What's up Puta?" Tito asked, "Where are you going?"

"Huh?" Dooky said trying to figure out what he just called him. "I'm going up the block."

Dooky picked up the basketball that he had left in the front yard to take with him to World's house.

"Where are you going with my ball puta?"

"This ain't your ball. My mother bought me this ball."

Tito stepped close to him and mushed him hard in the face

.

"Gimmie my fuckin ball puta!"

Dooky stumbled backwards and used his hands to break his fall. The ball he was holding rolled over towards Tito's feet and Tito picked it up. Dooky sat there on the pavement watching, fear and shock froze him. He felt the moisture begin to dampen his butt cheeks and a silent fart escaped his grippers.

Tito turned to walk towards his house and attempted to bounce his new ball. When the ball didn't even come halfway back up, he realized that the ball needed air. He turned back to Dooky who was still on the floor, and with a running start, he threw the ball at Dooky. The ball came at Dooky so fast that he didn't have time to put up a defense. All he could do was close his eyes as the ball hit him square in the face.

Tito laughed. "I said catch puta, didn't you hear me? You supposed to catch with your hands, not your face puta."

Dooky felt his lips beginning to swell and felt like he was about to cry. He held back his tears, picked up his ball and shamefully went to World's house without mentioning what had just happened.

As weeks turned into months, the torture had only gotten worse. Tito took whatever Dooky had that he wanted and would punish him for it. Dooky would come home bruised or swollen and would make up lies to account for his injuries. He began to sneak out of his own house or travel through backyards just to go to World's house or the store. On his way home from school one day, Tito snuck up behind him.

"Where have you been puta?" Tito said, grabbing the back of his collar with a devilish grin "Are you duckin' me pendejo?"
Dooky let out a whole Uzi clip of silent gas and like the smell of a skunk, the gas immediately broke the fresh air.

"Did you step in shit puta? Or did you just shit ya pants? Conyo! Tu Apesta como mielda!" Tito yelled as he covered his nose.

Dooky tried to take off running but Tito shoved him hard and caused him to fall.

"Where the fuck you trying to run to maricon?"

Tito hit Dooky hard in the stomach and the punch knocked the wind out of Dooky - all of the wind. And the fart Dooky released sounded like he had just stepped on a frog.

"Conyo! What the fuck was that puta maricon?!" Did you just shit or did a mouse just ride by on a mini-bike?"

Tito laughed at his own humor then punched Dooky hard in his right eye. Dooky cried out in pain and rolled around on the floor holding his eye.

Tammy had been walking up the block not too far behind them when Tito had jumped out from behind the parked car and surprised her brother. She slowed down just so she could see if her brother knew how to handle himself. But after a few minutes of watching her brother do nothing to defend himself, she stepped in to break it up. She reached them seconds after Tito had punched her brother in the eye. She kicked Tito in his back and he turned around like he was about to do something, instead he just got off of her brother and ran.

Tammy helped Dooky up and took him home. She told Nana and her parents what Tito did to him.

They were all upset and Dooky had to beg his mother not to press charges.

He was sitting in his room with ice over his black eye when his dad walked in.

"You alright son?"

"Yeah, I'm okay dad."

"That's one helluva shiner you got there, it kind of reminds me of a Cadillac Coupe De Ville."

They both laughed.

Dooky's resemblance to his father was unmistakable. He looked almost exactly as his father did at that age. His father's skin complexion was a shade or two darker but the head, nose, and deep features of his eyes were almost mirror-like. His dad looked at him and spoke to him softly.

"Son, it is almost impossible to win every fight, sometimes you have to lose in order to gain. What matters is how much effort you put into whatever it is that you do. You may have lost this one, but now you know how it feels to have a black eye. Don't worry, it will heal, and it may take a little longer for the emotional scar to scab, but you gonna be

alright." His father looked behind him then closed the door a little.

"Now let me tell you a little something about equalizers."

"What's an equalizer?" Dooky asked curiously.

"This... is an equalizer, well, it's one of them," his father said showing him a 6-inch folding blade. "But anything can be use as an equalizer son, like I said, it's all about how much effort you put into it." Before Dooky's father could continue, World came storming into the room.

"Hi Mr. Douglas, what up Dook? Yo, dammit man! What happened to your eye? You look like you got kicked by a horse!"

"Well..." Mr. Douglas said cuffing the knife, "I'm gonna let you two cats shoot the breeze. Son, I will finish our conversation later. But! Remember what I said about the 'Equalizer'." As Mr. Douglas turned to leave the room he said, "And after you understand the importance of an equalizer. I'll teach you about my 'neutralizers'." He winked at his son and said, "You can't lose with the shit I use," as he left the room.

World watched Mr. Douglas leave and closed the door. "Ayo, what's your pops talking about equalizers for? You trying to learn how to dee-jay or something?"

"Nah," Dooky said, "He was just schooling me about something."

"Your pops is mad cool son, but yo! What the fuck happened to your eye? You need to put a Fred Flintstone steak on that shit! What you get hit with?

"Tito's fist." Tammy said coming into Dooky's room unannounced. "Tito punched him in the face and he didn't even fight him back!"

"What!" World said looking from Tammy to Dooky confused.

"I ain't lying," she said, both hands on her hips, "Am I lying Dooky?"

Dooky just sat there saying nothing. Tammy wasn't trying to make fun of her lil brother; she was trying to get him angry enough to go back out and fight Tito. But instead, her psychology missed Dooky and struck World's bravado.

"I'm gonna kick that nigga's ass tomorrow! OOOH Yeah," World sang "I'm gonna fuck himmmm uuup!"

The very next day World and Dooky sat in front of Dooky's house waiting for Tito to come outside. World was practicing his jab and when he saw that Tammy was in the window, he started shuffling his feet like Sugar Ray Leonard. He hadn't even noticed that Tito had come outside until Dooky pulled on his shirt and pointed. World hyped because Tammy was watching, pulled off his shirt and ran up to Tito. Tito watched World and stood there waiting patiently until World was in striking distance and hit World with a straight right punch that dropped World to one knee.

Tito burst out laughing as World tried to maintain his balance with spaghetti legs.

"What's this?" Tito said between laughs, "A new dance? Big puta and lil puta. You putas do the same dances."

World shook off the dizziness as best as he could. He looked toward the window where Tammy was and saw that she was still watching. World jumped to his feet and rushed Tito who was still laughing at him. Tito threw a few punches that caught World, but he didn't feel them as he wrestled Tito to the ground. World realized that he was much stronger than Tito and began to dominate him. World picked Tito up, holding him head-locked under his arm and yelled, "Who's the puta noooowww?" As he DDT'd him.

Tito was still struggling to get free and World felt Tito's teeth sink into the side of his stomach. But World didn't let him go. He locked Tito's head tighter under his armpit so that Tito's forehead was exposed behind World, and with his other hand he grabbed a handful of the back of Tito's pants and dropped himself on his back. There was a loud thud that sounded like someone dropped a bowling ball and Tito's body was shaking like he was having a seizure. Dooky and World were both holding their breath. Everything was silent no car horns, no birds and no wind. The only thing that was heard was the sound of World's heartbeat. World let go of Tito and saw blood coming out of his forehead like a horror movie. He nudged Tito a couple of times, then looked up at the window to see if Tammy was still there before he ran.

Dooky stayed there stuck, looking at Tito's body lying there in the street did not scare him. He was amazed. He was about to go get a closer view when his sister came and pulled him in the house.

The fly that landed on Dooky's lip woke him out of his daydream. "*Damn!*" he thought as he realized he hadn't brushed his teeth this morning. Dooky sat up to get out of bed when his hand touched something slimy.

"Motherfucker!" he screamed realizing that either World or Doug had nutted on his bed, which meant one or both of them had sexed Queen La without a condom. He reached and grabbed a sock out of his dresser and wiped his bed off. Then he sprayed some lemon Pledge on the wet spot. Dooky silently plotted to repay both World and Doug by pissing in their bathtubs the next time he was in their homes.

Dooky brushed his teeth, showered, then made himself a sandwich. As he stuffed the last piece of the peanut butter and jelly into his mouth he headed for the door. "I'll be back Nana." Outside, he unconsciously stared at the house across the street. It was still lime green just a lot more raggedy. Since Tito's family had moved, it seemed that the house had a bad omen, because anyone else who moved in had stayed no longer than six months. Each time a family with daughters moved in, him and World would usually be the first ones they would hide the hot dog with. Joy, who's family now occupied the house, had hidden both World's and Dooky's hot dog on several occasions. Joy wasn't a dime, she was closer to a deuce and if it wasn't for those perky ass tits, she would've been in the negatives. But if you were able to see past her too long and too greasy baby hairs that made her forehead look like it had a long ass eyelash, her pancake flat ass, and her mouth that never stopped yappin' (unless you put a dick in it), then Joy was a cool girl that gave it up better than some of the professional cum freaks.

Dooky had been staring at her house and he had not even noticed that Joy was sitting there on her front steps.

"You just gonna stand there looking at me like I'm crazy and don't speak?" Joy said with an attitude.

"Go ahead with that dumb shit," Dooky responded, "I didn't even see your silly ass sitting there."

"Then you need to get your eyes checked," she said pointing a finger at Dooky.

Dooky said nothing and began walking down the block.

"Where you going?" Joy said.

"To the store. Why?" Dooky said without glancing in Joy's direction.

"Ooh," Joy said with excitement "Can you pick me up something while you there?"

"What?" Dooky asked getting annoyed.

Joy gave Dooky a list of things that she wanted from the store and Dooky waited for her to give him the money. When she didn't pull out any money Dooky got upset.

"I know your silly ass don't think that I am going to pay for all that shit!!"

"You's a cheap ass nigga," Joy replied with her own attitude. "Too damn cheap!"

"Whatever," Dook said "I'm out, see your silly ass later."

"Here!" Joy said giving Dooky a twenty dollar bill. "And bring me back my change!! All of my change!"

"This...is...change! Silly little girl! Chump change, at that!" Dooky said as he turned and continued on his way. Dooky walked right past thc store then traveled three more blocks onto Fulton Ave. to his boy SQ's house.

Squirrel was a robust, dark-skinned kid with thick nappy hair and thin lips. He had the fat cheeks that a grandma would love to pinch and he had an overbite to his pearly white teeth that gave his face squirrel-like features, which birthed his nickname, but all of his friends shortened it to SQ. SQ lived in a single parent household with his mother and his two older twin brothers, Lensey and Lewis. Very seldom could you catch both of his brothers home at the same time. One was always incarcerated. His real name was Dempsey Loggins, named after his deadbeat dad who he couldn't stand. And his mother constantly reminded him, and whoever she heard address him as Squirrel, that his name was Dempsey. "What are you? Some kind of rodent? Is that how you see yourself Dempsey?" His mother stayed on his case, praying that he would want something more since her son dropped out of school in the seventh grade believing that the streets would provide him with a better education. So his mom had given up and constantly reminded him not to call her when he goes to jail. SQ's house had become the hangout for anyone without any plans and a love for street dreams. His mother eventually found a man, remarried and moved out of their first floor rental, leaving her sons to fend for themselves.

Dooky walked into the front door without knocking. He walked into SQ's room and stood in the doorway. The room was just as junkie if not junkier than his. SQ was asleep on top of a pile of clothes, snoring loudly. Dooky pulled the pair of jeans that he had been using as a pillow from underneath him.

"Rise and shine," Dooky said.

SQ looked up and saw Dooky standing over him and tried to turn over and go back to sleep. Dooky hit him with the pants he had pulled from underneath him.

"Rise and shine fat boy!"

"Look nigga," SQ said with the killa in his voice, "I'm not gonna tell you this but once - don't fuck wit my sleep!"

"That's what I'm talking about!!" Dooky said with excitement. "Get mad nigga!"

SQ jumped out of bed "You think I'm playing nigga? This a game to you?? I'll show you what a thug about!"

"What nigga!?" Dooky said throwing up his hands.

SQ made sure that his boxer shorts were pulled up and then he threw his hands up in the air, smackin' his elbows trying to imitate the 52 block style. He faked a left jab and caught Dooky with a quick right open handed slap, "Whap."

The two of them slap boxed for the next 20 seconds catching each other with some good shots. "What was all that?" Dooky said.

"Nigga," SQ said, "That was 52 blocks nigga, 52 stops nigga, fuck around wit me I'll give you 52 shots nigga!"

"You ain't block nothing! Silly ass nigga!! I went right through that shit."

"You my boy that's why," SQ said. "Anybody else is not getting through this!" SQ said demonstrating his technique again.

Dooky was impressed, but he would never admit it. SQ moved pretty quickly for a fat boy and he hit hard too. Dooky had seen him knock a few niggas out cold.

"Ahiight," Dooky interrupted "Calm your silly ass down Ali. I came over here to buy some weed, where's your brother at?" SQ stopped shadow blocking and he was now out of breath. "If he home he's probably in his room, let's go see."

Dooky and SQ walked down the hallway to Lensey's room. SQ pushed the door open and they saw his brother's girlfriend bouncing up and down on his dick in the reverse cowgirl position. Her yellow titties were flying around all willy-nilly, when she looked up and saw them standing there. She stopped, grabbed the sheet and tried to cover herself as she told her man that the two of them had opened the door.

"Close my fuckin door before I fuck you the fuck up!!" his older brother yelled.

"Fuck who up??" SQ said showing his 52 block skills, "Dooky wanna buy some weed."

"Close the fuckin door!!" Lensey yelled again.

SQ slammed the door shut and they walked back to his room. "That bitch got my brother nose wide open! She think she all that but she's just a deuce. She on my dick too," SQ lied. "I could've fucked her a long time ago but for real, I don't even want that pussy son."

Dooky didn't believe a word of what his partner was saying. In fact, he had never even seen SQ with a female.

"Nah son," Dooky said, "That bitch is badd! I saw the way she was fuckin ya brother, she was throwing that pussy nigga! I would fuck the shh.." The punch caught Dooky in his left ear and he fell on a pile of clothes.

Lensey stood over Dooky with nothing on except his boxers, "You would do what to my girl DooDoo?" Squirrel started warming up with his 52 block style in case his brother tried to punch him too.

"How many bags you want?" Lensey said looking down at Dooky.

"Two dimes," Dooky said handing him the $20 bill.

Lensey took the money and turned back towards his room. "I ran out of weed last night, but I'll take this $20 and put it towards what you owe me for the peep show," Lensey said slamming the door to his bedroom. Dooky sat on the floor feeling stupid.

"What the fuck is up wit your brother?!"

SQ shrugged his shoulders and said, "He be trippin but he's either gonna give you some weed or your money back. He's not gonna jack you - you know that."

"I'm saying," Dooky said. "Fuck he hit me for?"

"Ah man," SQ said. "He just tapped you, stop crying. You should've 52 blocked it."

Dooky wasn't in the mood for the jokes because Lensey popped him in his ear kind of hard. Squirrel thought the shit was funny, but Dooky was thinking about a neutralizer.

Squirrel walked past Dooky and headed towards the kitchen. Dooky got up and followed him. Every time Dooky took a step his nuts felt irritated and he was trying to readjust his boxer shorts when squirrel offered him a bowl of cereal. "Want some Honeycombs?"

"No! I don't want no fuckin Honeycombs!" Dooky almost screamed, "I just want you to go and talk to your crazy ass brother about my money!"

"Nigga I done told you to chill," SQ said seriously, "and wait til he come out the room... but if you that impatient then go in there and talk to him yaself."

Dooky knew better than to go back into Lensey's room but he was mad because SQ was acting all nonchalant about everything. Dooky sat there and watched Squirrel pour himself a gorilla-sized bowl of cereal and when he saw that there was no milk in the refrigerator he used the tap water from the kitchen sink.

Dooky silently prayed that Squirrel would choke on his food and after watching him drink the water out of his second bowl, he knew that his prayers were not going to be answered.

Squirrel got up from the table and put his empty bowl in the sink. He let out a loud belch and rubbed his fat stomach. "So, what's up for tonight?"

"I don't know," Dooky said "I'm probably gon' get up with Doug and World."

"You still be hanging with them bozos?" SQ said trying to make his little lips snarl. "World, he ahiight but that other nigga is a clown!"

Dooky knew that SQ was talkin about Doug and got a little annoyed.
"You talkin about my boy Doug?? Man, Doug would probably fuck you up if he heard you say that."

"Okay," Squirrel began, "Now I believe you. My brother must've hit you in your head real hard nigga!"

"Keep sleeping on my boy Doug if you want to," Dooky said enjoying the instigating he was doing.

"You can't be serious Dooky," SQ said. "I will fuck your boy Doug up!"

"Yeah whatever nigga," Dooky teased. "Wait until I tell him."

"Tell him nigga!" SQ said getting mad. "Matter of fact, go get him right now!" Squirrel screamed.

Dooky couldn't hold it in any longer and bust out laughin. He told SQ that he was only playin but Squirrel didn't think that the shit was funny. In fact, Squirrel had already made up his mind to fuck Doug up the next time he saw him.

Ten minutes later Lensey came out from his room with his girl in front of him. Dooky tapped Squirrel and Squirrel yelled, "Yo Lens, what up wit Dooky shit?"

"Fuck Dooky!" is all Lensey said as he walked out the door.

"He just fuckin wit you." Squirrel said, "He'll be back."

Dooky was beyond mad. "What the fuck am I s'posed to do, sit around here and wait for the nigga?!!"

"Yeah," SQ said. "Chill nigga, he'll be back - be easy - I got a blunt in my room - I'll smoke that with you – but! You gotta hold on 'cause I gotta take a shit first. I'll be right back."

When SQ disappeared into the bathroom, Dooky crept up into Lensey's room. Lensey's room was strange, but it was neat and hooked up nicely. The bed wasn't made but all his sneakers and shoes were lined up against the wall wrapped in plastic bags, he had shirts neatly folded and laid on a chair, the top of his dresser was filled with different soaps, baby oils, and lotions all neatly stacked in vertical and horizontal rows and he had a lot of naked women posters covering his walls. The only thing Dooky found odd was the clothesline he had tied from one end of the wall to the other that had socks and underwear hanging from it. Dooky thought that was strange but quickly released the thought and hurried to look under the bed. He pulled out three shoeboxes. The first shoebox he opened contained a Ziplock bag full of loose vials of crack cocaine.

Dooky guessed at about 5,000 vials. He quickly opened the bag and grabbed two handfuls and stuffed them in his pocket. He closed that box and slid it back under the bed and opened the next box. As soon as he opened it he smiled at what he saw. The box contained more than a pound of some sticky green weed, "*You lying motherfucker*!" Dooky said to himself as he took over an ounce and stuffed it into his other pocket. Dooky heard the toilet flush in the bathroom and knew the jig was up. He pushed the third box back under the bed and hurriedly made his way back into the kitchen. Less than a minute passed before SQ returned.

"I feel a hundred pounds lighter, you know what I'm saying Dook? I had to feed the fish my nigga... C'mon," SQ said, "Let's go blow this blunt in my room."

Dooky felt uneasy now, he didn't want to be there when Lensey came home. Not that he would notice that somebody tapped his stash, but if in the event that he did notice, Dooky would have a real problem. All he wanted to do was leave without drawing any tips. "Nah Squirrel, you go on and smoke that to the head," Dooky said. "I don't even feel like getting high now."

"Ah man," SQ said. "You still trippin off my brother??! Don't let him catch your vein, smoke this wit me and I'll holla at him for you when he gets back."

"Man fuck that! I'm good," Dooky said trying to sound upset. He was really getting nervous and he wanted to leave. The gasses in his stomach started bubbling and he knew that he was about to start passing gas. "Nah, I'm good Squirrel for real, I ain't trippin... I just got things to do so I can't hang around but I'll call you later though... but try to get that from ya brother when he comes back."

Dooky had unconsciously been scratching his nuts in front of Squirrel, so when Dooky went to give SQ dap before he left SQ dapped him with his elbow.

"Ahiight yo, stay up."

"Yeah," Dook responded. "Stay up."

Dooky was in a rush to get back home so he walked quickly trying to avoid anybody he knew with long-winded conversation. Police in Mount Vernon had a thirst for harassing young black and Latino teens and he was not trying to get caught with the drugs he had on him. When he was about 30 ft. from his front door, he looked across the street and was happy to see that Joy was no longer sitting in front of her house. But just as he got to his door, he heard Joy's voice.

"Where the fuck you been?! Where's my shit at Dooky?"

"Joy listen... you will never believe what happened," Dooky said in his smoothest voice. "Yo, I got robbed."
"Stop fuckin playin with me nigga!" she screamed "Gimmie my fuckin money!"

Joy was clearly upset and Dooky didn't feel like going through the bullshit over $20. His mind was on the drugs in his pocket, plus his nuts were burning and itching like a motherfucker. He knew that all he had to do was give her some attention, but he felt like he desperately needed another shower, so he said "I got you joy..." as he tried to get inside his door. "....Tomorrow."

"Hell naw nigga!" Joy said as she ran up on Dooky with lightening speed. "Gimmie mines right now!" she demanded.

Joy continued ranting and raving when Dooky turned to her and put his arms around her waist, pulling her close to him. He reached both hands down to her flat ass gripping what little flesh she had. Although Joy was "all pockets" in the ass department, her skin smelled like fresh fruit mixed with honey and her scent sparked his arousal. His dick grew hard and he pulled her closer as he grinded his groin into hers. He kissed her on the nape of her neck and she confirmed her submission by releasing a soft moan. Joy tried to make her lips meet his but he smoothly escaped her invitation by nibbling on her ear. The way they were grinding made it appear as if they were dancing to reggae music. Dooky slid his hand into the back of her pants to see if she would allow him to put a finger in her asshole. His finger found the button and pressed it, and Joy responded by pushing her ass back against his finger until it was in all the way in to the knuckle.

"OOOOH," she moaned as she reached and grabbed a handful of his dick. "Let's go inside your hou—"

"BITCH! If you don't get your hot nasty ass in this got damn house I am going to beat the brakes off you! Out here in the middle of the damn street with a fist up your ass!"

The voice was unmistakably coming from Joy's mother who must've come out of the house looking for her. Joy did a Jackie Joyner, Evil Canevil type sprint as she darted and ducked a flurry of blows before she made it into her house. Her mother stood there for a moment wearing a long T-shirt type of nightgown with a pair of furry character slippers giving him the evil eye. Dooky looked at her two watermelon sized titties then politely said "How you Doing Ms. Brown?" She rolled her eyes and went into her house and slammed the door. Dooky laughed, smelled his finger then frowned.

After he got inside and washed his hands he thought about Joy and her mother's titties. "I bet both of them are some cum freaks." He debated on whether he should pop in a porno before he tallied up the drugs in his pocket but dismissed both thoughts when his nuts started itching again. He undressed and headed for the shower.

Chapter Six

It Gets Greater Later

Doug had been at home since he left Dooky's house. He was feeling miserable. For one, his testicles were on fire and for two, he was still uptight about getting roughed up because he had voiced his opinion about Dooky's "so-called" legendary idiotic hero.

"Who," he thought, "other than some pea brain idiot would commit suicide just because he wanted to chase after someone who had just committed suicide? I know some people do crazy things over love, but for money?? Fuck outta here! And how do you know you gonna see this person? Huh Dooky? You couldn't answer that question could you - you fuckin dickhead!! Yeah nigga! Your man Get Mines to Me was a fuckin asshole! And you're a butt plug for thinking the motherfucker is legendary!"

Besides that, Doug had to hear his grandmother's mouth. He smelled the liquor once he stepped inside the house, and from the looks of his grandmother he determined that she started throwing them back the moment he left this morning. He heard his grandmother's footsteps approaching. "Where the fuck you at dirty nigga?!" Doug remained seated in the living room ignoring her and watching the television. His grandmother positioned herself in front of the television as she spoke. "Who... said you...," pointing at Doug, "could watch my...", pointing at her chest, "Teee Veee?"

Doug looked in his grandmother's direction and immediately noticed that she did not have any under clothes on beneath her nightgown. He could also tell by the way she was leaning back and forth that she must've been drinking doubles. "Excuse me please grandma, I'm trying to see the game."

"You trying to watch what? Get outta your way?? Get the fuck outta your way???" She jerked her head so hard trying to emphasize, that she caused her wig to tilt to the side like a Kangol. **"Not on my motherfuckin' Teee Veee! Hell no. I'm tired of you burnin' up all my got damn tricity nigger!"**

Doug was trying to control his temper, but he felt himself loosing control. There had been plenty of times in the past when he'd cursed his grandmother out and it almost always led to her dialing 911. He was desperately trying to avoid this confrontation, but his patience was so low that his reserve tank was on fumes. His grandmother did not know, nor did she care about his problems. He was at home because he needed peace, but he felt that even at home, he was not at home. "Grandma please... please, I am not in the mood for this shit right now."

His grandmother raised her eyebrows, adjusted her stance so that she was positioned close enough to him that he could smell her breath. She pointed her index finger less than a centimeter from his face and poked him in the nose each time she spoke. "What... you... mean... you... not... gonna move nigger?! You... don't... pay... no... tricity... in here!! I... pays the... bill!! And I say turn... my... got... damn... Teee Veee off!!" She spun around and clicked the off button on the television.

The steam was coming out of Doug's head, ears and nose as he rose from the couch and turned the television back on. Before he could sit back down, through his peripheral, he saw his grandmother's arm cocking back and he caught her wrist right before she made contact with his face. His anger got the best of him and he unconsciously twisted her wrist with more force than intended.

"Oh Lord! He done broke my arm. I'm calling the Po-Leese. You trying to kill me!!"

Doug released his grip letting her go as she swung a wild blow hitting him on the side of his neck and causing her wig to fall off of her head. Doug focused on the hole in the back of her stocking cap as she ran into her room, slamming the door.

Doug knew that he didn't break his grandmother's arm, but he was definitely trying to hurt her for making him feel so unloved and unwanted. All his life he had shared a roof with his mother and grandmother.

He had never met his father and most of his step-dads and step-granddads were just snapshots in his life. His mother got married and moved to Washington D.C., leaving her only child with her mother and an empty promise that she would send for him as soon as she was settled in. That was fourteen years ago. Besides the occasional visits his mother made to New York, Doug hardly ever saw her.

His grandmother raised him, she was the one who nursed him when he was sick, cheered for him at his baseball games, taught him how to cook and held him when he cried for his mother. When his grandmother started drinking after a car accident killed his most recent step-granddaddy, things got awry. She began to verbally and physically abuse Doug until it consumed their whole relationship. He often prayed for her to stop drinking, hoping that it would bridge the gap between them. Despite all the abuse she put him through, he loved his grandmother to death. She was all he had and right now she was probably in her room calling the police and telling them that he was trying to kill her. The police had been to their residence on so many different occasions that they knew both Doug and his grandmother. Most of the time noticing how intoxicated she was they would just ask him if he could sleep elsewhere for the night or go out and get some fresh air until she sobered up. But there were other occasions when his grandmother put on such a performance that he had almost been put in jail.

Doug was not taking any chances. He knew that he didn't break her arm, but it was a possibility that she might have a bruise, which was enough for him to have to explain his story to a judge. Doug grabbed his keys and his jacket and headed to Dooky's house. Before he left, he eased up to his grandmother's door and listened.

She was on the phone talking to one of her "Bingo-Buddies". "He tried to kill me again Dorothy! He has the devil in him! He almost broke my arm and I want him out of my house!.......... (sob)... mmhmmm, oh yes Lord, the Po-Leese are on their way." That was all Doug needed to hear before he left.

World was in his bathroom naked. He was sitting on the side of the bathtub examining his groin. After already taking three showers he still felt unclean. Something had to be wrong. He had vigorously scrubbed his groin with soap, body wash and shampoo and it was still itching. "What the fuck?!," he mumbled pulling a bug out of his pubics. "I know this bitch ain't give me crabs!" He examined the bug closely and saw that the shit looked like a tiny monster with claws. "Ah fuck nah!" He flushed the mutant in the toilet and got back into the shower. After 15 minutes of more washing and scrubbing he got out of the shower and poured a handful of some cheap cologne in the palm of his hand hoping that the alcohol filled fragrance would cure the problem. He rubbed it all over his groin. Two seconds after the flammable liquid settled into all of the irritation and broken skin caused by all of his scratching and scrubbing, World let out a piercing scream. The sound was so high pitched that a dog started barking two blocks away.

World's mother knocked on the bathroom door. "What happened? Are you okay in there?" World could not find the strength to talk. All that came out of his mouth was "OOOOHWEEEEAAAH." Despite the pain, he prepared himself for a few more splashes of the cologne before exiting the bathroom unto the watchful eye of his mother. She had a look of concern when she asked, "What is going on with you World?"

"Nothing Ma, I dropped something on my foot." World lied.

His mother looked at him suspiciously. She knew a fish story when she heard one. "Why do you have on so much cologne? It's way too strong." She pinched her nose to avoid the smell.

World didn't respond to his mother's remark as he headed toward his bedroom. His mother stopped him, putting a hand on his shoulder.

"Are you going out tonight?"

"I'll probably go down to Dooky's house or something."

"World Jr.," his mother's tone was sorrowful. "Please don't stay out drinking and carrying on and come home like you did last night. All that alcohol is bad for your liver baby."

"I know Ma," World said. "We're just going to chill tonight, that all."

His mother was not convinced. "Please, don't drink tonight." She was basically begging him.

"I won't Ma, I swear."

"Alright then," his mother sighed silently praying that her son was telling her the truth. "Before you go out make sure that you eat. Your dinner is on the stove."

"Thanks Ma," World said as he continued to his room.

World got dressed and ate his dinner. His groin hadn't bothered him since he used the cologne and he was relived. He picked up the phone and called Dooky. Tammy answered the phone on the second ring.

"Hello". The sound of Tammy's voice hypnotized him and he began thinking about her nakedness. He wondered if she had intentionally showed him her body.

"HELL-LOOW??!" Tammy yelled into the receiver snapping him out of his trance.

"Hey, what's up Tam?"

There was an awkward silence and this time it was World's turn to repeat himself.

"What's up Tammy??"

"Oh, hey World. I thought that was you." Tammy said with a trace of excitement. World was stuck. Did she just say "*Oh hey World?*" That's some new shit there, he thought. He wasn't used to this friendliness and it caught him off guard.

World quickly regrouped and shot back, "Yeah it's me... What up? What you doing?"

"I'm not doing nothing World," Tammy said seductively. "I'm just sitting here painting my toenails."

World loved the way she just said his name. It sounded like she said it with a lot of passion and devotion. He held the receiver tight against his ear as though he could hear what she was thinking. He pictured her sitting on her bed dressed in a T-shirt and panties. Her chin was resting on the knee of the leg she had clutched to her chest as she painted a toe and admired her work. Her other leg was spread open exposing the mound of love joy hidden inside of her cotton panties. World's dick began to grow hard as he said,

"So what color is your panties?"

"WHAT?" Tammy yelled.

"I meant." World said, "What color are you painting them... you know your toenails?"

"Oh," she said still somewhat confused. "Umm, hot pink."

World was only half listening because his mind had drifted back off into "La La Land" picturing her sitting on the bed in her panties, when he said, "That's my favorite color." Shocked by his response Tammy just said "Huh?" Then cautiously told World to hold on as she went to give her brother the phone.

World couldn't believe how he just played himself. He had been awaiting the opportunity to get past her defenses and the first shot he got he put his foot in his mouth.

Dooky spoke into the receiver loud and full of energy, "Yo son, I think that dirty bitch Doug brought over here gave me crabs!" World heard Tammy's voice in the background calling her brother disgusting.

"Mind your business shit mouth," Dooky shot at her before he continued. "Yo, your balls ain't itching son? I know I ain't the only one who got these shits."

World heard Tammy make another noise in the background and he knew then that Dooky's big mouth just killed whatever progress he had been making with Tammy.

"Yo! You hear me silly nigga? I said I think I got crabs!" Dooky exclaimed.

"Yeah man I heard you". World said feeling depressed. "My shit was itching too, put a bunch of cologne on your shit to get rid of them."

"Word?"

"Yeah," World answered. "That all."

"Okay bet, I'm right on it. But check it, I made a power move a little while ago and I need to talk to you on some real shit. What you doing now?"

"Ain't shit." World said. "I was about to come over there."

"Come on over then. Oh yo World, what's up with that white boy that live across the street from you? What's his name again?"
"Who you talking about?" World said. "Which one, Gus or FrankMike?"

"Yeah," Dooky answered. "That nigga FrankMike."

"Why? What up?"

"Nah, I'm sayin," Dooky began. "That nigga FrankMike smoke crack right?"

"I don't know what that nigga smoke." World said kind of agitated. "The way he looks he probably will smoke anything... why?"

"I'll tell you when you get here," Dooky said, then added, "Cologne right?... Any kind?"

"Yeah," World said with a chuckle. "Gotta use a whole lot of it though."

15 minutes later World was walking towards Dooky's house and noticed Doug Diddy boppin' in the same direction. Instead of waiting for Doug, he rang the doorbell hoping that Tammy came to the door. Instead Dooky pulled the front door open with a frown on his face.

"Yo that motherfuckin cologne ain't no joke! I damn near burnt my nuts off with that shit!"

World laughed. "Yo Doug is on his way up the block."

"Oh yeah," Dooky said with a devilish grin. "I'm gonna teach him about bringing them dirty bitches to my crib."

World laughed again. "What you gonna do?"

"You'll see, just chill and go along with me."

"You ain't shit." World said with a chuckle just as Doug walked up.

Doug looked at the two conspirators and his gut told him that they were plotting on him. So he tested the waters.

"Yo what up Dooky, yo what up World, yo?"

"What up yo," they both responded.

"Ayo, yo Doug," Dooky began, "Word yo, I think that bitch you brought through earlier gave me some shit son." Dooky opened the door so his two partners could come inside. "Matter of fact, I know she gave me some shit b'cause I saw one of them shits before I got rid of them."

"How you got rid of them?" Doug said, "Cause yo, I got 'em too. I've been scratchin' the skin off my nuts all afternoon!"

World couldn't keep a straight face. He burst out laughin. Doug gave World a strange look. "What's so funny?" World fixed his face then explained how him and Dooky went through the same shit. "What you gotta do is used some..." Dooky cut World off and finished the sentence "...rubbing alcohol."

"Rubbing alcohol?" Doug said, "Word... you got some in here?" he asked.

"Yeah," Dooky said. "Hold up, I just put it back. Let me get it."

Dooky disappeared for a moment and came back with the rubbing alcohol, a coffee mug and a towel that he had on his shoulder. He filled the coffee mug more than halfway with rubbing alcohol and passed it to Doug. "Here hold this." He put the bottle down and took the towel off of his shoulder.

"Let me give you a demonstration Doug, pay close attention because you have to make sure you kill all the crabs before one of them crawls in your dick." Dooky continued, "Now look, go in the bathroom, pull your shit down and stand over the toilet. Take this towel and hold it under your nuts like this..." Dooky demonstrated how to hold the towel. "... Make sure that your nuts and your hotdog is on the towel like a plate of food. Then...,"

Dooky continued, "... You splash everything in the cup on everything, and that will kill em."

World was turning red trying not to laugh. He had to pretend that he saw something interesting on Dooky's dresser so that he could turn his back and try to contain himself.

"You got that?" Dooky said.

"Yeah, I got it." Doug said nonchalantly.

"Remember..." Dooky reminded him, "...Stand over the toilet."

Doug disappeared into the bathroom and less than a minute later they heard the sound of breaking glass followed by and earth shattering scream, "EEEEEEE.......EEEEEEE...EEE... EEEE." Doug sounded like an opera singer in labor. Both Dooky and World were on the floor hurting from laughter when Nana and Tammy came running into his room. Nana looked around her grandson's room suspiciously.

"What in heaven's name is going on in here?"

Tammy heard moaning coming from the bathroom. "It came from in here Nana," she said pointing to the bathroom door.

Dooky and World followed Tammy and Nana to the bathroom. Nana pushed the door open and everyone got quiet. Doug was standing over the toilet with his pants and boxers down to his ankles, facing the bathroom door. He was still holding the towel underneath his nutsack and the first thing that all of them saw was Doug's 11 ½ inch dick propped on top of the towel like a dead snake. Everyone was speechless. Dooky was the first one to speak.

"Got damn Loafer, put that fuckin python away man!! My grandmother is here!"

"Watch your mouth!" Nana said as she did a double take to Doug's member.

When World saw Doug's dick size, his first reaction was to look at Tammy. He saw the lust in her eyes, while she bit her lip and was immediately heartbroken. Her eyes were glued to Doug's dick and World was imagining what she was thinking. He nudged Dooky and gave him a head nod in Tammy's direction. Dooky peeped his sister lusting on Doug's dick.

"Damn Tammy! Why you staring at it like dat? What are you some type of snake charmer??"

Doug was embarrassed, but the alcohol stung him so badly that he was scared to move.

Nana smelled the alcohol. "What's going on here?" She spoke to anyone and everyone.

"All of these fools caught the crabs Nana," Tammy blurted.

"And you put alcohol on your penis?" Nana said, "Doug are you crazy? What possessed you to do something that foolish?"

"I thought...," Doug swallowed his words as he realized he'd been herbed again.

Nana saw that Tammy was still looking at Doug's penis and stepped in front of her. "Get dressed Doug," Nana said. She looked at Dooky and World, "Yall itchin' too?"

They both nodded their heads.

"Good lawd! What am I going to do with these boys? Tammy, get my purse... Tammy!" Nana yelled, bringing her granddaughter back to life. "Go and get my purse... Now!" Tammy was so busy watching Doug put that anaconda away that she didn't hear Nana the first time she spoke. Before she left to go get Nana's purse, she gave Doug a wink on the sly.

Doug was already accustomed to the special attention he received when the ladies saw his meat. He read Tammy's face the minute she saw it. He had seen those invitations on many occasions. He even detected an invite from Nana on the low. But now was not a good time for any action. He felt that his meat would be out of commission for a while. But he made up his mind that he was going to put all 11 ½ inches into Dooky's sister for all of the shit he put him through.

World watched Tammy's actions as she stared at Doug's dick. He watched her shift her legs, bite her lip and he even caught the wink she shot at Doug on the low. As she went to get Nana's purse, she walked past World as if he didn't exist. World tried to thrust his pelvis out a little to try and get a tasteless dry hump as she walked past but as if she sensed his move, she avoided any contact with him. "*Man fuck her!*" World thought as she slid by him with her back hugging the doorframe like he was contagious.

Moments later... Nana and Tammy left the house and Dooky called World and Doug into his room.

"Yo look, yo," Dooky began. "I have something serious to discuss with yall."

"Man!" Doug complained. "That's fucked up! Why you tell me to put that shit on my dick? I thought I was about to die in there... I probably did internal damage and need medical attention! Yall niggas is on some bullshit!"

World laughed. "Yo Doug, I ain't know that you could hit notes that high."

"Yeah," Dooky cut in. "You sounded like a lil bitch."

"True dat," World said then continued. "But yo Dook, did you peep this nigga Doug's dick? His shit looks like an elephant trunk. He must drink a lot of that peanut punch."

Dooky looked at World suspiciously. "Ayo, fuck you still thinking about his dick for nigga!? I'm really starting to believe that you're a fuckin' fag!"

Dooky examined both of his buddies closely. The three of them were still scratchin and talkin shit when Dooky got serious. "Look yall, check this out," Dooky picked up a sock and turned it inside out spilling a bunch of tiny crack vials onto his mattress.

“Where you get that from?” Doug asked.

“Don’t worry about that silly nigga, all we got to do is sell it and we straight.”

“We?” World spoke, “I ain’t no fuckin’ drug dealer.”

“Me either,” Doug added.

Dooky looked from World to Doug like he was disgusted. “I ain’t no motherfuckin’ drug dealer either, you silly ass niggas! But we got what we got and we’ll get what we get when we get rid of this shit.” Dooky looked from World to Doug and continued. “All three of us is broke niggas, but I don’t plan to stay broke. We get rid of this and we’ll all have some paper in our pockets... I need yall niggas help. You with me or not?”

Doug and World looked at one another to see who would answer his question. World spoke first. “Yo Dook dig, you my boy and all that but I don’t know if I want to get involved with selling crack.” World paused, then added, “Let me ask you this, where did you get this shit from, and how much do you have to pay your connection?”

Dooky explained where and how he got the drugs and immediately regretted it.

"Ah man". World sighed "Dooky you're a crazy ass nigga you know that?! First of all," World continued, "do you realize you're talking about crack cocaine? It is a felony to sell that shit in N.Y. A felony nigga! Not no Mr. I didn't mean it." Word said, referring to a misdemeanor. "Besides, what happens if Squirrel's brother finds out?" Doug nodded his head in agreement when World mentioned Squirrel's brother and Dooky got angry.

"Man fuck Squirrel's brother!" Dooky yelled, "He ain't gonna find out shit! And by any chance that he does... what he gonna do?? I ain't scared of that nigga. I'll put that nigga on the brown side of the grass!" Dooky exclaimed convincing no one. "Look, there's 371 $10 vials here, that's about $1,000 a piece after we sell them."

"There you go with that '*we*' shit again." World said emphasizing the "we". "I ain't agreed to nothing nigga! If it was weed it might be a different story but..." Dooky reached into his dresser and pulled out a Ziplock bag more than half full of weed and threw it at World's chest.

"Remember when I asked you about FrankMike?"

"Yeah... oh, that's why." World said unconsciously reaching into his pants to scratch his nuts.

Dooky said, "You think that white nigga fuck wit crack?"

"I told you..." World said, "... I don't know what the nigga fuck wit. I know the nigga gets high off of..." World stopped and examined the little mutant that he just pulled out of his pubics. He unsuccessfully tried to crush it between his fingertips, then he plucked it away before he continued, "yeah yo, that nigga probably smoke anything."

Dooky was losing his patience with World, "Ayo you stupid ass silly nigga! How the fuck you just gonna pull a fuckin crab out of your nasty ass nuts and pluck that shit somewhere in my room? Fuck is wrong wit you?!"

"My bad." World said, "the shit was dead before I plucked it though."

Dooky had already turned his attention to Doug, who had been silent for most of the conversation. "Yo Doug, you know any crack heads?"

"Nah," Doug said, "1don't know any, but maybe them Portuguese niggas that live in the buildings down on Lorraine Ave. might fuck wit that shit."

"You mean them Brazilian niggas?"

"Brazilian?" Doug said laughing, "There might be a brazillion of them niggas in that building but I'm pretty sure they're Portuguese."

"Who gives a fuck what they are?!" Dooky said getting agitated, "Do them niggas smoke crack? That's all I wanna know."

"Probably so," Doug said.

"Good," Dooky said rubbing his hands together. "Yall wit me or not?"

It took close to an hour but Dooky finally convinced his partners to help him sell the drugs. They felt it would be easier if they split the drugs up and work at their own pace. Doug was gonna try and reach the Portuguese, while World would see if he could get some customers through FrankMike. However, Dooky was going to try his luck on 3rd Street, which was one of the most seasoned drug blocks in Mount Vernon.

Dooky heard a car pulling up in front of the house and he peeped out the window to see who it was. "Yo, my moms and pops is home. Put all that shit away." World and Doug each had 100 vials a piece. They quickly stashed the drugs in their pockets and Dooky stashed the weed and the remainder of the vials in his dresser.

When his parents entered the house, he heard his mother call his name.

"I'm in my room Ma."

Mrs. Douglas stuck her head into the door; both World and Doug greeted her with hellos.

"Hey guys," Mrs. Douglas said to her little soldiers. "Dooky where is Nana and Tammy?"

"I don't know where they went Ma, but they left about 30 minutes ago."

His mother looked around his room, "Dooky you really need to do something about this room, it stinks in here. I don't see how you entertain company in here." She added, "at least make your bed and straighten out the top of your dresser, pick those socks off the floor and empty the garbage." Mrs. Douglas stepped inside the room when she saw something, "And is that my good dishes you got over there on your floor? What did I tell you about eating in your room? Get my dishes off the floor and do something about this room!" His mother left without closing his door.

Dooky sprayed more Lemon Pledge around the room and some of the mist landed on World's face.

"Yo! Watch that shit son!" World yelled.

"My bad," Dooky mocked, "You act like it was gonna kill you or something."

"I don't want none of that shit to get in my eyes." World said as he fanned the mist from in front of his face.

Doug jumped in, "You need to get some of that in your mouth cause your breath smells like shit!" Dooky and Doug laughed. World said, "Oh yeah? I can imagine what your breath smells like Doug cause you know you be suckin' your own dick."

Dooky looked at World like he was fuckin crazy. Doug said "Huh?"

Dooky jumped in, "Yo World, you wanna tell us something man?... You one of those undercover trench coat homos or something?"

"Fuck outta here." World said.

"Fuck you mean, fuck outta here man? That's like the second time you mentioned something about the nigga dick!"

"Ayo I ain't no fuckin homo!" World said defensively. "I just ain't never seen a nigga dick that long, that all."

Dooky raised his eyebrows at World's statement.

"Oh yeah nigga, so how many dicks you seen World? Dooky asked.

"Stop playin wit me." World said seriously.

"Then stop acting like a snake charmer." Dooky said playfully.

Dooky's father stepped into the room and all three heads turned to his direction. "Hey fellas."

"What's up Mr. Douglas," World and Doug responded.

"Hey Dad," Dooky added, "You going out tonight?"

"I don't think so," his father responded. "I think me and your mother is in for tonight."

"Can I hold you car?" Dooky asked.

Mr. Douglas looked at his son and smiled. There was no way that you couldn't see their resemblance. Dooky had the same 5'11" frame with broad shoulders, brown eyes, brown skin and full lips. They even had the same crooked front tooth. The only difference in appearance was the way they wore their hair. Mr. Douglas embraced the short Afro, while Dooky kept a Caesar.

"Listen Dooky," Mr. Douglas said stepping further into the room. "I don't have a problem with letting you use my car. I know you fellas like to hang out - but!" Mr. Douglas was looking for a place to sit until he noticed the stains on the bed. He decided to remain standing. "I don't want to have to clean out my car every time I get it back... and this morning," Mr. Douglas said, "this morning I got in my car and the seat was all the way back here." He leaned back so far trying to demonstrate that he almost lost his balance. "And my gas tank was on 'E'. My tank is full now and that's how I want it to be when I get in it tomorrow."

"Alright Dad," Dooky said before adding, "Dad, can I um, borrow a couple of dollars?"

Mr. Douglas laughed, "I tell you what," he reached in his wallet and gave his son $20. "I got a couple of things I need you to do around the house tomorrow." He handed Dooky the keys to his car. "Be careful... you hear me?"

"Okay, thanks Dad."

"Alright fellas."

"Later Mr. Douglas."

Dooky, World and Doug were on their way out of the house when Tammy and Nana pulled up. Nana got out of the car followed by Tammy.

"Where yall boys off to?" Nana asked anyone and everyone.

"We might go to the movies," Dooky said.

Nana frowned at the three of them. "How you boys expect to sit and watch a movie with your privates itchin' like that?"

"Cause they just nasty!" Tammy answered.

"Hush Tammy!" Nana yelled. "I just came back from the pharmacy and got yall boys something to put on that itch." She held up the brown paper bag for them to see. "It will only take a minute so c'mon back inside."

They all went back inside and nana gave the boys fresh towels and instructions on how to use the razor and the cream. One by one they went in the bathroom to handle their business.

Nana pulled Tammy into her room and pulled out another paper bag.

"Chile, there ain't no reason for you to be walkin' round here with your breath smelling like that. Now you take this floss and make sure there ain't no food stuck in your teeth, and wash your mouth out with this Listerine after you brush... twice a day."

Tammy cupped her hand over her mouth and nose trying to see if her breath was stink. It didn't stink to her, so she blew her breath in Nana's face then asked, "Nana you sure it was me you was smelling?"

Nana got mad, "What you trying to do chile, burn my face up? Take this and do what I say!" Nana passed Tammy the bag.

Embarrassed, Tammy went to her room and slammed the door. Nana looked up to the Lord when she said, "*Please help these chirren.*"

Chapter Seven

Don't Hate The Playa

The three of them got in the car. World was riding shotgun and Doug was in the backseat.

"Ayo," Dooky said adjusting the seat back almost sitting in Doug's lap. "Yall wanna go by the nigga FrankMike's house first?"

"We can see if he's out front, but I ain't finned to ring the niggas bell son," World said as he tried to find a station.

They drove in front of FrankMike's house, but no one was outside. The house was built like a brownstone and FrankMike spent most of his time sitting on the steps.

"Blow the horn right quick." World instructed.

Dooky went crazy on the horn like an impatient cab driver. Several people in other houses looked out of their windows. World looked to his right to see if his mother was curious enough to look out of her window. He was relieved when he didn't see her.

"Chill wit the horn nigga!" World said pushing Dooky's hand. "Fuck you tryna do, make the whole block come out?"

Dooky was about to say something slick until he saw FrankMike appear in the window. "There he go." Dooky pointed and waved at him to come outside. FrankMike looked at Dooky confused until World leaned over and showed his face.

"When he comes out let me do all of the talking." World instructed. "You just chill."

"Whatever," Dooky said leaning back into his seat.

FrankMike stepped out of his house and stopped far enough away from the car just in case this wasn't a friendly visit. He was an averaged looking white boy, just a lot more raggedy. Stringy brown hair that almost covered his eyes, long crooked nose that must've been broken one too many times, his clothing was outdated by at least 3 years and his body was tall and slinky almost frail. He kind of looked like "Shaggy" from Scooby Doo. But nevertheless, FrankMike's family had money. At least the BMW and Mercedes that was parked in the driveway suggested it.

FrankMike looked into the driver's side window at an unsmiling Dooky.

"What up nigga?" Dooky said straight-faced.

"Er... Ah... How's it going?" FrankMike responded.

"Fuck happened to your teeth?" Dooky asked, noticing how fucked up and rotten his teeth looked.

World interrupted, "Yo FrankMike, come on this side so I can ask you something." World had known FrankMike for a long time. He was one of the first people he met when he moved onto the block. Frank smiled as he approached the passenger's side window, and World had never noticed how fucked up his teeth were until today.

"What up Frank?" World greeted. "Listen, my boy here...," pointing at Dooky, "got some crack... you interested?"
FrankMike looked at the unsmiling Dooky, then he glanced at Doug who was staring off into space. "How many does he have?" He whispered.

'That depends." World said. "How much you spending?"

FrankMike's pants were so tight that he struggled to get his hand in his pocket. "I got fourteen dollars."

"I will give you three for fourteen." World offered.

Dooky hit World with an elbow.

"Chill!" World shot back. "This is my boy."

Dooky let out a sigh as World gave FrankMike the three vials of crack. FrankMike quickly disappeared as if he thought World would change his mind and none of them saw where he went.

"Fuck he go that fast?" Dooky said looking around the area, then opening the car door and looking under the car.

"Beam me up Scotty," Doug joked. "That nigga went up to '*The Starship Enterprise*'."

Dooky was making a U-turn when he looked and saw World smiling and counting the money he had gotten from FrankMike.

"You's a silly ass nigga World! Three for fourteen dollars?"

"Why you always trippin'," World said only counting twelve singles. "I looked out for him dat all. Now stop at the store so I can buy some beer."

The three of them rode to the 24 hr. Arab store a few blocks over. Dooky parked in front of the store and World jumped out and went inside. It was almost 6 pm and it was still kind of quiet around the store. Dooky was trying to call World and tell him to pick up some cigars and some loose cigarettes but World was already inside. Dooky got out of the car to go into the store, and Old Man Walt appeared out of nowhere and startled him.

"Dooky Dook, my man fifty grand pots and pans..." Walt sang. "... How's my favorite mack daddy wit fifty ho's and fifty caddies? Peppermint Patty daddy waasuup youngin?"

"What up Walt, Ayo, where the fuck you just come from yo?"

"You see me, I'm here, I'm there, I'm everywhere Dooky Dook."

Walt was one of the older players that probably had a good run in his younger day. But he eventually got played by the game he once embraced. Walt had a million stories that Dooky enjoyed listening to. All of that old school pimps and hustlers, ho's and gangster shit... had Dooky amazed. That was the life Walt claimed before he became a full-time dope fiend. Walt was the one that told Dooky the story about Get Mines to Me.

But Walt was all washed up now and looking bad so Dooky didn't come talk to him as much as he used to. It seemed that any drug of choice was Walt's choice now. He was real dirty and dusty and no matter the weather, he kept his long dirty coat on. Dooky guessed that Walt had to be at least fifty but he was only 41. He was really, really dark with green eyes. His eyes made him look like an alien. His beard was thick and un-groomed and his long dusty trench coat made people cross the street to avoid him.

Dooky gave Walt some dap and headed towards the store.

"Ah Dooky Dook booty, if I had your hand, I'd cut mines off." Walt jived, "Let me get a couple of dollars b'fore them ho's get ya."

"Walt Shaker your boy is fucked up right now, I ain't got it," Dooky said.

"C'mon mannn, don't do Ol' Walt Shaker like that Dook booty... help a brother from another mother."

That's when the light went on in Dooky's head. He thought that Walt might be able to help them sell some of the crack they had. Of course crack heads know other crack heads.

"Yo Walt, check it, I got a couple of vials of some good crack I'm trying to sell, maybe you can help a brother out and find me some customers."

Dooky watched Walt's facial expression brighten and Walt did what appeared to be a tap dance routine before he answered.

"You know Walt Shaker already know where to go Dook booty. How many of them do you got, and you gotta give ol' Walt a sample right 'o' right?"

"297 vials," Dooky said, "and ain't none of them samples."

"That's all?" Walt said. "I thought you were gonna say a bigger number youngin. Walt Shaker can move that for you in a heartbeat daddy o."

"That's what I wanna hear Walt, so we gonna do business right?"

"Ah Dooky Dook booty, it won't take but a minute. All I gotta do is go see the white boy over there in the building. He parties all the time."

Walt pointed to the building diagonally across the street from the store. Dooky got excited.

This was going to be easier than he expected. He was already spending the money in his mind.

"Yo, hold on Walt, wait here, let me run in the store right quick."

Walt did that tap dance step again. "Dooky Dooook, I'll be right here, right here baby."

Dooky stepped into the store just as the Arab man behind the counter was putting World's two beers in a bag.

"Yo Ay-Rab, give him a box of cigars and four loosies," Dooky said.

The Arab man looked at World for confirmation before putting the four loose cigarettes on the counter. He reached for a box of White Owl cigars.

"Nah man!" Dooky said. "I want Dutch Masters."

"We doonut have Dutch Master...," the Arab said. "... You take the White Owl."

"How the fuck you gonna tell me what I gotta take?" Dooky said raising his voice then turning to World. "You hear this shit?!" Dooky continued, "If you don't have Dutches then give me a box of Phillies."

The Arab man got offended. He did not like blacks. He felt that they were all undesirables and a disrespectful race that could not come together and lived beyond their means. He had noticed Dooky in front of his store conversing with Walt who had constantly tried to steal from his store. He knew Walt was on drugs and he considered most blacks to be anything but honest. So he automatically associated, by the contents of their purchase. World, Dooky and Walt as “Two Peas in a Pod”.

“We only have White Owl! You take White Owl or get thee fook outta my store muddafuk!”

Dooky laughed. He knew the Arab man didn’t like black people so he always gave the man a hard time.

“Fook you too muddafuk! Gimmie the White Owl!”

World and Dooky laughed as they walked out of the store. They heard the Arab call them crack heads as they exited which made the both of them laugh harder.

Outside the store Walt was still doing his dance when Dooky told him to get in the back. World looked at Dooky strangely but Dooky ignored him.

World had seen Walt plenty of times but had never once spoke to him. Doug saw that Walt was getting in the car and he moved closer to the window. When they were all seated in the car the first thing they noticed was Walt's body odor.

World rolled down his window then looked at Walt like he had dog shit on his face. Dooky ignored the smell.

"Listen yall, Walt Shaker is gonna help us get rid of these vials. He's gonna take us over to this white boy who's gonna buy them all."

World turned around and looked at Walt, then he looked at Dooky and laughed. "Yeah right," World said.

Doug said nothing; he just shook his head and stared out of the window.

"What's wrong with yall silly ass niggas? Walt, tell my partners what you just told me... tell them about the white boy in the building."

"Well," Walt began, shifting in his seat "you see, this whitey white bread that I'm talkin about, you see, his daddy is a big suit that owns a lot of these banks here in these parts... you see, and little whitey white bread done went out and caught himself a crack habit. But you see, he ain't got a problem buyin' it all, cause you see they don't call him whitey white bread cause he's broke. But you see Dooky Dook booty, I can't bring you youngbloods up there with me cause whitey ain't gonna let you cats in there with all that money he sittin' on."

"But!" World said, "He gonna let your dirty old ass inside right?" World hissed.

"Now you see, youngin ya just run ya mouth too much without thinking. What's wrong with ya partner Dook?" Walt looked from World to Dooky. "You see, I knows the whitey since he was a snot nose cause I knows his daddy."

Walt tried to reach behind him to adjust his drawers that was wedged in his ass. "You see, I'm tryna do yall youngins a favor you see... Dooky," Walt said, "why ya partner here wanna be a ball-breaker to old Walt Shaker? All I'm tryna do is help my boy Dooky, Dook booty dat all..." Walt looked at World, "You don't trust Walt Shaker?"

"Fuck naw!" World said heated.

"Chill the fuck out World...," Dooky cut in, "He gonna help us."

"I know you ain't stupid enough to believe this nigga and his fish story," World said in disbelief.

"Walt ain't gonna do me like dat."

"Yeah oh kay?" World said pulling out his 40 oz. bottle of Old English 800. "Whatever you say son... tap this." World put the bottle in front of Dooky and Dooky tapped it on the bottom of the bottle. Then World extended the bottle towards Doug and Doug tapped the bottom too. Walt reached and tried to tap the bottom and World moved the bottle away. "You ain't gottaa tap it...," World said to Walt. "...You ain't getting none." World opened his door and poured a little beer on the ground before taking a long gulp. "Alright then...," World said, "...let's get it jumpin'."

"Gimmie the rest of your vials," Dooky said to World.

"What!!!?? For what? Man fuck that! I don't need no help son," World said. "Give the nigga your shit," World said before taking another long gulp.

Dooky looked at World like he was embarrassing him. "You such a silly ass nigga you know that?" Dooky said, "Just a minute ago, you was bitchin about not being a drug dealer."

"Whatever," World replied.

Dooky wasn't even upset. "What about you Doug?"

Doug hadn't said much of anything since leaving FrankMike's house. He had other shit on his mind but he had heard everything the dirty old man had said and he didn't trust him either. Plus the old man smelled like he slept in a dumpster, and here he is trying to make them believe that he knew a white boy that had all this money.

"For real Dook...," Doug said speaking up for the first time in the whole conversation. "...It kind of sounds like some fish market shit to me. I would rather go see them Portuguese niggas."

"Ah man later for yall two silly niggas!" Dooky said frustrated and tired of trying to convince his partners. "Here Walt," he said passing Walt a sock containing the 171 crack vials. "I'm gonna be parked right here, go do your thing..."

"You about a dumb ass nigga!" World said as he shook his head in disagreement.

"We'll see who's dumb you silly ass nigga...," Dooky said trying not to let World get to him. "How long you gonna be Walt?"

"Dooky Dook Booty, dig what I'm sayin..." Walt sang as he put the sock in his inside pocket. "Why don't you slide me some change so I can page Whitey and let him know that I'm on my way."

Dooky gave Walt some change and Walt got out of the car. There was a pay phone less than two feet from where they were parked, and Walt jumped right on it and did a dance as he picked up the receiver. They all heard Walt finger fucking the phone and pressing numbers before he hung up. Walt started dancing again and World said he looked like a smoked out James Brown.

World's comment broke the tension in the car just as the pay phone began to ring. Walt picked it up on the second ring.

"Walt Shaker... Yeah it's me the one and only... anyone else gotta be a phony... Wassup Daddy O??... Right on, right on." He continued to babble a little while longer before the three of them heard him say, "listen, I'm right outside with three heavyweight players and they got it good... straight from the fields in Columbia." Walt looked at Dooky and winked, then he started dancing again. As he spoke into the receiver beads of sweat formed on his head. "MMMHMMM... you know that Daddy O. No, no! I'm not gonna bring nobody up, I got you. How's ya old man?... Right on, right on. Okay sit tight, I'm on my way...," he said as he put the receiver back into it's cradle and sticking his face through World's window. "It's all set baby," he said to anyone who was listening. "You already know Walt Shaker is a move maker."

World gave Walt a "*get the fuck outta my face*" look, and Walt moved to the backseat window. Walt looked at Doug. He had peeped Doug studying him while he was on the phone. His first thoughts when he saw Doug was, "*Square as a flag, queer as a fag.*" He turned his attentions to Dooky who was looking anxious.

"What that cracker nigga say?" Dooky questioned.

"Dooky Dook boo - tay," Walt sang. "You know youngin...," Walt said examining Dooky's face. "You look like my baby pictures. If you ain't no yo daddy, I would ask you who yo mama is." Walt laughed. He was the only one who thought his joke was funny.

"Man fuck all that!" Dooky said getting angry at Walt, "Tell me what that cracker nigga said!"

Walt jumped back and threw up his hands like he was blocking punches. "Hold on Dook Booty baby, calm yo nerves. You already know that Walt Shaker is a move maker!" Walt sang. "Whitey asked if yall had $20 rocks? So we are gonna double up on whitey with these here." Walt said tapping his inside pocket.

"Dat's what I'm tawking about... yeah!" Dooky said with excitement. "You da man Walt."

"You know Walt Shaker ain't no undertaker... Dooky Dook Booty."

World had been quietly watching and listening to Walt while he spoke into the receiver. He was surprised when the phone actually rang and then, after hearing him tell Dooky that he was gonna sell the vials for twenty dollars a piece made him want to be a part of the movement. Maybe Dooky was right. Maybe this dirty old stinkin' mafucka had some potential after all. Fronting like he didn't give a fuck about what he just heard.

World said, "Ahiight old head, I got 97 more to put with the shit Dooky gave you."

"Listen to the ball-breaker...," Walt sang while looking at Dooky. "...Now, he respectin' Walt Shaker."

"Don't get it twisted...". World shot back with the quickness. "I respect your hustle dat all." World was beginning to feel the effects of the beer that he had yet to pass to anybody. "You want this shit or not?" He said as he passed Walt a crunchy cheese doodle bag containing the 97 vials.

Doug had heard and observed everything as well. Still, his gut told him not to trust Walt. But if he was wrong about his feeling then he would miss out on the opportunity to double up. Greed got the best of him. "Fuck it yo...," Doug announced. "...I got a hundred." Doug reached in his pants, down towards his crotch area and pulled out a winter hat containing the drugs. He passed the hat to Walt. Walt smiled, and Doug's instinct told him to snatch his shit back but he ignored it.

Walt put the sock and the cheese doodle bag inside the hat. "Walt Shaker is gonna walk to the building right there..." He said pointing diagonally across the street. "Yall sit tight, I ain't gonna be but ten - fifteen minutes." Then we can talk about whatcha gonna give Walt Shaker for being ya money maker." Walt sang.

"Make sure you count dat money!" Dooky said as they watched Walt walk to the building. Walt pressed a buzzer and seconds later he was buzzed in.

"Yo, we should follow dat old nigga," Doug said.

"Word up!" World concurred.

"I got a funny feeling about this cat," Doug added as he watched the building.

"Ah man, yall niggas is worrying about nothing," Dooky pronounced. "Walt ain't like that." Dooky was silently hoping that he was right about Walt.

He watched Walt disappear into the building and shortly thereafter he saw a lady poke her head out of the building's entrance, then disappeared back inside. From the distance Dooky thought that the lady looked familiar, almost like the crack head that jumped out of his car last night. He disregarded his thought and turned his attention to Doug.

"Yo Doug... how you just gonna have my hat all in your nasty ass nuts like that? I'm sayin, I don't want it back now... but I used to sleep in that hat yo."

"My bad yo," Doug said. "I'll get you another hat... I just needed something to put the drugs in, dat all."

"I ain't sweatin it like dat...," Dooky said. "It's just the principle... yall niggas act like yall ain't got none... but anyway...," Dooky continued directing his words towards World, "I'm just glad that you two silly niggas came to your senses," he said extending his hand towards World's beer, "...cause this is easy money."

World passed him what was left in the bottle which wasn't much, "Ayo, where you know this old nigga from?"

"Who?... Walt? Ah man...," Dooky said. "Me and Walt go way back from when I used to buy guns from him."

World looked at Doug who just hunched his shoulders and gave him the "*don't ask me look.*"

"Nigga!" World said. "Stop lying! When did you buy a gun from him? You don't even have no gun!"

"That's how much you know silly ass nigga!" Dooky shot back. "And for your information I was talkin about way, way back in the days... before I met you, when I was livin' in Harlem." Dooky lied.

"In Harlem?" World laughed uncontrollably. "So you was selling guns when you was nine nigga?"

Dooky looked in the rearview mirror and saw that Doug was laughing too. "Man fuck yall silly ass niggas!"

Dooky drained the rest of the beer out of the bottle then passed it to Doug. Dooky broke open one of the cigars and passed it to World for him to dump the insides out of his window. World looked up to see the Arab man inside the store making faces and giving him the middle finger. Dooky rolled the blunt then closed all of the windows in the car. They did the "puff, puff, pass" until the entire blunt was gone. The three of them were high as kites, and World was sipping on his second beer when he said "Yo, what the fuck is taking that nigga so long?"

Doug added, "He been gone like 30 minutes yo."

Dooky gave no reply, he hadn't realized how long Walt had been gone until World said something. Dooky jumped out of the car releasing a cloud of smoke as he ran across the street dodging cars and making his way towards the building. What seemed like a beautiful day was becoming dark and gloomy. When he reached the building's entrance his eyes searched the intercom trying to distinguish any names that sounded Caucasian. There were only two Jacksons, a Brown, Taylor, Jones, James and an Abdul. The other slots were nameless and Dooky's stomach began to turn.

World and Doug strolled over to where he was standing. "Fuck is this old nigga at?" World asked, both angry and drunk which was a recipe for trouble. "I said... where the fuck is ya man at Dooky?!" World repeated.

Dooky was speechless. His mind was spinning in different directions, at the same time. He was hoping to see Walt appear from somewhere holding a pot of gold. But the knot in his stomach was telling him that he would need "Bob Hope" and his whole family if he wanted to find Walt tonight.

Doug read the names on the intercom and pushed three buzzers. Seconds later, without asking who was buzzing, someone buzzed them in the building. It was a four-story building without an elevator. Although from the outside, the property was well kept, the inside looked like it was hit by a tornado. The stairway stunk of urine and something empty, while the walls were decorated with graffiti. There were beer bottles and soda cans on the floor next to a couple of empty condom wrappers. The three of them went to every floor putting their ears to the doors looking and listening for Walt. They walked from the lobby to the roof then back down to the lobby. There was no sign of Walt and they all knew without saying that they had been beat. There was no way that a white dude with money would live here.

Doug walked down the hallway. "Ayo yo, come see this shit," he said pointing to the backdoor. Way in the back of the hallway was a door that led to the back alley of the building. The narrow walkway was littered with trash filled garbage bags on top of trash filled cans, which gave the narrow walkway a suffocating stench. As they stepped out into the alley, a few rats that were hard at work eating through bags of garbage stopped and looked at the trio as if they expected a handout. Realizing they were being ignored, the rodents went back to eating trash.

"Fuck!..." World said raising his voice suddenly conscious of the situation"... I knew that dirty motherfucka wasn't no good!" Doug had walked further down the alley examining a "cut-through" path that leads to the next block over. "He most likely went through here," Doug pronounced what they already knew. "We might still be able to catch him if we..."

"We ain't catching that motherfucka!" World said as he picked up the sock and the crunchy cheese doodle bag off the ground. "That nigga probably done smoked his way to west bubblefuck!"

“Let’s just take a ride and see,” Doug said trying to stay hopeful.

“Nigga! That nigga gone!” World said taking a step closer to Dooky and putting a finger in his face. “This nigga... Mr. I bought guns from him in Harlem...,” World sang in a girly voice “...done fucked us up again!”

“Fuck you nigga!” Dooky yelled, getting angry and smacking World’s hand from in front of his face. “If it wasn’t for me... you silly ass motherfucka... you wouldn’t have had shit!”

“Fuck you mean...??” World screamed in a drunken stupor. “...If it wasn’t for you...,” he said putting his hand back in Dooky’s face, “...we would’ve had shit!”

“Whatever nigga,” Dooky said lightly moving World’s hand away from his face. “You drunk.”

“I’m drunk??... I’m drunk??...” World screamed as he jumped up and down becoming overly excited. “...I ain’t drunk nigga!! Ya motherfuckin man talkin’ ‘bout you’s my baby picture Doo - kay, if you ain’t no’d yo daddy I’d ask you who yo mammy is Dooky Dooky Dooky Dooky Dook Booty!” World said imitating Walt’s voice. “That nigga dooked you in your booty nigga!!”

Dooky had been making his way out of the building when World made his last statement. He turned around in the lobby, facing World with his eyebrows raised. "What the fuck you just say nigga?" World had missed the threat in his tone, plus he was angry and drunk and really didn't give a fuck. He was frustrated that he had allowed Dooky to persuade his decision.

"You heard what I said the first time nigga! That nigga dooked you in your ass!" World yelled and threw the sock and the cheese doodle bag hitting Dooky in the face.

Dooky swung a hard right, striking World on top of the forehead. World took a stumbled step back then charged him like a bull. Doug tried to step in and break them up without holding just one of them, but he saw that World was about to get the best of Dooky so he stepped back. "*Justice*," he thought to himself.

World was bigger and stronger than Dooky, who was trying his hardest to get the drunken maniac off of him. But as hard as he tried, he was no match for the powerful World and his grappling ability. World had Dooky pinned to the floor. "AAAAGH!" World screamed like a caveman as he threw a barrage of jackhammer style punches at Dooky's head and face.

Dooky was trying to curl up like a shrimp and cover his face with his arms when World screamed and started his flurry. A few punches caught him flush and almost put him out, but he was able to get his defense up and block most of the punishment. Dooky unconsciously let out a silent fart. He was more angry than scared, but fear did have a temporary grip on him from trying to fight from the floor against the heavier, drunken World. But anything that fear had on him was used as fuel as he used every bit of strength that he had to get from underneath World and his jackhammer punches. Dooky grunted and roared like a lion "RRRRAAAAHHH!" as he came out from under World's assault and sprang to his feet.

World jumped to his feet just as quickly "AHH...AAHH... Yeah nigga whut!" he yelled. Spit flying out of his mouth looking like a madman, "you want some more? Cause I got some more pounding for that pussy!"

Doug had seen enough and stepped in between his two partners. "Yall niggas buggin man! Chill the fuck out wit the dumb shit and let's get the fuck outta here b'for somebody call 5 - OH."

Dooky was wiping off his clothes and checking his face for traces of blood while staring at World with anger in his eyes. World was standing opposite of him huffing and puffing while making strange animal sounds.

"Ain't nothing between us but air and fear," World spat.

Doug was still standing in between them with his arms stretched out like a referee. "Chill yall! Why don't yall niggas chill?!" Doug pleaded.

"Get the fuck outta the way Doug!" Dooky said reaching into his front pocket. "You wanna pop nigga?!" He said pointing at World with one hand and pulling something out of his pocket with the other. He put the hand that he pulled out of his pocket behind his back, "Let's get it then you homo-fag motherfucker!"

"Nah Dooky," Doug said getting scared. "Don't go there, it's over. It ain't that serious."

"Get... the... fuck... outta... the... way... Doug!" Dooky demanded coldly as he stepped closer to World with his hand behind his back. "What up?... Don't get scared now nigga! I told you earlier about putting your hands on me!"

World took two steps back as Dooky approached. He saw when Dooky went in his pocket and he caught a glimpse of something silver when he put his hand behind his back.

“You wanna play wit razors Dook?” World said reaching into his own pocket. “You scared to go wit the hands nigga?” he said as he pulled something out of his pocket and put his hand behind him. “You wanna cut mafucka?”... then let’s cut nigga!!”

Dooky peeped World pull out the shiny object and hide it behind his back, “Move Doug!” World said menacingly “Lets dance Dooky... what up nigga? I told you about pulling out razors, now I got something for yo ass...” World screamed like a psycho. “I got something for yo AAASSS!”

Dooky suddenly jumped at World startling him with a pump-fake of his hands and shoulders, causing World to jump backward like a scared cat.

World regained his composure. He stared at Dooky and nodded his head with a menacing smile. He burst towards Dooky growling like a German Shepard, pump-faking his head and shoulders as if he was having a seizure, causing Dooky to defensively jump backwards.

Doug stepped out of the way and watched the two of them fake each other about three more times before he said something.

"Why don't yall niggas stop frontin' and let's get the fuck outta here before somebody call 5-OH! Dooky, you know you still got all that weed in your pocket... if the police come running in here..."

"Fuck that!" Dooky said giving World another pump-fake. "I'm gonna cut this nigga!"

World jumped back a step, "C'mon wit it son..." he said giving Dooky a pump fake. "I got something for that ass!"

Doug got mad. He was getting fed up with the nonsense. Besides he knew that both of them were frontin'. At first he was nervous, worrying that the situation was getting out of hand. Then he noticed that Dooky's weapon was nothing but a cigarette lighter and World didn't have anything but a house key in his hand. "Dooky, put the lighter back in your pocket...," Doug said before turning to face World, "And you, put your fuckin' house keys away and lets go b'fore 5-OH come!"

Doug turned to leave. At this point he didn't care if they stayed there or not, he was outta there. He couldn't take a chance hanging around causing a disturbance not knowing what his grandmother had told the police about him. He was not trying to spend the night in booking, "I'm out! Yall niggas can stay and bullshit all yall want," he said as he left the building leaving them behind.

Dooky and World pump faked each other one more time before they both slipped their phony weapons back into their pockets. Dooky left the building with World following a few safe steps behind him.

Doug was casually standing out front when Dooky stepped out brushing off his clothes. "Yo...," Doug said looking around to see if the cops were coming. "Let's jus take a ride around the hood...," he said as he looked up and down the street. "...We might get lucky and run into the nigga."

World stepped out and stood next to Doug keeping his eye on Dooky. He didn't think that his bout with Dooky was over and he wasn't about to get caught slippin' and hit with a sucker punch. "I'm telling you Doug," he said catching the end of Doug's statement, "that nigga Walt ain't gonna be nowhere to be found." He looked over at Dooky who was still cleaning himself off, then continued. "That nigga just robbed us for all our shit! And you think he's gonna be chillin somewhere on a corner?? You can't be serious!"

"That nigga gone Doug," Dooky cut in. "But he'll come out sooner or later... and when he does... Whap!" Dooky caught World with a sucker punch that knocked World on his ass. "I told you nigga! Keep ya fuckin' hands off me!"

The blow shocked and embarrassed World more than it hurt him. He was so angry that he let Dooky catch him slippin' that he almost started crying. "I'm gonna kill you nigga!" World said jumping to his feet. Not realizing that his legs were unsteady from the impact of the punch. He tried to charge Dooky who had easily side stepped him and ran into the street laughing, "HAAA HAAA... Fuck you silly ass looking nigga!"
World found an empty bottle and threw it at him. Dooky ducked the bottle and it went crashing in the street. World found another bottle and threw it as Dooky laughed and back-pedaled to the car giving him the middle finger. As World searched for something else to throw, Dooky did a dance with both of his middle fingers in the air before he got into the car and drove away.

Doug stood there and watched. He knew, just as World knew that Dooky was known for the sucker punch. Doug watched as Dooky drove away. He didn't have the strength or the will to try and stop him. He was tired. Tired of all the bullshit at home and with his partners. He was tired of it all. Tired of being tired. He needed more and couldn't continue living his life like this. He had plans but he didn't have any support. His mother abandoned him and his grandmother hated him. Dooky and World just didn't know how good they had it. They both had family that loved, cared and supported them. They had a home that was filled with love and peace and here they are running the streets and taking it all for granted. Doug was envious. He wished he had what they had because they didn't deserve it. He did, and right now he wished that he could go home. Doug felt like killing Walt. Walt didn't just take 297 vials of crack cocaine; Walt stole the opportunity for Doug to get on his feet. Doug stood there with nowhere to go looking at World. If World wanted to, he could just say, "*fuck it*" and go on home.

Doug had nowhere to go though. He was stuck between a rock and a hard place. His plan had been to sleepover at Dooky's house and see how his grandmother was feeling in the morning. But Dooky just pulled off and it wasn't no telling if he was coming back or not. If worse came to worse he always had a place to stay on the subway, where he had spent plenty of nights riding from 241st to New Lots Ave or from Dyer to Ralph, but he just wasn't up to it tonight. He would rather spend the night in jail. *He would have to think of something*, he thought, taking a glance at World. They was cool but, He wasn't about to ask World if he could spend a night at his house... they wasn't that cool.

"What now?"

"What now... What?" World answered looking at him skeptically.

Doug hadn't realized he said that out loud.

"What now what?" World repeated then answered. "I'll tell you what I'm about to do now...," he said reaching into his pockets and pulling out his money. "I'm about to go across the street and buy me another beer."

Doug was about to follow World across the street when Dooky came speeding out of nowhere running them back onto the sidewalk. He had the music blasting as he drove past with his middle finger in the window.

"He's a fuckin' dickhead!" World stated as they watched him drive past. World stepped out into the street, grabbed his crotch and pumped it a few times while returning his middle finger to the back of his car. "Fuck dat nigga!" World said, "Let's go to the store."

After coming out of the store, purchasing two more 40 oz.'s they saw that Dooky was parked and waiting for them. He got outta the car and approached them. World put his beers down on the ground and put his two fists up like a boxer.

"What up?" He said straight-faced. "Round three? You ain't faze me son... you hit like a bitch!"
"You right, silly nigga," Dooky chuckled. "You right."

"Yeah, I know I'm right!" World said pointing in Dooky's face. "You don't want none of this! Straight up! I... will... fuck... you... up... Dooky! We can finish this right... now!"

Doug stepped in between them, "World chill... the shit is dead," he pleaded.

"Man fuck this nigga!" World said picking up his beers. This mafucka fucked everything up son!"

Dooky took a seat on the hood of the car and didn't respond to any of World's insults or complaints. He had taken a razor out of the glove compartment and had it palmed in his hand. If World made any attempts to do anything stupid, he was going to regret it. Dooky just sat there waiting; he smiled at World.

"Man fuck it! Fuck that shit World, it's done! It's over! Forget about it... just forget about it," Doug said.

"Ah nigga fuck you talkin about?" World said addressing Doug. "You always talkin' that peacemaker bullshit! Fuck you want, a peace prize? Just shut the fuck up cause nobody's talkin to you nigga!"

"You know what?" Doug said. "You right! You absolutely right! Yall niggas wanna kill each other? Go ahead, don't let me stop you or get in the way, I'm out!"

Doug turned and started walking up the block towards 3rd Street and neither World nor Dooky tried to stop him as he walked away.

Dooky was still sitting on the hood of the car smiling at World. He was just about to try and break the tension between them so they can catch up with Doug and move on when World spoke.

"You know what? I don't even wanna be around yo punk ass!"

"Silly ass nigga, you act like I'm holding your feet or something!"

"You right, you right Dook Booty. Fuck you nigga... I'm out!"
World started walking in the opposite direction of his house and Dooky mumbled, "fuck wrong wit his silly ass?"

He got back into the car and put the razor back in the glove compartment. He pulled another cigar out of the pack and quickly rolled another blunt. He started the car and drove in the direction Doug was walking. He caught up to Doug and slowed down beside him.

"Yo Loafer, come smoke this blunt with me yo," he yelled from inside of the car.

"Nah yo, I'm good."

"C'mon son, I hate smokin alone my nigga."

"I'm good yo," Doug said as he continued to walk. "I don't want none."

"Ahiight then, get in and ride wit me yo, let's go to Harlem and fuck wit some bitches or something. Or yo, I got a $20 bill, you can take a corner and I'll take a corner and we can fuck wit some ho's," Dooky said as he drove next to Doug at a snail's pace.

"Nah, I'm straight," Doug said never looking in Dooky's direction. "I ain't in the mood for none of that t'night."

"I'm saying Loafer, fuck is up?" Dooky said while stepping on the brakes. "You don't wanna chill wit a nigga?"

"I'm sayin yo," Doug retorted turning his head in Dooky's direction. Cars were driving around Dooky who had just about parked in the middle of the street. As other drivers went by, they were laying on their horns and shouting profanities.

"I ain't in the mood for none of that t'night, I'm just gonna stroll and clear my head."

"You ain't in the mood?" Dooky questioned with a shocked expression. "Stop the bullshit Doug and let's be out!" Dooky lifted the blunt and put it to his lips. "You got me driving next to you and trying to get you in the car like you're a cutie with a fat ass or something!"

Doug let out a loud sigh because he really didn't want to be bothered. "All you gotta do is step on the gas Dooky," Doug said calmly as he continued to walk up the block. "I already told you that I wasn't going."

"Say no more silly nigga!" is all Dooky said before he sped off.

Chapter Eight

If It Ain't Rough...

Doug watched the taillights of the Reliant-K car until they disappeared as he continued his trek up 3rd Street towards Mount Vernon's Southside. Being only four square miles, everything in Mount Vernon was in walking distance. It was a majority middle-class residential city and at such a small size it was easy to become familiar with its residents. But the Southside, which held most of the town's projects and tenements, was like the hood within the hood. But Doug didn't feel out of place. Although from his attire one would think that he wandered off of some Ivy League college campus and got lost. What they couldn't see was that Doug had problems.

He had nowhere to go and nowhere to be. The only people who were probably looking for him right now were the police. He was just walking with no destination looking and listening. Cars were zooming past him and his ears caught snippets of music, laughter and pieces of conversations as they drove by. He was passing a building where a bunch of dirty little kids were playing "Johnny on the Pony". He slowed down and watched as one of the rug rats ran and dived on the backs of the others trying to break the pony. He silently applauded when the pony didn't break, because deep inside he felt just like that pony. There were a few attractive older women that Doug hadn't noticed at first sitting on the front steps. Doug assumed that these were the parents. There were no men out on the steps with them so Doug thought it would be safe to give the women a courtesy nod. When he received no sign of acknowledgement Doug guessed that perhaps these women had x-ray vision and was able to see that the only things in his pockets were his keys and his bus pass, which made him invisible.

Doug wasn't the least bit affected by the treatment they gave him. He learned a long time ago that you can't charm them all. He walked into the next block and stopped in front of the Chinese take-out. He looked inside and saw that it was jam packed with black people. "*Don't nobody wanna cook,*" he thought. Doug loved to cook which is one of the reasons why he hardly ever spent his money on fast food, and if he did it certainly wouldn't be on Chinese. For one, he could never figure out what General Tso's chicken was. It didn't look like any chicken he had ever seen or cooked. And for two, he knew that Chinese people didn't spend their money on soul food. In fact, he didn't think they spent their dollar with anyone else - besides whites and their own kind. And what they spent with white people was simply out of necessity. So if

Doug was to spend his dollar with them that dollar would be forever gone from his people and community. With the amount of Chinese take-outs that's in his neighborhood, there was no need to wonder why all the mom and pop businesses were gone. Black folks just won't support their own. Doug had dreams of opening his own fish & chip restaurant one day. He liked the way "Sha's JackMack Palace" was set up, but that required the one thing he didn't have... money. He didn't even have a job, worse than that he might even be homeless. "*What the fuck am I gonna do?*" he thought.

The sight of a pretty light skinned female walking towards him interrupted his thoughts. She was wearing a pair of navy blue spandex and the outline of her shapely, stacked ass could be seen from the front of her body. As they approached each other, Doug greeted her "Hey wassup boo..." He charmed as if they were familiar. "Long time no see," he said pausing for conversation. The girl kept her pace and strolled right past him with a "*I don't know you look*" on her face.

"Oh, it's like that now?" Doug said watching her ass as she passed him. "You just gonna walk right past the good brother like you don't know him huh?"

His comment caught her attention and she stopped and looked at Doug for some kind of recognition. "Where I know you from?" she asked, as she looked him up and down.

Doug peeped her checkin' him out and he was glad that he had on the brown Polo sweater that matched his loafers. He just hoped that shorty didn't have x-ray vision. "That's kind of painful to know that I am not worthy of a fragment of your memory..." Doug charmed trying his best to sound like his favorite character from his "*Gentleman Jim*" novels. "I thought we had a connection but obviously I was wrong."

She looked at Doug puzzled and Doug continued, "You don't remember for real?" He paused, "Wow, I met you at that party!" He lied. "Remember?... those knuckleheads started shooting inside and we ran outside together and started talking? You gave me your phone number before you left and I must have misplaced it, but fate is truly a blessing sometimes because I was surely hoping to run into you again." Doug stepped a little closer into her personal space and hoped that his line about the party worked. *This chick is fine as hell*, he thought, as he was about to touch her hand.

She looked at Doug strangely and backed away from him before she spoke. "I'm very sorry young man, but it's obvious that you have me mixed up with your person of interest. Besides, I never give my number out to strangers. Plus you seem a little too young for me." She gave Doug a smile and was about to turn and walk away. The way she said "too young" sounded like something from the menu in the Chinese restaurant and reminded him that he was hungry, but Doug was determined not to let her get away that easy. Her body was just too bangin'.

"I'm Doug boo... you don't remember Doug?"

"Nah sweetie," she said as she left him standing where he stood and continued on her way.

Doug said a prayer to *Gentleman Jim* and tried to throw the net one last time before he let her go. "Matter of fact," Doug charmed to her back, "you had some other girl with you... I think she said her name was Linda," Doug lied.

The girl stopped, turned around and looked at Doug with a puzzled expression. "I am Linda," she said.

Doug couldn't believe his luck. I got her, he thought to himself as he thanked *Gentleman Jim*. "It was you!" He said happily. How could I have forgotten?"

Linda looked at Doug and could not remember ever seeing him in her life. “This shit is crazy,” she said. “Where was the party at again?” she asked.

“It’s all good,” Doug said switching the subject and spinning the conversation. “I’m saying, let me get that phone number again and I will call you later on this week for a get-together,” Doug charmed.

Against her better judgment, Linda wrote her number down and handed it to him. Doug studied her face and thought that she looked like a better version of Toni Braxton with a way better ass.

They chit-chatted long enough for him to learn that she was single with no kids and she had her own place. Doug was laying his Mack down extra hard trying to convince her that she needed his company for the night, when Squirrel and his two boys - Pat Daddy and Stutter approached him from behind.

“Well...” Linda said embracing Doug with a hug and a peck on the cheek.

“Lemme go, I see your friends are waiting for you,” she said pointing over his shoulder.

Doug turned around to see who she was referring to and immediately got nervous.

"Call me tomorrow sweetie," she said as she smiled and walked away.

Doug, Squirrel, Pat Daddy and Stutter all watched as she switched her ass extra hard making it dance in her spandex.

"Good Lord!" Pat Daddy exclaimed. "She got a brozillic ass son! You see that shit Stutter?"

"Mafuckin right I, I, I see it..." Stutter voiced. "I'll bus, bussa mafuckin ass too!" he stated with his nappy dreadlocks covering his face making him look like "*My Pet Monster*".

"You'll smash dat Stutt?" Pat Daddy asked, clowning. He already knew the answer, but he liked to make the hulkish looking man talk to hear him stutter.

"Mah... mah,.. mahfuckin right!" Stutter said. I'll bussa mah... mah, maahfuckin ass and have the ho... hoo... whole room smelling li, li, liiike shit nigga!"

Pat Daddy started laughing, "You crazy Stutt!"

Doug was silent. He was trying to figure out what they approached him for. When he heard them talking about fuckin' Linda he was relieved because he had thought that she had been one of their ex's or something. He did not want any problems with Squirrel or Stutter and he silently prayed that this was not about the drugs Dooky stole from his house. He had almost forgotten about that. Doug cautiously walked past the three of them, careful not to bump into anyone.

"What up Doug?" Squirrel said, placing a hand on his shoulder to stop him and giving him a rat toothed smile. "Where you headed?"

"I was just going up the way," Doug replied trying to check his nerves into place.

Stutter and Pat Daddy was staring at Doug like he did something wrong. "What up Stutter?" Doug said politely. "What's good Patrick?"

Squirrel and Stutter burst out in laughter when Doug referred to Pat Daddy as Patrick. Pat being eager to impress his two buddies got offended. "My name is Pat Daddy you lame! Pat Mafuckin Daddy!" he said while putting a finger in front of Doug's nose. Doug could not believe how Patrick was fronting on him trying to impress Squirrel and Stutter. He had known Patrick long before all this

"Pat Daddy" shit he was claiming. They went way back to grade school. When Patrick and his mother came to the states from Jamaica they had lived right next door to Doug and his grandmother. He was just plain ol' Patrick Brady and one of Doug's best friends.

"My bad," Doug apologized, refusing to look at Patrick.

"I'm saying Doug...," Squirrel said, suddenly serious. "I was wit Dooky earlier today and he spoke highly of your knuckle game 'n shit..." Squirrel looked at Doug and jacked his slacks, "... I'm saying, I didn't know you even had one of those."

As if on cue, Pat and Stutter started laughing.

"I don't," Doug said, relieved that this was not about drugs. "Dooky was probably trying to be funny... you know, clowning me."

"Yeah, I hear you...". Squirrel said stepping closer to Doug. "I thought that shit was real funny!" His face was inches away from Doug's, eyes cold and empty penetrating the center of Doug's fear. "Especially when he said that he thought that you could whoop my ass!"

Doug's armpits began to perspire, and beads of sweat formed on his forehead. He couldn't believe that even in his absence, Dooky still managed to get him into drama. Doug didn't want any problems and Squirrel was definitely bad news. Doug tried to be as cowardly as possible to avoid any chances of him not walking away from them unscathed.

"Now you know I wouldn't do that to you Squirrel," Doug said apologetically immediately regretting his choice of words.

Pat and Stutter both looked at each other, then at Squirrel and started laughing. Squirrel actually knew what Doug meant, but fed into the instigating laughter from his two cronies.

"Fuck you mean you wouldn't nigga?!" Squirrel said menacingly in a low intimidating tone. "... You couldn't mafucka!"

"You right," Doug said humbly. "You're absolutely right," he said and really meaning it because he really didn't think he could win in a fight against Squirrel. But Pat and Stutter started laughing again making it seem as if he was being sarcastic.

"You's a fuckin comedian, huh homie?" Squirrel said removing his jacket. "A real fuckin funny lil nigga! Let's see how funny this ass whoopin' is gonna feel!"

"This lame thinks you're pussy... SQ," Pat Daddy instigated.

"He think you bun, huhh... huhhnns son!" Stutter added.

"He think I'm buns Stutter?" Squirrel asked directing the question to both Pat and Stutter, then turning his attention back to Doug. "You think I'm pussy Doug?"

"Aw man naw... nah Squirrel. C'mon man," Doug said pleadingly. He could feel the sweat running down the side of his body from armpits. "You know I don't get down like that. These niggas is gassing you for no reason," he said as he pointed a finger at Pat.

"Fuck you pointing at lame?!" Pat Daddy exploded. "You ain't in court anymore." Pat barked implying that Doug was a snitch. Stutter and Squirrel both chuckled. Pat was acting extra tough with Doug and they were starting to take notice.

"C'mon Patrick man," Doug pleaded. "I don't want no problems," he said as he raised his hands in surrender. "What's this all about...?" he said looking at SQ and Stutter. "...Money?" Doug said while putting his hands in both front pockets and pulling them inside out. He looked at Squirrel as he held his hands up holding only his keys and bus pass. "I don't have any money, nothing, y'all can search me."

"I just told your bitch ass that it's Pat Daddy!" He said yelling, stomping his feet and going berserk like a spoiled child. "Get it right nigga!..." He spat mushing Doug in the face. "Pat... motherfuckin... Daddy!"

Doug stumbled backwards temporarily loosing his balance but regaining it before he fell. He stared at Pat and imploded in a deathlike silence.

"What's the matter Patrick?," young Doug asked worried from seeing his friend with tears in his eyes.

"Mi tired of people dem always makin' fun of mi," he sobbed.

Doug knew that kids referred to him as "Peasey Head Patrick" and teased him about his accent but it was nothing to cry about, they teased him too; everybody was being teased. "It's gonna be okay," Doug consoled him. "Don't cry Patrick."

"Doug," Patrick said in between sobs. "Will you help mi get rid of mi accent?" Patrick asked sobbing hysterically. "If I can speak more like you dem maybe dey wan bodda mi so much, seen."

Doug didn't know what to say so he just agreed to help his friend. Five months and one hundred and ten episodes of "What's Happening," later Patrick was running around saying "Hey Hey Hey and Waaasuup" like a true Yankee boy. He was no longer afraid to speak because he sounded like an American.

Occasionally, traces of his accent would resurface especially if he was scared or angry.

A few years ago, Patrick's mother passed away from a slip-and-fall accident due to a wet floor in the hospital where she worked. Pat was withdrawn for a long time. He ended up moving to the Southside to live in the projects with his mother's sister. The hefty compensation they received gave them a new life and Pat made a lot of new friends, which he used his money and materials to buy. The projects were filled with a lot of tougher less fortunate children and they all played Pat for a piece of his pie. Pat bought a brand-new Acura Integra when they first came out. Doug never been inside of the car but had always seen it zipping through the city blocks and if Patrick wasn't crammed up in the back seat, he wasn't in the car. It just disappeared along with the gold rings and jewelry that Pat once sported. Now he was standing here, after just mushin' him in the face, acting like some super thug mother fucker and demanding to be called Pat Daddy.

"Man fuck you Patrick you bitch ass nigga!" Doug exploded. "I don't know why you're trying to impress Squirrel and Stutter but you know, I know you frontin rude boy." He added the "Rude boy" to remind Patrick who he was shittin' on, "And if you put your hands on me again...," Doug let out a frustrated sigh and tried to calm himself with a breathing technique, *Blow out the candles...Doug breathed out... and smell the roses, he breathed in through his nose.*

Squirrel and Stutter were both on the sideline shouting "OOOOH" and laughing trying to instigate a fight. They both knew that Pat was a lame but let him stick around because of the settlement money. But lately Pat had been singing a song about how his aunt had taken control of his money and was giving him allowances and Squirrel was getting annoyed and scheming on ways to rob Pat's aunt.

Pat Daddy looked from Stutter to Squirrel for reassurance and they both gave him the "*don't look at me, what the fuck you gonna do?*" expression.

Pat turned his attention back to Doug trying to look as tough as he could. The face that he was making made him look about as tough as Gary Coleman.

"Who the fuck you think you talkin' to nigga?"

"I'm talkin to you, Patrick Brady!" returning his stare.

The "OOOOH's" coming from Squirrel and Stutter got louder as Doug returned Pat's stare.

"Yo, yo, Pat...," Stutter spoke getting everybody's attention. "...Ayo tuh tuh tell... jah jan and mmm... mmmaaahsher dat I wanna buh, buss day ass!"

Squirrel and Stutter erupted in laughter and Pat was furious. This is just how it used to be when he was young and someone heard his government name. That's why he adopted the moniker Pat Daddy. He refused to be teased. Hook or crook Pat was going to be respected. Infuriated and offended Pat stared at Doug and spat in his Jamaican accent, "Mi guh teach yee sum blood-clod respect!" Pat faked a punch and hurled a kick that caught Doug high on the left shoulder. "I mon a lion!!" Pat hollered faking another punch and launching another kick.

This time Doug was ready and he caught Pat's leg and yanked it causing him to fall on his back. Doug quickly rushed him striking him with numerous unblocked punches to his face. Doug was on top of Pat hitting him and saying his name "Pat" left punch "Daddy" right punch "Pat... Daddy... Pat... Daddy- left... right... left... right..." He was no longer in control of his actions because if he was, he would've stopped a long time ago.

Pat's nose and mouth was busted open and his eye was swollen shut and leaking blood from the corners like red tears. Pat had screamed and cried for help like a little girl as he unsuccessfully tried to block the first four or five punches Doug dropped on him like rainfall. But Pat had been unconscious for at least the last ten to eleven blows that landed flush to the center of his face and the damage being done was alarming.

Squirrel and Stutter stood on the side watching and laughing until Doug knocked Pat out. When they saw that Doug didn't let up they stepped in to break it up. Squirrel grabbed Doug from behind while Stutter pushed him from the front. Doug still not in control of his actions felt himself being grabbed and went wild. Releasing a flurry of kicks and elbows and catching Squirrel with a slanging left elbow to the temple that dropped him to one knee. Stutter saw the elbow that dropped his partner and reached for Doug, grabbing him by his throat and stepping on the still unconscious Pat Daddy. He hit Doug with a right hook to the jaw that sent him crashing to the pavement. The impact from the blow was like a bucket of cold water that brought Doug back to reality. Acknowledging the danger he was in, he sprang to his feet and tried to run. Squirrel grabbed the back of Doug's sweater momentarily stopping his getaway but Doug came right up out of the sweater leaving it in his hands as he ran.

Squirrel and Stutter chased him for a block and a half before accepting that they were wasting their time. "I'm gonna fuck you up when I catch you my nigga!" Squirrel screamed at Doug's back as they gave up the chase.

Doug was in "turbo-mode," hauling ass. He was low to the ground and he never looked back. His loafers were barely touching the ground and at the speed he was running one might mistake him for flying. He had no idea that he was no longer being chased. As he ran the next four blocks full speed like an experienced runner - in fact, as much as he ran you could honestly say that he was an experienced runner.

As he approached his fifth block he saw a car pulling up next to him through his peripheral vision and picked up his pace. Doug was running faster than the car and still picking up speed. He refused to look anywhere but forward as he bolted through block after block like a greyhound.

"Fuck you running so fast for silly ass nigga?" Dooky yelled from inside of the car.

Relieved, Doug finally slowed down and looked behind him. When he saw that no one was chasing him, he came to a complete stop and tried to catch his breath. Dooky pulled over beside him but remained seated in the car staring at him as he dragged in the smoke from a Newport. Doug was bent over with his hands on his knees heaving.

"Where the fuck is yo shirt at silly nigga?"

Doug hadn't even realized that he was bare chested until Dooky said it, but he was still trying to catch his breath and was unable to respond. Moments later after getting himself together, he opened the car door and got inside. He replayed everything that happened to Dooky starting from his conversation with Linda.

Dooky was heated. He made a U-tum and headed back towards the direction of Squirrel and Stutter.

"Where you going yo?" Doug asked nervously, hoping Dooky wasn't going back to try and find his attackers. "Leave it alone man," Doug pleaded.

"Man, fuck that Loafers!" Dooky spat sharply.

"You might be a silly ass nigga but them niggas know you my peoples! They violated! Plus," he added, "I never did like that stuttering muppet baby lookin mafucka!"

All Doug wanted to do was get away from the drama. He was tired of all the physical and mental abuse. His mind was hurting plus every time he spoke his jaw made a clicking sound. He needed to lay down and get some rest. He closed his eyes while he silently cursed his mother for leaving him and prayed that Squirrel and Stutter were nowhere to be found.

Dooky drove around for about an hour looking for the culprits but they were nowhere around. He stopped to get gas then called it a night. When he parked in front of Doug's house it was close to 1 am. Doug saw that his grandmother's light was still on and wondered why she was still up. He definitely wasn't in the mood for any of her shit right now. So he asked Dooky if he could stay over his house tonight.

"Of course you can stay over Loafer," he said snickering. "I understand... I'll protect you," Dooky giggled then added seriously, "but I don't share my bed with no men... the floor is all yours."

"Cool," Doug said falling back into the seat. He thought to himself, *the floor is way better than the subway.*

Chapter Nine

It's A Crazy "World" Out There!

World had spent the gist of his night standing in front of the 24-hour Arab store drinking beers. He had consumed a total of six 40 oz. bottles of malt liquor and he was pissy drunk. He had harassed every single female that came to the store and managed to get two phone numbers from females that *only* a drunk man would talk to. He almost got himself into three fights and received one death threat. When no one else came through and all his money was gone, he decided to call it a night. Trying to walk the three blocks to his house was a task. He kept stumbling and wobbling as if the ground was a seesaw tilting from left to right. A few times his steps looked like they were being taken on a tightrope and he had to stop for a minute to try and regain his composure. He was taking a short break, leaning against a fence when he saw Dooky and Doug drive past. "Ayo, yo whooay," World screamed. But neither of them heard him.

"Man fuck y'all niggas?" he yelled at the back of the car nearly falling on his face. "I don't give a shit!" He fought to regain his balance and continued his walk home, "Damn, I'm fucked up!" He said out loud, looking at the ground to see if it was moving.

World thought about his mother seeing him this drunk and tried to get a grip on sobriety. Even though the chances of his mother still being awake were slim, he didn't want to risk her seeing him in this condition especially after how he was this morning, so instead of taking the direct route, he detoured through a few back blocks to try to sober up a little before going home. He cut through Dell Ave, which was always dark and desolate at night. There was two auto body, used car lots that kept the block alive during the day and gave it a murkiness like a scene from a horror movie at night. But World grew up around here and knew every in and out, hole in the gate, backyard, front yard and any other escape there was in the area. So he always felt safe.

He stopped next to a parked car to take a piss. As the beer flowed out of his system he started to feel a little better. Still peeing he labeled the passengers side door of the parked car with a liquid "W". After relieving himself he took a moment to watch his "W" change into an "M" before he headed home. Halfway through the block he passed another parked car. He wasn't paying it any attention, but as he walked by he was almost sure he heard a moan - "uunh". He stood very still making sure not to disturb or startle anyone as he slowly turned his attention towards the sound. The sound had come from the inside of a dark colored

Toyota Camry. The passenger's window was open and there was a couple in the passenger's seat fucking.

He heard the sound again, "uunh", and his dick started moving in his pants. World crouched down to his knees and crawled closer to the window. He saw a woman on top of somebody getting her freak on. She was riding and grinding, humping hard on her partner at a steady rhythm causing a clapping sound... "Pap, pap, pap, pap." Her moans and groans was evidence that she was either enjoying herself or she was a helluva actress. Either way, the blood that rushed to his dick causing it to point like the arrow in a one-way sign was evidence that World was enjoying the show. From where he was, he couldn't tell if the woman was black or white or if he knew her or not. All he could see was her ass inside of a flower printed dress, bouncing up and down. He tried to position himself to see if he could get a peek under her dress. When he couldn't, he positioned his hand on top of her ass in a way that it would feel as though it were her lover touching her. Slowly, he placed his hand on her ass and gave it a firm squeeze. Her ass felt nice and soft as it bounced up and down in his hand. World lifted her dress exposing a big round white ass. "*Ooohwee*," he thought "*a snowbunny*." World could feel and smell the heat from the sex coming out of the car and it was making him horny.

She was still moaning and humping her lover without ceasing and World was still gripping and rubbing her white flesh, becoming more confident and giving her light smacks on the ass. World gripped her right ass cheek and squeezed it really hard, and then he slid his fingers down into the crack of her ass and rubbed her asshole. “Oooh yeah, I like that,” she moaned. World continued to rub her asshole as she cheered him on. He slowly pushed his middle finger deep inside her anus and gradually began to finger pop her ass. The lady slowed down her pace and began to grind her pussy on her lover as World’s finger rapidly went in and out of her asshole. By this time, half of World’s upper body was inside of the car and he was almost at the point of not caring but was still trying to be careful. By the sounds the lady was making, World could tell that she was about to cum. He pulled his finger out of her asshole and rubbed and pressed it for a beat or two. Then he put his whole hand in between her cheeks and squeezed her anus hard. She was moaning so loudly World thought that someone might hear her. She had him so excited that he was about to nut in his pants. World rubbed her anus faster and faster occasionally letting his finger enter her ass. He pumped his hand a little too hard and accidentally slid his hand down until the tip of his fingers poked her lover in the dick.

"What the fuck was that?!" the lover said sitting up quickly causing the lady to bump Into World whose whole upper body was bent inside the car. "What the fuck you doing mother-fucker?!" The black man said reaching for World, as the lady screamed.

World pulled his body out of the car and ran. No one chased him but he turned to see the man standing outside of his car looking in his direction. The man said something World didn't hear nor understand, and World gave him the middle finger before he took the backyards to his house.

World smelled the light scent of doo-doo on his fingers and laughed. No matter black or white, he thought all assholes smell like shit. He laughed to himself as he reached for his keys.

"Dooky ain't gonna believe this one," he said still checkin his pockets for his keys. "Fuck!" he exclaimed as he rang the doorbell.

*****

Doug was on the floor laying on his back and staring at the ceiling. Dooky had given him two pillows and a blanket and Doug got comfortable near the closet. Doug had spent the last 20 minutes telling Dooky about what happened between him and his grandmother earlier.

"You know what?" Dooky asked as if he had a solution. "You should let me fuck your grandmoms."

"You know man..." Doug said seriously. "I try to have a serious conversation with you... but everything is a joke to you."

"I'm saying Loafer, for real, would you be mad if I fucked your grandmoms?" He laughed, "I'm serious, and suppose you came home and I had your grandmoms bent over the couch hittin' it like this...?" Dooky demonstrated how he would be humping and smacking her ass then burst out in laughter.

Doug started to make a slick remark about how Nana was staring at his dick earlier but Dooky continued, "Yo, you ever peep Joy's moms?" He said all joking aside, "You know who I'm talkin about right?... Joy from across the street. Yo her moms, yo, she got some big ass titties son! Them joints look like two big ass missiles stuffed in a t-shirt! Them shits is out here son!" Dooky indicated by putting his hands out past his knees.

Doug no longer felt like talking. He laid back and tried to figure out a way to orchestrate his life. He knew that he had to find himself a job. That was the first thing he had to do. Then, he would try to save enough money to put him through culinary school. He was going to do something, even if it meant he had to pop-in on his mother out in D.C. for a long surprise visit. Something had to give. Doug was drifting off to sleep as he was thinking. He could still hear Dooky babbling... "Yo, I would put some baby oil on them shits and titty fuck her... them shits is so big son, you can fuck one titty at a time. I'll put my nuts all in between..." Doug wasn't paying his friend any attention. His last thoughts were about Linda as he drifted into sleep.

"Why don't you come a little closer?"

"Is this close enough?" Linda asked seductively.

"Nah..." he said. "Come closer."

She snuggled up next to him and put her face against his neck. He could feel the warmth of her breath dancing on his nerves when she whispered, "Is this close enough?" She reached into his pants and began to massage his love muscle. Her hands were as soft as cotton candy as she gave his man-meat gentle strokes.

"Is this close enough?" she whispered.

"Get a little closer," he instructed.

She buried her face in Doug's lap and began to suck and jerk him at the same time. The moisture of her mouth combined with the softness of her hands made his toes curl. Saliva was dripping from her mouth as her movements progressed. She had his whole body shakin'. "Yeah..." He moaned closing his eyes. "Suck on that shit." He pulled his dick away from her and spanked it against her lips. She opened her mouth welcoming the weight of his meat as it jabbed against her mouth and tongue. She snatched his dick and rubbed it all over her face before putting it back into her mouth. She struggled to put all eleven inches of his sausage in her throat and Doug grabbed her head forcing the other half-inch inside. He held her head firmly in this position causing her to gag and her teeth bit down into his dick. It wasn't enough to hurt him but the sharp pain caused him to open his eyes. When he looked down, to his surprise Tammy was holding his dick in her hands. She put her index finger to her lips.

"Shhh, I'm sorry..." She whispered, "... did I hurt you?"

Shocked, Doug looked over at Dooky who was asleep in his bed snoring.

"Are you crazy?" he whispered trying to snatch his dick from her and put it away. "Your brother is right there," he said looking at the bed.

"He's knocked out." Tammy said snatching his meat from him. "He won't wake up, trust me," she charmed as she started suckin on his dick again.

The sound of Dooky snoring almost made Doug's dick go soft, but Tammy handled his rod like a porno star. She took him in her mouth deep throating his tool and licking his balls at the same time. His dick grew bigger and even harder than before. She smiled and admired her work before giving it a lick and playing with a thin string of pre-ejaculation that was attached to her tongue. She went down on him again pulling him out of her mouth with a loud "smop" noise.

Doug moaned then looked to see if he had disturbed Dooky's sleep, but he didn't move. Doug was ready to fuck but he didn't think he would be able to perform in this room next to Dooky. He reached and stuck his hand inside Tammy's pajama bottoms. She was so wet that he effortlessly slipped two fingers inside of her vagina. "Mmmm," she moaned, almost too loudly causing Doug to look at Dooky again.

"Not so loud Tam..." he whispered. "You gonna wake ya brother up."

Tammy momentarily stopped engulfing his wood long enough to respond.

"That nigga sleeps hard," she said as she slipped out of her pajama bottoms exposing her big round ass. "Stop worrying about him and put this sweet thang inside me... I need to feel it." She licked his cock a few times as she rubbed the juices between her thighs.

The thought of the crabs he had, had entered his mind. But as soon as it entered it was dismissed as he watched Tammy put her legs behind her head and tighten then release her pussy muscles making it snap. Doug submitted to temptation. There was no way he was not going to beat this pussy. Chaplain Ray-Ray and his whole congregation couldn't talk him out of it. You only live once, he thought, plus this was get-back.

Doug rubbed his beefsteak all around the outside of her wetness before he entered her. He made sure not to go easy as he pushed all of his wood inside her. "Mmmmmmm," she whined as he stilled himself filling her insides. "I can feel you in my stomach." He pulled his dick out leaving only the head inside of her, and then slammed it back in punching and pounding her pussy with powerful thrusts.

"Ooh nigga... yeah!" she cried out, "That's it... right there, right there! Oh my God!" she sobbed as tears ran from her eyes. "That's the, ooooh yeah...that's the spot! Hit it! Hit it! Hit iiiit!" She reached behind him and pulled his ass into her on every down stroke. "Fuck this pussy wit that fat ass dick nigga...fuck it!"

"You know I am!" Doug said beginning to break a sweat. "I know what you want bitch! Keep that pussy right there..." Doug demanded, "Keep it there!"

Doug was jumping up and down in the pussy trying to punish her for all the shit her brother put him through. Tammy was trying to talk shit but each time she tried to speak Doug crushed her cookies. The tears were falling from her eyes as Doug did his thing. He was staring at Tammy's face enjoying her expressions. She was still trying to speak, her lips were moving but no sound escaped from her mouth. When she finally found her voice it was deep and raspy.

"You's a nasty motherfucker just like World," she said roughly.

"What you say?" Doug questioned, stroking her as hard as he could hoping his dick would come out of her mouth for disrespect.

"Bong!"

Something hard and heavy hit Doug in the back of his head. When he opened his eyes, he saw Dooky standing over him.

"I said...," Dooky yelled looking down at Doug, "You's a nasty mafucka just like World!"

Instantly Doug snapped back to reality.

"What the fuck is wrong wit y'all niggas??!" Dooky went on. "First, this fruity ass nigga World was runnin' round here pointing his dick at me like a fuckin sniper and now I catch your silly ass laying here fuckin my mother's pillow like you trying to stab a hole in the mafucka! I think you need to take your hot ass home son!"

Doug was rubbing his head and looking at Dooky wondering how much he had heard.

"Yo, what the fuck you hit me with?"

When Dooky didn't respond Doug looked around the floor and saw a boot in close proximity and figured that it was the object he threw.

"Ayo, get the fuck up Loafer and go home!"

"You serious?" Doug said in disbelief.

"Yeah, I'm serious nigga! I don't feel comfortable sleeping around you knowing that you're some kind of hump freak! Suppose you started walking in your sleep or something? I would have to kill your silly ass."

Doug looked at the digital clock. "Ayo, its 4 am son... and your grandmoms is sleeping nigga! You only live up the block but if you want, I'll drive you home... but your freak ass is leaving here son!"

"Unbelievable!" Doug said putting on his shoes. "I don't need a ride homeboy... I'll walk!"

Doug got up and bounced. He wasn't even mad. In fact, he was happy that he wasn't talkin too much in his sleep. As he walked, he wondered what it would be like to bone Tammy and if she really gave it up like she did in his dream. Before he could ponder much of the thought, he was home. From the outside he could see that all of the lights inside were off and he was happy. He just wanted to get some rest without drama. As he entered the house, he almost tripped over a garbage bag by the door. He turned the light on and saw that all of his belongings were stuffed into three trash bags. As he began to move the bags back into the cramped space he called his bedroom, his semi-sober grandmother stepped out of her room smelling like vodka.

"Nigger! I... want... you... outta my got damn house!" She growled, pointing a finger at the front door. "You tried to break my arm!"

"Where am I supposed to go?" Doug asked as he felt the tears beginning to well in his eyes.
His grandmother didn't hear his question. She was anticipating him to argue about her arm.

"Yes you did break it! I can't move it!"

Doug looked at her arm. "Grandma, your arm isn't broken. I'm sorry if I hurt you, I didn't mean..."

"You broke it!" she screamed trying to wake up the neighbors. "I want your no tricity payin' ass outta her tomorrow! I can't stand your free loadin' ass! No tricity payin ass! You a low down dirty nigger and I hate you!! I want your ass outta here in the mornin'," she half stumbled back into her room leaving Doug standing there with tears staining his cheeks.

What his grandmother had said to him struck a cord. He was used to her cursing and yelling and calling him a dirty nigger but he couldn't ever remember her telling him that she hated him.
It hurt him so badly that he cried. He really boo-hoo'd. He cried about his life, he cried about how his mother abandoned him, he cried because all of his belongings fit into these three garbage bags and most of all he cried because he didn't have any love. Doug went to the wall unit and grabbed his grandmother's bible and locked himself in the bathroom. He opened the medicine cabinet and grabbed the first bottle of pills he saw. He swallowed 22 Tylenols and the remainder of a prescription that belonged to his grandmother. He sat on the toilet stool and opened the bible to the 23rd Psalm.

'The Lord is my shepherd, I shall not want..."

Doug thought about the kids he saw playing Johnny on the Pony." One by one, they jumped and screamed in laughter. They didn't have a care in the world. Life was all fun and games to them. If only they knew, Doug thought. Doug wished he was a kid again. He wished that he could do it all over. The tears were rolling down his cheeks and falling into the Psalm.

"*He makes me lie down in green pastures...*" Doug felt himself getting drowsy but he was smiling.

He thought about Linda. "*I'm sorry Linda...*" he whispered. "*I'm a low down dirty nigger.*"

Doug's body slipped off of the stool onto the floor. He felt tired and weak. The medication was running its course and filling his bloodstream.

"*He leads me beside the still waters...*" he was slipping in and out of consciousness.

"*I'm sorry grandma, I'm sorry.*"

Doug's chin was rested on his chest and he tried to read the rest of the Psalm.

"*He restores my soul...*"

"*I don't wanna die*!" Doug sobbed.

He called for his grandmother but he barely heard the words leave his mouth. He reached to try and open the door but he was too weak and he barely managed to unlock it.

"*Yea, though I walk through the valley...,*" was the last thing he read before everything went black.

Chapter Ten

Strictly Business

Walt Shaker pressed zero on the pay phone to reach the operator. After two rings, a female's voice responded. "Hello...operator assistance, my name is Joyce, how may I help you?"

"You see..." Walt began in a very low, fast talking song... "I'm tryna see if this here payphone rings before I page my friend..." His fingers were still moving as if he were still dialing a number as he continued. "Would ya mind dialing this number back for me?"

"No problem sir," the operator responded. "One moment please."

He hung up the phone and less than ten seconds later it began to ring. Walt picked up the receiver with dancing feet and started talking, "Walt Shaker..."

"Sir?? Is Everyth—" the operator started to ask, but Walt cut her off, "Yeah it's me the one and only..."

The operator was forced to listen to him run his game because her job forbade her to hang up on customers. She wanted a little break anyway; so she sat and listened trying to figure out the con. It didn't take her but a second to figure out that this was a crack head's fish story. You heard one, you heard em all, she thought.

Walt went through the bluff swiftly because he was determined to get all of their drugs leaving nothing behind. He kept his eye on World who seemed like the only potential problem. These youngins don't have no respect, no more, Walt thought He wasn't worried about Dooky and the fag. He read the greed signs all over their faces.

Walt spoke louder into the receiver looking for signals of assurance to appear as he peaked over at World. World was acting like he wasn't listening, but Walt knew better.

"Okay sit tight, I'm on my way."

Before he could hang up the receiver the operator said, "thank you sir...have a nice day," with a voice filled with sarcasm.

Walt was determined to get World to come up off his drugs. He didn't like World or his attitude. When he mentioned that he could sell their ten dollar vials for twenty, he saw the expression on World's face change. I got you sucka, Walt thought to himself, the only thing free is the price youngin... remember that next time."

After collecting all of the drugs, he hurried over to the building and pushed all of the buzzers. He knew someone would let him in without asking who it was. The hood was just like that. Hearing the buzz and pulling open the door gave him dancing feet again. His plan was to cut through the back alley and disappear but when he stepped out back he ran into Tracey who was inhaling the smoke from her last blast.

"Party for two... on you??" he asked amid the frown she gave him as she rolled her eyes. "Oh... you stingy now huh Trey??" Walt smiled getting no response. "It's okay Sugarbear, you ain't gotta burn no salt on Walt," he sang pulling out the sock and cheese doodle bag full of drugs.

He dumped the contents into the hat so Tracey could see, almost making her eyes pop out of her head. Walt pulled out his crack pipe and slammed the product of two vials inside the stem.

The giant flame from his Bic lighter disappeared into the tunnel of the pipe as he inhaled eyeing Tracey, then blowing smoke directly in her face. The look on her face said it all and Walt immediately took charge.

"Go to the door and tell me if you see three youngins sitting in a grey car parked by the store."

Without hesitation as if moving off of remote control, Tracey did exactly what she was told. When she peeked outside she saw the car and instantly recognized it. Then she saw Dooky look towards her direction and they briefly made eye contact. The bruises on her back began to hurt and remind her of the way he had treated her. She took a mental photo of him promising herself never to forget or forgive him until she got him back.

"They still there right?" Walt said sounding a little paranoid and interrupting her thoughts.

"Yeah," she said silently pleading for a blast. Seeing Dooky's face was fucking with her head. "They right across the street."

"Well, you see Sugarbear..." Walt sang, "Ol' Walt here is bakin' them youngins a cake and while they waitin', I'm gonna need a place to kick my feets up for a while, you see?"

Tracey knew what he was insinuating - everything he was insinuating. But she needed to get high and didn't want to work the streets, it was too dangerous, plus she was still shook-up and bruised from what she went through last night.

Against her better judgment, she agreed to assist Walt.

"I live right in the next building, we can go there."

Walt smiled letting her lead the way as he gave her a light smack on her ass.

*****

Since leaving the building, Walt and Tracey had been cooped up in her apartment getting high. Walt smiled as he thought about Dooky. He really had a liking for Dooky but this was business. Risky business, shady business or funny business... you can either get the business or give the business, but it's all business. And business was business. It wasn't personal. He caught the kid slippin and it's the price you pay. The next time he'd run into Dooky he figured he'd try and explain this to him. Give him a little lesson in hustling. On the other hand, worst case scenario he'd probably would have an ass-whooping to deal with and Walt wasn't worrying about that. In fact, he would take two ass whoopings for the amount of crack he smoked so far. He dismissed all thoughts of Dooky, convinced that he'll deal with him when the time comes and focused on Tracey who was getting on his nerves. When they first entered her studio apartment, Walt preyed on her thirst to get high and demanded that she give him a blowjob before he shared any of his drugs - business is business. She obliged by giving him probably the best head that he had since he became a nobody.

Now that she was high, she was acting like she didn't know what the word blowjob meant. For the last three hours he had been trying to get her to give him another dose of that world class head, but she was so high and tweaking so bad that she couldn't keep still. Every two minutes she looked under her bed or checked to see if someone was hiding in the closet. Then, she would go into the bathroom and look behind the door and open then close the shower curtain.

And now, Tracey was standing at the door to her apartment looking through the peephole and Walt was getting annoyed.

"Bitch' I wish you would keep your crack head ass still and stop running around here tweakin'-n-shit!! This ain't no got damn mansion! Ain't nobody coming up in here without us seeing them." Walt patted the empty space on the couch beside him. "Come sit over here and relax..." he enchanted, "You makin Ol' Walt Shakers nerves bad."

Tracey turned and looked at Walt wide-eyed. She had her index finger up to her lips. "Shhhh...I think somebody is hiding in the hallway."

Walt slam dunked another vial in his pipe. The residue alone that was jammed and caked up in his stem was enough to get him high for a day. He flicked the lighter and the four-inch flame came to life. Walt refused to let her fuck up his high.

Tracey heard the sizzling sounds of burning crack and turned around to watch him inhale the smoke from the drug and she suddenly came to life. The anticipation of taking another hit of the wonder drug made her feel like she had to take a shit. She pulled out her little piece of car antenna that she used as her crack pipe and held out her palm indicating that she wanted a vial... or two.

"Not so fast sweet Sadie," he said blowing out a cloud of smoke. "I still need you to take care of something first," he voiced, grabbing his crotch while blowing out a smoke ring.

Tracey looked at Walt's crotch and a bitter taste formed in her mouth. She knew she shouldn't have sucked his dick as good as she had done but she figured if she got his nose wide open he would get her high all night. She had sucked his little nasty dick despite the foul odor that arose from his crotch and ass and she told him not to cum in her mouth, but he did anyway. Now, listening to him ask her to go through all that all over again made her want to hurl.

"Why don't you let me jerk it? I'll lotion it up real nice for you," she said trying to improvise.

"Bitch! What I need you to jerk me off fo', when I can do that my damn self?"

"I'll tell you what..." she said, reaching for his zipper trying to locate his little dick.

"I'll let you put it in me okay? Just lemme get another hit so I can get right first." She felt his bite-sized dick begin to stiffen.

"Oh hell nah Sugarbear..." Walt said, as he grabbed her hand helping her massage his miniature meat.

"You know that once you take a blast you start tweaking-n-shit. Lemme slide this stud trunk in your love hole b'fore you take a hit... I'll be quick..." He winked, "I promise."

Tracey faked a smile and nodded. She got up and went into the bathroom to lube the inside of her vagina with Vaseline. Although his baby dick couldn't do any damage, she knew she wouldn't get wet and she wanted this to be over as quickly as possible. After she was sure she was properly lubricated, she grabbed a condom from her stash under the sink and re-entered the room.

To her surprise, Walt was standing there naked. He had nappy grey hairs covering his chest and crotch. He was looking at her and smiling while he massaged his three inches of cub-scout dick. Tracey thought, *"fuck is he smiling about with that tiny dick,"* as she held back her laughter and almost gagging at the same time.

"You alright Sugarbear?," Walt asked. His green eyes looked like they were turning grey as he tried to charm her. "C'mon outta them rags sweet Sadie," giving her another wink.

The bad taste in her mouth was now forming in her throat and rising as she stepped closer to him. The stench of his body filled her nostrils and she didn't want to touch him or even worse, let him touch her. She thought of killing him and taking all of the drugs but it was just a thought. She didn't have that type of courage. She was trying to think of a way to out-slick him, but she had to admit that if he wasn't nothing else, he was definitely game-tight. He was standing in front of her butt-ass naked and the only thing he had in his hands was the hat full of crack.

"C'mon over here and bring that baby maker to Walt Shaker," he rapped still rubbing his microscopic meat. "I've been wanting to give you a piece of the rock for a long time."

"Rock," she thought. "*He must mean pebble.*" She handed Walt the condom.

"What's this for?" He said surprised.

Shocked, she said, "What the fuck you mean what's it for? It goes on your little ashy dick!"

Walt was looking at her like she was crazy. "Walt Shaker don't make love with no glove Sugarbear."

"Well..." Tracey said agitated, "I know you ain't think you was gonna stick your nasty ass dick in me without putting on a rubber."

Walt had been wanting to get with Tracey ever since he found out she was hooked on crack. He had wanted her before she fell victim to the drugs but she was out of his range acting all high sadditty and turning her nose up to Ol' Walt. Now that he finally had his chance, he wasn't gonna blow it.

"Easy there Sugarbear," he sang. "I understand you loud and clear. Gimmie the condom, I know you don't want to get pregnant," he added giving her a better excuse besides the obvious one.

Tracey watched closely as he put the condom on before unfastening her pants and slipping one pant leg off. She walked past him trying not to make her ass jiggle and got on her bed lying on her back.

"If you ready then let's get it over with," she said sounding a little agitated.

Walt was mesmerized by what he could see of her body. She wasn't as thick as she was before she started smokin', but she wasn't all skin and bones like other crack head chicks he had sexed. Her ass was still nice and plump with that cuff in the bottom giving her butt the illusion that it was connected to her body like a titty. The hairs on her vagina were trimmed finer than Barry White's beard, and the one ebony leg she had exposed looked smooth and toned, almost athletic.

Walt had taken several mental photos to store and use at another time, but it was now time for the experience and he was excited. His dancing feet came alive and he did a little dance step before dropping to his knees and trying to put his face between her thighs.

"Unh Uh!" she closed her legs quickly blocking his advance and pushing his head away. "You trying to go down on me? Nah-Uh, that ain't happening nigga! Let's get this over with... let's go!"

Disappointed by her rejection, Walt suggested that she let him fuck her doggy style. Tracey hesitated then obliged thinking that he might've tried to kiss her or something crazy. Plus this way, she didn't have to look at his face. She turned over and assumed the position. When she turned around, Walt saw the raspberry scar running up the side of her leg to her back.

"What happened here?" he asked somewhat concerned.

"Listen..." she said heated, tired and wanting to get high. "Are you writing a book? If you are, then leave this chapter out of it and let's get down to business! I had a little accident, that's all you need to know... now let's go!"

What a bitch, Walt thought as he slid his tiny tool inside of her business. He moaned cumming after four strokes.

Tracey didn't realize he came so quickly, had she noticed he would've been done. Walt kept pumping, happy with his ability to stay hard. His dick slipped out and he accidentally poked her on the anus causing her to jump.

"Watch that shit nigga!" she warned giving him her killer look. "And hurry up!"

"I ain't mean to put it there, Sugarbear," he said apologetically while he slyly slipped the condom off his cock.

"This pussy feels so good sweet Sadie," sliding his dick in raw dawg.

"Oooh yeah," he sighed feeling that feeling he had been craving. "This that good shit here, Sadie!! Oooh motherfuckin yeah! Make that kitty cat snap Sugarbear."

Tracey was ignoring him and trying hard to block out this whole experience. She wanted him to hurry up and get from behind her. She could barely feel his lil dick inside of her but she felt his thrusts. She started to fuck him back and talk a little shit to get him to cum quickly.

"Ooh damn daddy! That feels so good... unh unh. Pump that dick in me daddy... grab on that ass!" she demanded pounding her ass against his pelvis.

Walt was trying to control the overwhelming sensation that was rising in his body. He wanted this pleasurable feeling to last for at least ten minutes but he just couldn't fight any longer. "Aaaagghhh!" he grunted releasing his load into her vagina.

"Damn Sugarbear..." he said smacking her on the ass. "You gotta get a permit for this shit!"

Whatever, she thought getting up and rushing into the bathroom. All she wanted to do was wash the whole experience off of her body, but she knew that there was no way, to scrub off the way that she was feeling. She caught her reflection in the mirror and almost didn't recognize the person staring back at her. Her habit was out of control and she looked at herself and asked, "*What happened to you?*"

*****

Tracey was born in the latter part of 1973 to two middle class black parents. Her dad was a cop and her mom had a decent paying public service job in the small suburban town they lived in. Her parents never married. Actually Tracey's dad was already married to another woman who had given birth a mere 9 months before Tracey was born and had another child exactly 9 months after with another woman. Simply put, Tracey's dad was a fuckin' whore!

The affair between her parents ended after a few years, but not soon enough. Tracey was often subjected to watching her father go off at the drop of a dime and whoop the shit out of her moms. At a very early age, Tracey thought that this shit was normal.

Tracey's mom had a kid 10 years earlier and this broad was off the fuckin chain. Tracey's older sister Mona hated her guts. Mona had been her mom's one and only for 10 years and then this spoiled little bitch (Tracey) came into the picture. Mona definitely put Tracey through it. She would lock her in the bathroom when their mother went to work at night at her second job.

Meanwhile, Mona and her friends would get high and drink Pink Champale and often get fucked in the back room. It was no surprise when Mona ended up dropping out of high school at age 14 and ran away to Las Vegas. She returned home 8 months pregnant. Tracey's mom had three kids to raise now.

Tracey was a straight A student but she was bad. She had a filthy mouth and had turned into a very angry and violent little girl. Her mouth got her into a lot of bullshit but she didn't care. She wasn't afraid of anything or anyone. For a girl, she had a mean knuckle game and mostly came out on top in any altercation.

She didn't look her age either. At 10 years old, she had grown ass men approaching her. Yeah, she was cute and had curves in the right places but if them older fellas was really paying attention, they would've realized that she was just a shorty. But most niggas was only paying attention to those big titties and that extra fat ass. Tracey was all that and she knew it.

Her behavior worsened and the more she fought and cut classes, the more she was suspended from school. The days she was suspended were the days she spent with him - Unique.

Unique was fairly good looking - tall, brown skinned with dimples and straight up hood, which was exactly how she liked them. Unique was more than 5 years older than her so at age 12 she was doing a bunch of shit she had absolutely no business doing. She preferred to keep their relationship on the low because of the age difference and she often referred to him as her cousin, which most people believed to be true. Although Unique was a bad seed and a bad influence on Tracey, she thought she was in love. But what she didn't understand was that she was just strung out on the dick and he could get her to do anything he wanted her to do. She later learned that if she did not comply with his wishes, she got her ass beat. Over time, the beatings became more and more severe so whatever he asked she did, including smoking crack. And now Tracey was in over her head and she needed help... she needed help badly.

*****

Not knowing the answer to her question, she stared at herself with pity. She hated the person that she had become. Instantly she felt dirty. She wanted to soak her body in the tub and then try to wash away all of her guilt and pain in a hot shower. But the over-whelming urge to get high invaded her thoughts and whispered in her ear. The calling from the drug became priority but she held back long enough to wipe her putty with a rag. It suddenly dawned on her that she felt particularly wet inside. Her first thought was the Vaseline, but when she gave a little push and the thick sap-like secretion dripped from her vagina she almost had a stroke. When she saw that it was semen she panicked. "How could this have happened?" The absoluteness of what he had done caused her fear to submerge and her anger to heighten. "This Motherfucker!!" she shrieked as wrathful tears began to roll down her cheeks. She reached into the cabinet under the sink and grabbed a bottle of bleach. She emptied the contents of a foot basin on the floor and filled it with the noxious liquid. She stepped out of the bathroom crying, dragging her pants on the floor. But to her surprise, Walt Shaker was gone. On the bed next to the condom, he left her ten vials of crack cocaine. Tracey put the basin down and reached into her pants to find her antenna. She desperately needed a blast to forget about all of her problems. She slammed two vials inside her make-shift pipe and sparked a flame. The smoke filled her lungs and she no longer cared, nothing mattered as the drug embraced her awareness. She smoked one vial after another until she no longer remembered, as she fell deeper and deeper into oblivion with her eye glued to the peephole.

Chapter Eleven

Just Say No!

World woke up with a headache but he was grateful that he wasn't sick. He rolled out of bed to go to the bathroom and came upon the watchful eye of his mother who was entering the kitchen.

"Mornin Ma," he said as he leaned forward giving her a kiss on the cheek. His mother smelled the alcohol coming out of his pores before he said a word. She was still upset by the way he leaned on the bell last night after coming home drunk and losing his keys. It wasn't the fact that he came home so late that bothered her, because she couldn't comfortably go to sleep anyways until she knew that he was in the house. It was the alcohol that she was witnessing destroy her only son.... And it was breaking her heart. She had begged, pleaded, cried and prayed but he still continued to drink. She didn't know what else to do or say so she left it all in God's hands.

"You mean, good afternoon," she said, walking towards the front door.

"Where you going Ma?" He asked hoping that she was going to the store and coming right back.

But his mother left, slamming the door without answering him. World knew why his mother was mad and felt guilty. He tried to shake it off by convincing himself that he was going to quit drinking, but he couldn't fool himself.

After he put some food in his stomach, he visualized the events from last night. He laughed aloud as he thought about putting his finger in the white lady's butthole. He smelled his finger for a trace of her scent.

"I should've slipped my phone number in her ass so that bitch could call me." He laughed to himself and started to call Dooky to boast about his crazy episode, but when he thought about it he said, "*Fuck Dooky*!" He was still tight about getting hit with that sucker-punch. Plus World thought, "*That nigga let that funky ass crack head mafucka gank them for all their cra... Oh shit*!" World thought, as it dawned on him... he remembered the argument he got into with the fine ass red-bone honey that stopped at the store.

"Im'a get my boyfriend to buss yo ass... believe me!" she yelled.

"Oh yeah"? World responded with a slur, "Fuck your boyfriend!... Who's your boyfriend?" he questioned.

"Lensey" she spat, hoping his name evoked fear. "I'm gonna tell him to whoop your mother fuckin bitch ass!"

"Lensey??!... Lensey?" World laughed, "Bitch, fuck Lensey! He can't whoop nothing over here...!" World pounded on his chest for emphasis then continued, "Matter of fact bitch, my boy Dooky just robbed your pussy ass boyfriend for his crack and weed.......... Bitch!"

"Bitch??" She said insulted, raising her eyebrows and shaking her neck. "Who the fuck you calling a bitch? You drunk ass crack head motherfucker!" She responded coldly before she spit in his face.

The spit landed between his nose and upper lip. He reacted instantly and slapped her hard across her cheek. The sound of his hand hitting her face was so loud that it sounded like a sound-effect. Her body spun around so fast that she almost drilled a hole in the ground before she fell to the hard pavement.

"My name is World the Pearl bitch! I'll fuck up a nigga or a girl!! I don't give a fuck!" He yelled before cock spitting on her.

His spit landed on her forehead and was drooling down toward her eyes as she stared at him without blinking or wiping it off. Her body was still sprawled out on the pavement and she was smiling wickedly as she said, "You dead motherfucker! You dead!"

A chill went through World's body as he thought about the repercussions from what he did and he reached for the phone to call Dooky.

*****

Dooky opened his eyes and looked at the digital clock. "Damn," he mumbled, seeing that it was almost two o'clock. He got out of bed, stretched as he let out a lengthy machine-gun sounding fart before going to drain his bladder. Once he started pissing the phone began to ring.

"*Fuck that!*" He thought. "*I ain't running for that shit.*" He pissed for so long that the ringing had stopped then started again. He rinsed his hands and ran in the kitchen to answer the phone but it stopped again as soon as he reached it.

He saw that his mother left him a note telling him that they all went to church and there were sausages in the oven. She also let him know that his room smelled bad and he needed to clean it.

Dooky made a bee-line to the oven and grabbed the sausage links. He went back to his room and sprayed some more of the Lemon Pledge throughout the room. He pressed play on his boom box and the sounds of his old school Kid Capri tape boomed out of the speakers.

"I want to thank you, heavenly father, for shinning your light on me..."

He turned the volume up full blast and looked out of his bedroom window. He was happy to see that his father's car was still there and nana's car was gone. He was about to close his shade and smoke his "top of the morning" blunt when Joy's mother came out of her house wearing a jogging suit. Dooky eyeballed her titties from his window and rubbed his dick. "*You should let me put my meat between those motherfuckers,*" he whispered. As if she had a bionic ear, she looked directly at his window and gave him a hateful look.

Dooky smiled charmingly and licked his lips. "*Don't jog too hard...*" He said more so in thought than with sound. "*If you hit yaself in the face with one of them titties ya might get a concussion.*" He laughed to himself as he went into his pants and pulled out a half of blunt. The music was playing so loudly that he didn't hear the phone as it began to ring again.

*****

"I know this nigga don't sleep that hard!" World said slamming the receiver back into its cradle. "Fuck!" He had already gotten dressed but he didn't want to face Dooky and tell him what he'd done. He would much rather prefer to explain it by phone, but it seemed inevitable that he go down to his house b'cause no one was answering the phone. "Fuck it... I'll wait a little longer, then try one more time."

*****

Lensey grabbed his cell phone and turned it off. It had been ringing all night disturbing his flow as he long stroked the dark-skinned stallion that he met when he got down here. He loved the attention he received every time he came to Raleigh, N.C. They made him feel like a kingpin down here. But he was far from kingpin status, in fact he was just a mule that knew how to flash - but he loved it. He escorted the dark-skinned broad out of his room in the Motel 6 and pecked her on the cheek. "Call me later uh... er.. um.."

"Sonya!" She answered for him.

"Yeah Sonya baby, call me later on okay?" He said giving her a wink while trying to get away from her.

"But I thought you said we was going to the mall... I thought you were gonna..."

"Call me later!" He said raising his voice and looking at her violently before re-entering his room and slamming the door in her face.

"Yeah ahiight you bunk ass nigga!" She mumbled as she turned to leave. "I'll make that call alright... to the Po-Lice!"

Lensey entered the room feeling a little agitated. "Fuck is wrong wit these broads?..." He said as he plopped on the bed. "Fuck outta here with that shit!" He reached for his cell phone to call one of his boss' workers, who he was supposed to deliver the drugs to. As soon as he turned, the phone on it rang. He looked at the number and sighed "Fuck does this bitch want now?" He thought about ignoring it, then decided to answer.

"What the dealy yo?"

"Boo," her voice rattled in his ear. "I've been calling you all night... this nigga World was out here disrespecting you, calling you all types of names... I told him he should watch his mouth... because you're my man and I ain't gonna let nobody disrespect mines…!"

"Who??" Lensey said confused, not knowing who or what she was talking about.

"World!" she said.

"Who the fuck is World??" He said still confused.

Ignoring his question she continued rambling "… and then he said fuck Lensey! He ain't nobody but a worker," she added knowing how much her man wanted to be a boss. "And that's why him and his boy Dooky robbed you for your drugs."

"He did what?!" Lensey said reaching for the drugs he had stashed in his suitcase, dumping the vials on the bed and started counting them.

She continued with her yammer, "I told him that he is a hater and I didn't have time for his child's play. And when I tried to walk away, he grabbed me by my hair and started punching me in my face… I couldn't do nothing boo… I tried but…" she sobbed "…I tried. Now my face is all bruised and swollen."

Lensey heard what she said about getting her ass kicked, but he didn't give a fuck about that. He was worrying about his own ass as he continued counting the vials. When he finished, he realized that he was short close to 1,000 vials and got nervous.

"... You should see my face boo," she said sobbing uncontrollably. "... It hurts so bad boo,"

"I'm gonna kill that motherfucker!" Lensey exploded.

"That nigga stole my shit! I'm gonna kill his motherfuckin ass!"

Lensey hung up on her and immediately called his little brother.

"Who dis?" Squirrel answered on the first ring.

"Ayo who the fuck is World? And how the fuck did him and Dooky get they hands on my shit?! Lensey yelled infuriated

Squirrel removed the receiver from his ear and looked at it like it licked his ear. "Lens... what the fuck you talking about?"

"I wanna know who went in my room and stole my shit!?" Squirrel swallowed hard. He knew that one day his brother would get hip that he was pinching him for drugs. He paused to make up a lie when his brother yelled back into the receiver.

"Hey dickface! I said, I wanna know how the fuck did World and Dooky get into my shit? ... When I left you and Dooky there earlier... did that motherfucker go in my room?"

"Nah," Squirrel answered, still trying to think. "World ain't been over here..." he said, then added, "Whatcha missing?"

"You fuckin stupid motherfucker! I'm short a thousand pieces! Did you leave Dooky alone for any period of time?"

"A thousand?" Squirrel said almost too loudly. He knew that he only took less than one hundred vials. Then he thought about it and remembered how strange Dooky was acting after he came out of the bathroom. And how he left without smoking the weed he'd offered him... Dooky had never turned down no weed. "That greasy ass nigga Dooky! I knew he was acting funny! My fault Lens... I will take care of it!"

"You fuckin right it's your fault you little prick! And I will deal with you after I deal with your lil friends... I'll be home Wednesday. Be around b'cause I need you to show me where they live!" Lensey said hanging up the phone.

Once his brother hung up. Squirrel called Stutter. "Yo get the tooly's son and call the nigga Pat and tell him to get his aunt's car... we got work to put in!!"

After smoking his "top of the morning" and eating the sausages, Dooky was fiending for a Newport. After checking through all of his pockets and stashes and coming up empty, he decided to drive up to the store. As he was walking out the house the phone started ringing. "*Man, fuck that! Nobody's home.*"

Dooky walked into the Arab store "Habeeb-Bop what up?"

"Fook yoo! Yoo buy, yoo leave dassit!" The short-tempered Arab man voiced.

"Yeah, yeah, yeah sandface," Dooky said between laughs "Just gimmie four loosies so I can roll out."

The Arab yelled at Dooky in a sing-song voice that must've been a mixture of Arabic and English. All Dooky understood was "Fuck" and "Black" as he passed Dooky the loosies and Dooky paid him his money.

"Next time don't touch my filters..." Dooky scolded. "I don't know how many camel dicks you been touching."

The Arab let out a slew of curses. And again, all Dooky could understand was "Fuck" and "Black".

As he turned to leave, Dooky pissed the man off one more time. "I hope you don't kiss your wife and kids with that mouth... Ay-Rab!!"

Dooky stepped out of the store and lit a Newport. It was a beautiful Sunday afternoon. The sun was out and people were going to and from enjoying the day. As he exhaled a cloud of smoke from his lungs, a strange feeling overwhelmed him. Suddenly, the day didn't seem so beautiful anymore. It felt like there was something dark and evil behind the sunshine – watching and waiting. Dooky looked at his Newport thinking that perhaps the Arab sold him a Kool or Salem. When he saw that it was a Newport he plucked it in the street, "Shit must be stale." He looked back at the Arab man who was eyeing him from inside of the store. Dooky gave him the middle finger and Habeeb-Bop sent two middle fingers back his way.

Dooky got in the car and drove to Doug's house. He beeped the horn a few times, then got out and rang the buzzer. Doug's grandmother's voice boomed out of the intercom.

"Yeah... who is it?!"

"It's me, Dooky granny..." he spoke into the intercom. "Is Doug home?"

Her voiced boomed out of the speaker even louder as she said, "I ain't yo got damn granny you no good nigger"" She screamed, "Doug is dead and gone!... Dead!" she yelled "...Nigger swallowed all of the..."

Doug's grandmother must've let go of the "talk" button. So Dooky rang the buzzer again.

"What nigger?!" she hollered "You trying to run up my tricity on my intercom bill ain't you?" I done told yo nappy headed ass... he's dead!"

Dooky thought he detected her sobbing as she spoke. But it was hard for him to believe what she was saying. He knew that Doug's grandmother stayed drunk and talked a whole lot of shit but... how could this be true? How can Doug be dead? It didn't make sense.

Dooky rang the buzzer of Doug's next-door neighbor.

"Helloo, who is it?" the upbeat voice poured out of the speaker.

"Um... hi... hello... ug, my name is Dooky and I'm a friend of your neighbor's... Doug. I was hoping that you could tell me... um... if uh what happened to him last night?" The door buzzed and Dooky stepped inside. He ran up one flight of stairs and was met by an older full-figured Spanish woman.

At first glance Dooky figured, "late 40's early 50's, thrifty, but likes to cook and definitely likes to eat"... and when he got a little closer he added, "but doesn't like to wash."

"Hi... er Ms. My name is Dooky, I'm Doug's friend. I just spoke to his grandmother and she said that Doug is dead and I find that hard to believe because Loafer... er... uh... Doug left my house early this morning and... and I just don't... believe what she's telling me."

The woman smiled softly, "okay Dooky, let me explain... is that your real name? ... Dooky? I've never heard that one before." She stared at him expecting an answer. When he didn't respond she continued to wait.

Finally getting the hint, he answered "Yes, that is my real name."

"Wow!" she openly admired, "Such a beautiful name for such a handsome young man." She smiled "My name is Marcia, but you can call me what Doug calls me Mamita Azuca, which means Sugar Mama in Spanish."

"*Okay, this bitch is crazy!*" Dooky thought. "That name fits you well," he voiced "but... what happened to Doug?"

"Oh, yes, Doug."

Dooky was thinking, "*I bet Doug fucked this broad before,*" but he said "Yes... Doug, what happened?"

"Well..." she started "I really don't know. The ambulance came early this morning and that's all I know."

"Unbelievable!" Dooky said aloud. "What time did the ambulance get here?"

"Oh, it had to be at least 12 am."

"*This woman was nuts,*" Dooky thought, he turned around and knocked on Doug's grandmother's door. She opened her door and saw Dooky, then looked and saw her neighbor and slammed the door. You could hear the sounds of chains being secured coming from inside.

Dooky was leaving, when Ms. Azuca invited him into her place. He ignored her and decided to take a ride over to Mount Vernon Hospital. He was driving past his block when he saw World in the street trying to flag him down.

Chapter Twelve

Critical Thoughts

Doug woke up in the hospital feeling beat-up. His mouth was painfully dry and chalky. It didn't take him long to figure out where he was or why he was there. He remembered taking the Tylenols but everything else was a blank. He tried to sit up but the pain that shot from his abdomen to his head made him lay his ass back down. He found a button attached to a cord and gave it a squeeze. Shortly after, a petite young Italian nurse was at his attention. She looked just like the daughter from the show "*Married with Children*" in a nurse's uniform.

"Good afternoon Mr. Campbell. I'm so glad to have you back with us again. How are you feeling?"

At that moment Doug was happy to be alive. He tried to force a smile, "I think things are about to get better."

"I see..." she said smiling. "Certain parts of your body are obviously very happy to be alive as well," she joked, giving a little head not at his erection.

Doug looked at his flagpole that was at attention, "Down boy," he said and they both laughed. He felt the pain shoot through his body when he laughed and calmed himself.

"Don't worry..." she explained kindly patting him on the arm "... it's normal for these things to happen. At least you know..." she gave him a smile and nodded at his member "...that things are still working in that department. For now get some rest and the doctor will be in to see you momentarily... I'm nurse Angel Gentilli but you can call me nurse Angel."

Doug was picturing her naked with a set of wings coming out of her back. Then he immediately felt embarrassed for sitting there in front of this fine ass white lady after trying to commit suicide - the courageous cowardly sucka's way out.

"Thank you," he mumbled.

When she left, Doug started to press the button again. He had got so caught up in her beauty that he forgot to ask her how he got to the hospital. He decided that it could wait until later and was about to try to go back to sleep when a tall "Magic Johnson" lookin doctor walked into his room.

"Good afternoon Mr. Douglas. My name is Dr. Irving Jordan. How are you feeling?"

"My head feels like it's been kicked by the women's soccer team and my mouth is so dry I can barely talk."

"Well..." Doctor Jordan said, "You will probably be feeling a bit of pain in your abdomen too. Aside from the stomach vacuum, the discomfort you feel comes from the overdose of Acetaminophen acid in your body."

"Acety-what?" Doug asked confused.

"Asprin," the doctor said, "to be specific... Tylenol. We also found traces of birth control in your system."

"Birth control?" Doug said shocked and embarrassed.

"Yeah," the doctor said. "Had we'd been unsuccessful in saving your life, two things you wouldn't have had to worry about in heaven... a headache and an unexpected pregnancy."

Doctor Jordan burst out laughing but Doug didn't crack a smile. *What was amusing about him trying to kill himself? What's funny about that? Was it funny when his grandmother said she hated him? Was it funny when his mother abandoned him? Is it funny being homeless? Nothing was fuckin funny!* It was obvious that the doctor thought it was funny because he was still laughing.

"When can I get the fuck outta here?" Doug said, getting angry.

Doctor Jordan ignored Doug's profanity, he was used to it. "You're gonna have to stick around for a few days Mr. Douglas. We have to keep you here for observation and of course you have to see the psychiatrist before you can be released. Oh, and the dryness along with the bitter taste in your mouth comes from the charcoal that was used as a coating to help remove most of the dosage from your abdomen." Doctor Jordan smiled at Doug, "You will be okay Mr. Douglas."

"Campbell." Doug voiced.

"Excuse me?" Doc asked.

"My name is Doug Campbell... not Doug Douglas."

Doctor Jordan picked up Doug's chart and looked at it. "I apologize, Mr.
Campbell." he said sincerely. "I know that it has been stormy for you and it feels like a losing battle, I've seen many people like yourself Mr. Campbell that thinks that committing suicide is the solution, but it's not. Death is final. No matter what you go

through in this life, as long as you are alive you still have a chance. You are young, strong and you will get better. I didn't mean to upset you, if I did, I apologize. I am just trying to cheer you up and help you regain your will to live. Remember this Mr. Campbell, *The man with one leg thought he had it rough until he met the man with no legs.* Now get yourself some rest okay."

"Okay" Doug said, feeling bad realizing that the doctor was only trying to lift his spirits. "Thanks doc," he said in a way to show that there were no hard feelings.

"Hey doc," he called before Doctor Jordan left the room. "I was wondering as tall as you are, why didn't you try-out for the NBA or something?"

Doctor Jordan laughed, "The NBA? Nah, that wasn't going to happen... besides I can't wear shorts."

"You can't wear shorts?" Doug said puzzled. "Why not?"

Doctor Jordan laughed as he headed towards the door. Before he left, he turned and faced Doug who was still looking at him puzzled. "I can't wear shorts Mr. Campbell because my dick is too long." He burst out laughing as he left the room.

Doug woke up a few hours later with an uncomfortable taste in his mouth. His throat was still painfully dry and he desperately needed to use the bathroom. He thought about nurse Angel as he pressed the "call" button and ten minutes later, a very big, very strong-looking Jamaican nurse entered his room.

"I'm hungry and I gotta take a leak," Doug spat, apparently disappointed because she wasn't nurse Angel.

"Das wha fi call me far?" The nurse asked agitated. "You doan push di button if fi have to pee, you jus go pee... di bat troom right dere... an ye food, ye food is right in front ta ye face." She pointed to a tray that was next to him on his left.

"My bad," Doug apologized.

"Ye not bad..." She said, "...first time me ave ta tell ya."

After he used the bathroom and ate as much as he could Doug forced himself to take a stroll to see who else was on his floor. As soon as he stepped out into the hallway he realized that he was sharing the floor with a bunch of bug-outs... he was in the psychiatric ward of the hospital. The entrance, exit door was buzz-locked with two security guards standing post. Most of the nurses he saw were as strong-looking as the Jamaican nurse, but the orderly's were as huge as wrestlers, and they eyed Doug suspiciously, as he walked past. At first he thought it was the paper gown and slippers he had on, especially since he wasn't wearing any underwear. But then he noticed that the muscle head bullies were staring at everyone suspiciously, so he ignored them. Anyway, his main concern was to find someone who he could talk to and hopefully get an idea of how long he'd have to stay in this place. But everyone that he saw or tried to talk to were either already into deep dialogue with themselves or too medicated to notice him, so he just sat in his room and rested.

Shortly after he laid down, the Jamaican nurse came into his room to inform him that he had visitors.

World and Dooky stopped arguing as soon as the security guard buzzed them into the ward. After they entered, the door was key-locked and secured.

“It smells like Pine-Sol in here,” Dooky said.

“Man, what the fuck is this??” World said, looking at the two security guards.

"You mean to tell me..." Dooky cut in, "...that they just lock us on the floor with these crazy motherfuckers?" The two of them stood still and watched as four heavily medicated patients stared at them.

"Look at these fuckin zombies..." Dooky said as he pointed at the four patients that was staring at them. "I'm glad I got my razor, for real yo, anyone of these nutsacks that get outta line..." Dooky mimicked using his finger like he was cutting his throat "...They're in the right place!"

A loud noise followed by a scream coming from somewhere down the hallway ambushed their attention. World and Dooky both watched bewildered when a man with one leg came rolling towards them in a wheelchair, screaming at the top of his lungs.

"Grilled cheese! Gimmie my grilled cheese!" he screamed almost rolling right into World.

World jumped back and the man rolled his chair in front of Dooky, "Do you have my grilled cheese?" Dooky bent down so he could look the man in the eyes, and without fear, without blinking he said, "Do I look like I got yo grilled cheese you silly ass coo-coo motherfucka?"

The man backed away from Dooky eyeing him suspiciously before quickly rolling towards World again. World jumped again, "Yo fuck this shit... I'm out!" Dooky laughed but he was pissed off at World, the shit he did could get them killed.

"Yo chill out you scary ass nigga! How your silly ass gonna be scared of a man in a wheelchair?" Dooky grabbed the back of the man's chair, and with a running start, he pushed him down the hallway.

A nice looking Spanish lady greeted them politely then escorted them to the waiting room. The room was spaciously furnished with colorful couches, television sets, and both ping-pong and card tables. Dooky guessed that the room also dubbed as the recreation area. Besides them, there were three heavily medicated patients situated on a couch being watched by the T.V.

The Spanish woman smiled courteously and invited them to have a seat. She adjusted her clipboard before she spoke.

"My name is Maria... and I just have to ask you gentlemen a few questions. First things first," she said adjusting her clipboard, "who are you gentlemen here to see?"

"Douglas Campbell," Dooky answered.

"Mhmm, well..." She eyed him, "...And do you know why he's here?"

"I think it was a suicide attempt, but I'm not positive," he responded.

"I see... well, how old is his parents?"

"Huh?" Dooky said looking at World for help, but World just shrugged his shoulders with a "*Don't ask me expression*" on his face. "I don't know," Dooky answered.

She made a notation on her clipboard before continuing, "Does he have any children?"

"Not that I know of," Dooky responded.

She made another notation then directed her attention to World. "How did you get to the hospital, sir?"

"Huh?" World said confused, "How did *I* get here?"

"Yes, how did you get here?" She asked, pointing her pen at him.

"I rode over here with him," he answered pointing a thumb at Dooky.

"Car or motorcycle?"

Before Dooky or World could answer, Doug walked into the room with his arms stretched out like he wanted to hug both of them. He was smiling brightly until he saw who was sitting with them.

"Ayo, break-the-fuck out lady," he spat at the Spanish woman, then he turned to his partners. Yo, what up yall?"

"What up Loafer? Yo, what the fuck man?!"

"Wassup Doug? How you feel?" World asked.

Doug had never been so happy to see them ever in all the years he knew them. He was overwhelmed with emotions. He was about to tell them that he loved them when he noticed that the Spanish lady with the clipboard was still sitting there taking notes.

"Ayo!" Doug yelled then balled his fists, "Didn't I just tell you to get the fuck outta here?! Get the fuck away from us!!" Doug yelled.

"Yo be easy Loafer," Dooky said trying to calm him down. "Don't go crazy on the nurse like that, she was just asking us some questions."

Doug burst out laughing as much as it hurt him to laugh, he just couldn't stop.

"Wow Dook, I guess that you're the silly ass nigga today yo, because she ain't no motherfuckin nurse... that bitch is a patient!!"

World and Dooky looked at each other in disbelief as they watched the lady scurry away with her clipboard.

"Yo fuck this!" World said, "It was good to see you my nigga, ...get well and come home soon... Yo, I'm outta here!"

Doug convinced World to stay, and Dooky told Doug about his grandmother and his crazy ass next-door neighbor. After Doug admitted to having sex with Mamita Azucar, Dooky filled him in about the shit World did.

"Aah man!" Doug cried out feeling dizzy. He didn't need any more problems - especially problems like this. "I just can't escape it," he said burying his face in his hands. "What are we gonna do?"

"Well..." Dooky said calmly, "I'm not too worried about SQ, Pat, or that my pet monster looking mafucka Stutter... It's Lensey that's gonna be a problem."

"I fucked up." World voiced feeling guilty "...So I will step-up and deal with the consequences."

"What?!" Dooky said heated, "Who do you think you are, the last patriot or something? You silly ass nigga! You think you gonna save the day? Fuck outta here!"

"No, I'm not sayin that." World responded, "I'm just sayin..."

"You sayin what?" Dooky challenged.

"I'm sayin it's my fault so I'll handle it... dat all!"

"Silly ass nigga! Do you know how crazy you sound?" Dooky looked at Doug and pointed at World. "This grilled cheese-screaming, wheelchair rolling, one-legged coo-coo ass nigga had this scary ass nigga ready to leave!" He turned and faced World holding his two fingers to his head like a gun, "What the fuck you gonna do when Lensey puts the tooly to your head? Bang! Bang!"

"Aah man!" Doug cried out again, "What we gonna do?"

"Don't start that snot and booga shit Loafer. We just gotta think and not panic."

The three of them sat in silence, each one in their own thoughts. Dooky was first to break the silence.

"Okay... I got it. We're all in this together right, like Earth, Wind and Fire, right?"

"Yeah no doubt." World and Doug agreed in unison.

"Ahiight then, we're just gonna pay the nigga Lensey back... dat all."

"Aah man!" Doug cried out, "That's your plan? How we s'posed to pay him back Dook? With what?"

"We gonna rob a bank!" Dooky said calmly.

"Man Doug, get this crazy nigga a room!" World demanded. "He done lost his mind!"

"Listen silly, I know we can do it."

"Here you go..." World said, "Once you start talking that 'we' shit..."

"You got a better idea?" Dooky asked agitated.

"Yes, matter of fact I do." World replied, "We go talk to him and apologize."

"Listen to this silly nigga... you hear him right Doug? He's the one that needs a room! Go talk and apologize? Are you dumb, drunk or Dominican? You done smacked the man's chick, stole the man's drugs and now you wanna talk? You can't be serious!"

"Hold up." World said, opening up both palms. "*You* stole the drugs."

Dooky looked at World with disgust, he was really starting to dislike World.

"You right yo, *I* was the one who stole the drugs, but you might as well had been right next to me when I did it b'cause you're in it just as deep. If anybody is safe in this shit *yoouu* got us into, I would say that it would be Loafer, but I doubt it, because SQ and his two nut buggers tried to jump Doug last night.

"For real? What happened?" World quizzed. Doug explained what happened and World got quiet.

"We gonna rob a bank!" Dooky reiterated.

"I ain't robbing no fuckin' banks!" World screamed.

"Fuck your silly ass screaming for? You trying to tell security?"

"I don't give a fuck who hears me!" World yelled getting irate, "Cause I ain't doing it!"

Doug was quiet. He had been sitting there listening and contemplating whether or not robbing a bank was a good idea. If they pulled it off he would probably be able to open up the fish and chip restaurant he dreamed about. He pondered, imagining how it would look inside and out, how people would come from everywhere just to eat his food. It didn't take long to convince him...

"Yo, I'm wit it Dook! I'm wit you!" Doug said overly excited.

Dooky smiled, "Good, cause I'm gonna set it up properly," he looked at World before he added, "Because we gotta do it ASAP."

"Yall niggas is crazy!" World yelled becoming hysterical, "Fuck it! I gotta better idea, lets just kill Lensey and them niggas!... This way we don't have to pay shit back!"

Dooky was considering what World just said but, before he could respond World continued.

"And while we're at it, I can name a few other people I wanna kill!! Like that bitch at *Chubby Burgers* that forgot to put the bacon on my double chubby cheese!" World suggested sarcastically.

"Listen World..." Dooky said seriously, "...If you ain't wit the program then... cool, but all that other shit you talking and getting stupid with... now is not the time!"

"Yall the niggas that's getting stupid!" World retorted. "Oh wait, excuse me, stupider! Do yall dumb ass niggas realize what you're planning? Do you?? No, lemme put it to you this way..." World sat straight up as if it made them hear the consequences? "Prison time!... And Doug, I can see you now tucking that dick and being sombody's prison bitch!"

World's words made Doug conscious to the fact that he had on a paper suit with no underwear.

"I don't give a fuck what you say World..." Doug voiced, "What if we pull it off? What if we get paid? What if..."

"Your ass goes to jail for following this dumb ass!" World said finishing Doug's sentence and pointing a finger in Dooky's face.

Dooky smacked World's hand away.

"I told you to get outta here with that scary shit! Besides, it's your fault that we're in the middle of this shit anyway! Your silly ass wanna get drunk and fight females!"

World was about to swing on Dooky but Dooky gave him a nod that said, "*I wish you would.*"

"Do it World! Go ahead," Dooky encouraged.

"Try it! Go for it my nigga! You're in the right place!"

"Yeah whatever, fuck it! I ain't gonna waste my time trying to convince yall dumbass niggas!" World exclaimed as he got up to leave. "Doug, write me when you get to prison and let me know what color lipstick you want. And Dooky, I'll see your stupid ass in ten to twenty! I'm outta here!"

Dooky was pacing back and forth in Doug's room. He picked up a piece of Salsbury steak off Doug's hospital tray, smelled it, then tossed it back on the tray.

"Man, fuck World!" He exclaimed. "He's out there runnin' his fuckin' alcoholic mouth and fighting chicks-n-shit! And outta all the bitches in the world, this silly ass nigga had to fuck wit Lensey's chick! I can't fuckin believe it! Why? Why her?"

Doug was silent. He just nodded, then shrugged his shoulders. A cold draft shot up his hospital gown, giving him a chill.

"F'real though Doug," Dooky said, "I don't give a fuck about Lensey. You know how I do..." He imitated a gun by pointing his finger, "Bong, bong, bong!... And that would be a wrap for Lensey."

Doug tucked his gown underneath his legs as he nodded. He was only half listening to Dooky and his cowboy imagination.

"Yeah I hear you Dook, but we don't wanna do that, right?"

"Not if we don't have to," Dooky answered, still pacing back and forth. "But I'm saying, it's one of our options."

"A yo, man," Doug said, tired of hearing anything about murder. "I ain't killing nobody, so that ain't no option for me. Besides, I thought we already agreed on the bank. I'm wit that."

"Yeah, yeah, no doubt. We gonna handle that soon as you get outta the hospital," Dooky stopped pacing and turned to face Doug. "Matter of fact—what made your silly ass do some dumb shit like that in the first place?"

Doug sat quietly, looking down at his legs like he was being scolded. When he didn't respond, Dooky raised his voice. "A yo, what the fuck is up with you, loafer? You sitting there looking crazy in your paper dress... what up?"

Dooky paused for a moment and stared at him. Doug was looking like he was really troubled and Dooky kind of felt sorry for his partner.

"Seriously my nigga, what made you do that shit? Why did you try to body ya'self?"

Doug knew these questions were coming, and he thought he would be prepared when they came. But it was hard for him to explain the pressure, pain and abandonment that he had to deal with on a daily basis, without sounding like a weakling. Dooky was staring at him expecting an answer and Doug knew he wouldn't let it rest until he got one. Doug let out an exasperated sigh then took a deep breath before he spoke.

"A yo, it's my grandmother. She be stressing me man, and I just couldn't---"

"Your grandmoms? You can't be serious, Loafer! That old lady got you under that much pressure? Why you ain't tell me?" Dooky said, balling his fist in front of Doug's face. "Why you ain't tell me yo? I would've got you a dog, a pit bull or a rotti. Old people are scared of dogs son... everybody knows that." Dooky looked at Doug and grinned. "Or, my nigga, I could've just put this dick in her right quick, that would've calmed her ass down, yo." Dooky grabbed his crotch and laughed. "But I heard you could catch worms from fuckin' old people though, but fuck it! You my nigga, my silly ass nigga, and I would catch the worms for you, yo."

Doug laughed for the first time without pain since being in the hospital. Dooky always put him through a lot of shit, but he loved Dooky like a brother.

"A yo," Doug said seriously, leaning close to Dooky and lowering his voice. "You serious about hitting the bank right? Cause I'm wit that shit, f'real yo."

"Yeah, son, I'm dead serious," Dooky said.

"Y'know," Doug said, "We're gonna need a lot of shit? We gonna need guns, masks, gloves, um... a stolen car... what bank we robbing? We gonna need a good getaway plan and a back-up plan, just in case. And you know they got that exploding money, right?

We gotta watch that. And yo, no stashing! keep it real, Dook, 50/50, I know how niggas---"

"Slow your silly ass down, Loafer! You sound like you medicated! We'll figure out all that shit when you get outta here. When did they say you getting out?"

Doug said. "First chance I get, I'm outta this spot!"

*****

World left the hospital angry. He couldn't stick around any longer and listen to them talk about robbing a bank. "Dooky think he know every fuckin' thing," he mumbled aloud. "And Doug stupid ass... hmph!.. . Yall two dumb ass niggas go right ahead and do your stupid thing! I'll see yall niggas on the news!"

Because the hospital was on the other side of town, World had a long walk home. He stopped at the first store he came to, to buy a bag of chips, but when he got inside he changed his mind and decided to buy a beer. *I'm only going to buy a can.* He thought as he walked to the beverage section. World glanced at the old Spanish man behind the counter busy stocking cigarettes.

When he saw that he wasn't being watched, temptation overwhelmed him and he quickly grabbed a 40 oz. bottle of beer and stuffed it down his sleeve, just like Dooky showed him. Then instead of a can, he grabbed another 40 oz. bottle and approached the counter. "How much?" World asked as he put the bottle on the counter.

"Two-fifty," the man answered, as he put the beer in a bag.

World put the exact amount on the counter and was about to grab the bag when the man pulled the bag out of his reach and snatched the money that World put on the counter.

"This," he said, putting the money in the register, "is for the beer you put in your sleeve." The man tapped the beer that was in the bag on the counter, then reached below the register and pulled out a wooden baseball bat. "If you want this one, you pay for it! Or get the fuck out of my store before I call the cops!"

Shocked and embarrassed, World paid the man for the other beer. He was too embarrassed to ask for another bag, so he left the store with the other beer still in his sleeve.

*****

Squirrel, Stutter, and a very badly bruised Pat daddy had just pulled away from an ATM machine that was around the corner from the hospital. Pat had just given them some money to help fund their arsenal.

"Good lookin out, Pat," Squirrel said, nudging Stutter.

"Yo, g..g...goooood lu... lu... luuh... lookin, Pat Brade... Braydee... Ha."

"Oh shit, look!" Squirrel pointed, spotting World as he came out of the store. "Would you look at this straight-outta-the-movies shit, here!"

"It's only 3'o'clock in the afternoon and that nigga is drinking a 40," Pat added from the back seat of the car.

"Nigga, fuck what he's doin', it's a wrap for this clown...he's done off!" Squirrel growled, silencing Pat by looking at him through the rearview mirror.

"Now let's see if Dooky and that other clown is gonna come outta the store so we can body these three stooges, right now!"

"D. . . d... dass... dass wassup, my nigga!" Stutter agreed, tapping the gun he had tucked in his waist.

*****

Pat Daddy shivered in the backseat. The thought of him being an accessory to murder frightened him. He definitely wanted to get back at Doug for mercilessly beating him the way he did.

Especially since he, of all people, should've known that he was just trying to establish an edge and had no intentions of fighting him. "*So what if I mushed him a lil bit*," Pat thought.

"*Common sense should of told him I wasn't trying to hurt him, besides, that's no excuse for what he did to my face.*"

Pat's lip was split in three places, his left eye was swollen shut and the rest of his face looked like it was attacked by bumblebees. He looked worse than a "*Rocky*" movie. So yeah, he wanted revenge. He wanted to go another round, and maybe this time his kick would work... but he didn't want to kill anybody.

He would've still been in his house licking and nursing his wounds if Squirrel hadn't come to his house and put a gun to his head, forcing him to get his aunt's car and come outside. He even withdrew $500 from the ATM because Squirrel and Stutter gave him some fish story about buying some switch blades.

Now he was trapped, sitting in the backseat of his aunts Maxima, which he was supposed to have returned over an hour ago, listening to Squirrel and Stutter conspire about committing a drive-by shooting. Pat felt like jumping out of the car and running.

"Yo, yall, I don't think this is a good idea."

"Who told you to think... Patrick!" Squirrel said eyeing him through the rearview mirror. He doubled parked the car across the street from the store and watched World.

"Yo, it's broad daylight, Squirrel. Plus, this is my aunt's car. S'pose somebody see the license plate?"

"Don't worry about that?" Squirrel said disregarding Pat and turning his attention to

Stutter. “Look at this nigga, Stutter...look how he just standing there in front of the store.” Squirrel expressed his rat toothed smile. “This nigga is sweet as deer meat!”

“I, I see ‘em,” Stutter said, watching. “I ssss... seeee ‘em.”

*****

World was standing in front of the store when he opened his beer and took a long swig. By the time he finished gulping, half of the bottle had been drained. He took another swallow before he started walking. His stride and swagger came alive as the alcohol began to inebriate him. He no longer cared about Dooky, Doug, Lensey, or anybody because the confidence that alcohol gave him made him feel invincible.

With his third swig, he emptied the 40 oz. down to suds and placed the bottle on the ground without breaking it. When he looked up a cute, chubby, brown skin girl was about to walk past him. The way she popped the gum in her mouth made her look approachable. World tapped her on her arm politely.

“Excuse me love, but I just had to let you know that you---.”

She snatched her arm away from him hard and fast, as if he were contagious then rolled her eyes and continued on her way without losing a step.

World became upset by the way she exaggerated her rejection towards him, especially since she wasn't all that.

"I don't know why yo fat ass is rushing... Chubby Burgers is open 24 hours," he shouted, but the girl ignored him and kept walking and that really got him mad. "I told yo fat ass, I ain't paying for no more abortions!"

His last comment hit a nerve and the girl turned around and stuck her tongue out at him then rolled her eyes. Then she looked around to see if anyone was watching before she gave him the finger.

Satisfied with her reaction. World went back to his stride. He walked up second avenue towards the library, hoping to find one of those pig-tailed, mini-skirt wearing, lollipop sucking freaks that you only find in porno movie libraries, but was disappointed when he saw that it was closed. "*Damn*," he thought, forgetting that it was Sunday.

As he continued his walk he noticed a familiar looking, funny walking character, about a half block ahead of him. World rubbed his eyes with his fist, he could only see the persons back. But he was sure that he was seeing who he was seeing. World got excited.

"Ain't this a bitch! I got yo ass now mafucka!" He ducked down low, creeping close to the parked cars as he ran towards Walt Shaker. "Ain't no sneaking out the back door this time! Not this time, nigga!"

*****

Squirrel, Stutter and Pat drove slowly behind World, waiting for the opportune time to attack. Squirrel looked at Pat through the rearview mirror.

"Yo, Patrick! You are gonna take care of this clown right here, son! It's time for you to put in some work, nigga!"

Squirrel looked at Stutter who was staring out the window daydreaming. "Yo, Stutter... Stutter!" He yelled, nudging him with his elbow. "Give Pat your gun so he can put the work in on this buster."

Stutter pulled the .357 revolver out of his waist and passed it to Pat. Pat pushed the gun back towards Stutter.

"I can't! I can't do this yall. I can't go through with this," he pleaded, trying not to put his fingerprints on the weapon.

"Fuck you mean you can't?" Squirrel yelled turning around to face Pat. His face was twisted into a frown that made him look like an evil, deranged rodent. He lifted the tech-9 that he kept concealed by his side and pointed it at Pat's face. He waved the gun from side to side as he spoke. "Either you or him, bitch ass nigga! You make the choice!"

The way that Squirrel carelessly maneuvered the weapon even caused Stutter to flinch.

Snitches Get Stitches

Walt Shaker was higher than a kite that was stuck in the engine of a 747 traveling to Japan. He was twitching and tweaking like the bonafide basehead that he was. He hadn't slept since taking the drugs from Dooky and his crew, but yet, his eyes were wide open like he had just seen a ghost. Since he'd left Tracy's apartment, he had been stepping in and out of buildings and taking hits in the staircases. It had been a long night and he couldn't stop his feet from dancing. He had never been this high off of crack cocaine, then again, he had never had this much crack at one time. He didn't like to be this high in the daytime because it made him too paranoid. The darkness of the night was like a shade, a cover for him to hide himself. Right now he was walking around looking for a place to lay low and get him off the street for a few hours. He had just finished smoking the last seven vials of his stash and his heart was racing so fast that he was scared that it might burst. He tried to balance it by speeding walking and singing songs, hoping that it would help calm his nerves.

"I came through the door, I said it before... I'll never let the pipe magnetize me no more, now wooly Willy got a pair of my sneakers... slow, slow down."

*****

Staring at the hole in the barrel of the mini-machine gun, nearly caused Pat to wet his pants.

"Alright! Alright!" Pat pleaded. He closed his good eye and raised his hands to surrender. "Please! I'll do it! Please!... Put the gun away, I'll do it."

Stutter offered him the gun again and this time Pat reached for it nervously, praying that it wouldn't accidentally discharge. The realization of what he agreed to do broke his body out in goosebumps. The weight of the weapon felt scary in his hands and he held it gently, as if it were an infant.

Squirrel glared at him menacingly before removing his weapon from in front of his face, and focused on World, who appeared to be harassing the chubby girl that walked past him.

"Look at this thirsty motherfucker! Look! That girl he yelling at can't be more than thirteen years old."

"She d... d... dooon't look like shhhee f... four... fourteen! Shit I,I,I might havta... I thing, think, I would b... b... beeet dat p... p... pusssee up, son!"

"Nigga is you crazy! How old are you again? You can't be fuckin' serious! Let me find out you one of those Chester-ass, freak niggas running around with candy in your pockets! You one of them '*you remind me of my jeep*' type of niggas, ain't you?"

Squirrel looked over Stutter's dreadlocks and saw World duck behind the parked cars.

"Oh shit! The nigga is trying to get away!"

*****

World was three car-lengths away from Walt and gaining momentum, when Walt turned and saw him coming. Fear momentarily froze him as he vigorously tried not to panic. He was trying to get a good look at the face of the person who was running towards him because he wasn't sure if the person was coming to attack him or going to run past him. The runner was filling the gap quickly, giving Walt only a few seconds to decide whether he was going to run or reason. He stepped closer to a parked car, just so the runner would have enough space to run by. There was no one chasing the runner, as far as Walt could see, and that gave him a bad feeling.

"Slow, slow down, youngin," Walt sang nervously, just as the runner reached in his jacket, while his face displayed a mask of pure evil. It was then that Walt recognized World. "Somebody!" Walt shrieked, spinning on his heels. "Somebody help meee! He's got a gun!"

*****

When World ducked behind the parked cars and started running up the block, Squirrel assumed that he had spotted them and was trying to get away.

"It's showtime, son! Nigga trying to run! Pat! Don't fuck this up mafucka! Just reach out, aim, and squeeze the trigger! If you miss, I'm lighting yo ass up!" Squirrel turned up the volume of the music, then stepped on the gas. "Let's get this bozo! Remember what I said, Pat. Aim and squeeze! Don't fuckin' miss!"

Pat was scared and visibly shaking. He thought about putting the .357 to his temple and pulling the trigger. He did not want to do this, but he felt that there was no way out of it now. He was trying to think about what he would tell the police when they arrested him. Surely they were not going to believe, "He made me do it," again. He thought about jumping out of the window and running until Squirrel, as if he read his thoughts, pointed the mini-machine gun at him with his free hand and yelled.

"Get ready nigga! If you miss, you finished!"

Pat began to cry as he leaned his body out of the back window and aimed.

*****

World charged towards Walt silently and was almost as close as his shadow, when Walt turned around and saw him. As soon as Walt recognized him, he tried to take off running. World reached and pulled out the 40 oz. bottle of malt liquor and grabbed the collar of the back of Walt's coat.

"Where you going, you crack head motherfucker?" Walt was able to pull away, ripping the coat, leaving a dirty piece of rag in Worlds hands.

World tossed the piece of material and laughed, "You ain't getting away old nigga!" World yelled, enjoying the cat and mouse game. "Not til I whoop yo old ass!"

He easily caught up to Walt and tried to clip his feet. Walt weebled and wobbled sideways like he was doing a new dance, but was able to keep his balance.

World let out a deep homicidal laugh at Walt's footwork, as he closed in for the kill. He raised the bottle to strike the back of Walt's head, when the sound of screeching tires distracted him.

*****

Squirrel pulled the car as close as he could to World and jammed on the brakes, narrowly avoiding hitting a parked car. The sound of screeching tires sliced the air as the teary eyed

Pat Daddy hung halfway out of the window, pointing a gun. He aimed the .357 Magnum in World's direction, closed his good eye in fear and squeezed the trigger four times.

Boom! Boom! Boom! Boom!

The thunder from the weapon activated a few car alarms of the parked cars. Squirrel didn't wait for the results. He stepped on the gas, causing the tires to screech, as he sped off.

*****

Dooky had just stepped off the elevator and was about to exit the hospital when paramedics came rushing through the side doors, pushing a patient on a stretcher towards the emergency room. There were two medics attending to the patient, one was vigorously pumping the patients chest, while the other was giving oxygen and simultaneously checking for a pulse. Dooky wasn't but a few steps away from the stretcher and his curiosity got the best of him. He stepped just a little closer to see if he could get a better look at the face or the damage. They were just about to push the patient right past him and Dooky was able to see the patient's bloody face. He almost didn't recognize who he was staring at because the patients head had swelled to the size of a pumpkin.

"Ohhh shit!" He voiced a little too loudly, "What the fuck happened to you my nigga?"

A man in a flashy suit that had walked in right behind the paramedics responded.

"He's been shot... do you know this person?"

Dooky looked at the man that answered his question and automatically knew he was a cop. He was dressed like *Miami Vice* was his favorite show and had an air of confidence that said, "*he was a bad ass white boy with a gun.*"

He was tall and slim with a square jaw line and a pointy nose. His eyes were cold and recording information that was probably being fed into a built-in lie detector.

Dooky stared him up and down as the stretcher disappeared behind the swinging doors of the ER.

"Nah, I don't know him," he answered as he attempted to walk away. He desperately needed to get to a phone. Before he was able to take a step, he felt a heavy hand grip his shoulder, and when he turned around the cop was flashing his badge.

"My name is Detective Ford, and I would like to ask you a few questions... please come with me."

His hand never left Dooky's shoulder, which indicated that he didn't have a choice.

*****

Squirrel was driving fast and recklessly, as if they were being chased by the law. Stutter was sitting in the passenger seat, bracing himself with his hands and occasionally his knees against the dashboard as if it were going to stop him from flying through the windshield if they crashed.

Pat was silently sitting in the back seat with an eerie calmness. He was no longer crying, in fact, except for the bruises, his face was expressionless, and his good eye looked vacant. The first shot he fired, his eyes were closed and he opened them after he heard the sound of breaking glass. The power that he felt from the gun gave him a rush that was electrifying and intoxicating. He no longer felt scared or weak. This was the feeling that he had been searching for. The second shot that he fired left the barrel of the gun in slow motion as he aimed at World's head. He noticed that World had company and decided to kill them both. His eyes followed the back of the bullet as it traveled through the air, hitting its target and leaving a hole about the size of a penny where it entered his head. His third and forth shots went through the windows of the parked car that his other target had ducked behind. Pat wanted to get out and finished the job. Not because of Squirrel's threat, but because he had a blood thirst that made him want to kill. But Squirrel had pulled off before he could get out.

Now Pat was sitting in the back seat thinking about what he had just done. He felt empty. He felt like his soul was missing. But at the same time, he felt powerful. He didn't even notice how fast and wild Squirrel was driving until a sharp turn made his body sway to the side. He looked at the back of Squirrel's head and cursed him under his breath. He turned to look out the back window to see if someone was following them before he spoke.

"Slow the fuck down b'fore you hit something nigga! Ain't nobody chasing us!"

Squirrel slowed down and pulled over on a side street behind the projects. He turned to face Pat.

"A yo, son, you popped that nigga top, son! You seen that shit, right Stutter?"

"Suh, son... I suh, suh, son... word!"

In fact, neither Squirrel or Stutter saw anybody get shot. As soon as the first shot was fired Squirrel was ready to get up out of there and Stutter was nudging him, telling him to drive away.

Pat was silent. He stared at the two of them for a long moment before he got out of the car. He tucked the .357 in his waist then opened the driver's side door. With a nod of his head, he motioned for Squirrel to get out of the car.

"Yo, what up?" Squirrel questioned, looking at him strangely. "What you doin', son?"

"I'm taking the car! Now get out!"

"Chill nigga! We gotta get our stories straight just in case we..."

"Aye bwoy! Get de fuck outta mi bloodcot kear! Now!"

"Oh!" Squirrel said, unimpressed with Pat's accent. "So now, all of a sudden, you some type of tough Jamaican killa, gangsta, rude-boy, ass nigga, huh? That tough talk don't scare me...Patrick! You still pussy!"

Squirrel twisted his lips making his angry rodent face look rabid. He jumped out of the car pulling out his tech-9 and put the barrel underneath Pat's chin.

“I'll murder yo bitch ass Patrick, if you ever talk that tough shit again, nigga!”

Just as Squirrel finished his threat, Pat snatched the .357 from his waist and pulled the trigger. The bullet tore through Squirrel's hip, blowing most of his hip bone up the block. Squirrel fell to the floor in pain, screaming and holding his hip.

“Aagghh! You motherfucka! Aagghh! Fuck you shoot me for? Aagghh! You fuck! You fuckin crazy!”

The tech-9 Squirrel was holding was useless and unloaded. The clip of the gun was in place, making the weapon look dangerous, but it didn't have a firing pin.

Squirrel threw the empty weapon at Pat's head, and it barely managed to hit him in the shoulder. Pat picked up the empty weapon and examined it in his hand. He liked the way that this gun felt too. He pointed both weapons at Squirrel and laughed.

The car door opened then slammed shut. Pat turned around just in time to see Stutter doing a great rendition of Carl Lewis's 100-yard dash. He pointed the tech-9 at Stutter's back and pulled the trigger, when there was no thunder from the weapon, he laughed.

"Fuck bwoy, carry 'em a dead gun."

Pat studied Squirrel for a long moment, debating if he should put a bullet in his head or mouth. He reached down into Squirrel's pocket and removed the $450 that he gave to him earlier. Then Pat kicked Squirrel in the hip, and Squirrel screamed like an opera singer.

The tables had now turned and Pat felt the power. Hearing Squirrel scream gave him another adrenaline rush.

"Poosy bwoy!" He screamed. "I mon a lion!" He yelled, as he beat the shit out of Squirrel with the tech-9.

*****

World had the bottle raised high above his head and was preparing to strike the back of Walt's skull when the sound of screeching tires distracted him. The sound was too close to be ignored.

"What the fuck?" He said startled, he thought that it was an unmarked police vehicle that had pulled up beside them until he saw the driver and noticed the awfully battered Pat Daddy leaning out of the back window, pointing a gun at him.

World screamed as the first shot blasted from the gun shattering the 40.oz bottle that he still had held above his head. He actually heard the hum of the second bullet zip by his head before he ducked. Beer was rolling down his back and face, stinging his eyes as he crouched beside a parked car. World stayed low and bolted in the opposite direction, followed by the thundering of two more gunshots and screeching tires.

*****

"Help me!" World yelled hysterically as he burst through the doors of Mount Vernon police station. "They're trying to kill me!"

A few officers in the precinct almost reached for their weapons when World burst through the doors, but the more seasoned officers just glanced at him and went back to whatever they were doing. World was still screaming for help when a young uniformed officer approached him.

"Calm down, son... whoa." The officer backed up a step. "Have you been drinking?"

At that moment World realized he smelled like beer.

"No... well, yes... but! I was drinking but, the bullets went through my beer when they shot at me."

"Hold on," the officer said confused, "who was shooting at you, and where did this incident take place?"

"Their names are Squirrel, Pat Daddy and Stutter, and they all tried to kill me right there on second avenue... up the block from the library."

The officer whipped out his notepad, hoping to get his first collar. "Um... can you repeat those names again," he said politely, as he pulled out his pen. "What did you say your name was again?"

"Worldin."

"Okay, uh... Mr. Worldin, tell me what happened."

Once World started talking he couldn't stop. He told the officer everything. He told about the drugs Dooky stole from Lensey and how Walt had tricked them into trusting him, he told the officer about Doug's suicide attempt, and how him and Dooky were planning to rob a bank to pay Lensey back. He explained how he was about to fight Walt when Squirrel and Pat drove up and tried to kill him. He told the officer everything... except for the drugs he sold to FrankMike and the smack he gave to Lensey's girl. The officer wrote it all on his notepad.

The officer was happy that he approached World, he was still a rookie and hadn't seen any action, so this was big. He hoped that the captain would let him stay on the case instead of the boring desk job he had been assigned to.

"Have a seat, Mr. Worldin." The officer instructed before he walked into the detectives offices. "I'll be back in a sec."

Moments later, Detective Ford and his partner, Detective Reeves, along with the uniformed officer approached World. The three of them stared at World like a science project, before
Detective Ford took the initiative.

"What is your name, son?"

"Worldin Jr." World answered, feeling intimidated by their stares. The officer passed his notepad to Detective Ford. Ford took the notepad and studied it briefly, then passed it to his partner. A strong stench of alcohol invaded Detective Ford's nostrils.

"Have you been drinking, son?" He asked emphatically.

"Yes, but, um... like I told the officer, I... um."

"He said," the officer interrupted, "that one of the suspects bullets went through his beer bottle causing the alcohol to soak his clothing, sir."

Detectives Ford and Reeves both looked at the officer impatiently. "Thank you, that will be all officer." Ford said dismissing him.

"You don't need me to---?"

"No!... Thank you. We will take it from here."

*****

As the detectives escorted World into their office, World was nervously trying to convince himself that he was doing the right thing by talking to the police. *Why shouldn't I tell the police? Shit! Them mafuckas was really trying to kill me! They're murderers!* Before they were able to sit down, a call came over Detective Ford's radio about shots being fired on second avenue and both detectives turned to look at him. World was standing there mumbling to himself as Ford responded to the call. When he finished he whispered something to his partner, gesturing towards World, then left. Det. Reeves approached World casually.

"So, Mr. World... have a seat. Would you like some coffee and doughnuts?"

"I'll take a doughnut... but, I don't drink coffee."

Det. Reeves sat a box of *Donnies Doughnuts* in front of World and he grabbed one.

"So, let me get this straight, who was planning to rob a bank?"

*****

"Man, for the third time, I don't know anybody named Worldin! I told you, I came here to visit a friend. Dat all!" Dooky said, becoming angry and annoyed with Det. Ford's questions.

"Tell me about Squirrel and his brother Lensey," Det. Ford persisted.

"Who?"

"You know! Where do they keep the drugs?" Ford said, getting upset.

"What drugs? Listen, I don't know what you're talking about, man! Can I go now?"

Dooky's obnoxious behavior was almost enough to provoke Det. Ford to punch him in the face. If there hadn't been so many people around, he would've just beat the information out of Dooky... a technique that he had practiced and perfected, that guaranteed results. Instead Det. Ford stepped closer to Dooky and grabbed two handfuls of his shirt. He pulled him so close to his face that he could smell the fear leaking out of Dooky's pores.

"Let me remind you of '*what drugs*' I'm talking about, you nappy headed, son of a bitch! I'm talkin about the drugs you stole from Lensey and Squirrel! The same drugs that Pat Daddy just shot and killed crack head Walt for! You wanna play games with me, Dookiah Douglas? You wanna play games, huh Dooky, you fuckin scumbag? Let me tell you what kind of games I play, you little prick! I will lock your black ass up for distribution of a controlled substance, interfering with a murder investigation of a confidential informant, and conspiracy to commit bank robbery! You wanna fuck with me, you little piece of shit? Try me!"

Det. Ford shoved Dooky towards the side doors of the hospital.

"You see that apple tree in the middle of the parking lot?"

Dooky looked outside at the parking lot, then shook his head. All he saw out there were vehicles.

“By the time you get outta prison, you little prick, there’s gonna be one out there! Now, give me some fuckin answers!”

Dooky was shook-up by all the information that Det. Ford had. But he was trying to be cool. He figured that the police had somehow planted a bug or one of those FBI micro-chips in his clothes, and he wasn’t going to say another word. But he was scared to death.

“What the fuck is that smell?” Det. Ford said, more to himself than to Dooky. “It fuckin stinks like shit in here!” He added while checking his shoes. “You!” Ford said pointing at Dooky, “are coming with me! Let’s go, now!”

*****

Just as they were about to leave, paramedics came rushing through the emergency doors pushing a very badly beaten, swollen faced Squirrel towards the emergency room on a stretcher.

Dooky was trying to keep from being seen, he noticed two uniformed officers following closely behind the paramedics. The officers stopped when they saw Det. Ford and they exchanged words.

Dooky glanced at Squirrel, he was handcuffed to the stretcher and praying loudly, asking God to save him. Half of Squirrel's face was bashed in and obviously broken. Looking at him, all Dooky could think about was the 52 block style that he demonstrated. *I knew that shit didn't work,* he thought, as he turned his back so Squirrel wouldn't see him.

But Squirrel spotted him and called out. "Yo Dooky, Dooky...tell them! Tell these police how crazy Pat is. Ask Dooky, officer... he knows, he'll tell yall. He just shot me, and he shot World! I tried to stop him, but he had a gun. He's crazy! Tell them Dook!"

Det. Ford, the two officers, paramedics, and anyone else who was in earshot of Squirrel voice, looked at Dooky. He turned around and faced Squirrel, looking him dead in the eye.

"I don't know what you're talking about!" Dook said, backing out of the paramedics' way.

"Fuck you, Dooky! I never liked you anyway! My brother is gonna handle you; he's gonna smoke your bitch ass!"

Squirrel weakly tried to break the hold of the handcuffs as they rolled him towards the ER.

"It ain't over!" He yelled, "Watch! It ain't over!"

*****

Doug was trying to relax. He was thinking about how he was going to start his business when two uniformed officers entered his room.

"Douglas Campbell?" one of the officers asked. Doug sat up and slipped his feet inside his paper shoes. He immediately assumed the officers were there in regards to the dispute he had with his grandmother.

"Yes?" Doug said, instantly alert.

"We would like to ask you a few questions concerning---."

Doug dashed past the two officers, knocking one of them to the floor. He ran out of his room and down the hallway with the other officer running closely on his heels. The patients in the hallway who were witnessing the chase, clapped and cheered for Doug as he ran around aimlessly, trying to escape. The floor security along with the two muscle-bound orderlies joined the pursuit in attempt to capture and subdue him. Doug was running, dodging, and trying to knock anything over that was not nailed down to avoid them from catching him. One of the floor security guards managed to grab Doug's gown, ripping it from his body. Now Doug was ass-naked, running back up the hallway. Doug bulldozed two doctors that tried to grab him, and almost ran into the crazy man in the wheelchair who had rolled out of his room when he heard all of the commotion. He hurdled over the front of the wheelchair, barely missing it, but when he landed on his feet, one of the orderlies popped out of nowhere and hit him with a "one-hitter-quitter" that landed flush on the chin, knocking him on his back, hard and fast. One of the uniformed officers ran over and gave Doug a solid kick to his stomach.

"Now!,.. You crazy fuck! You're going to jail!"

All of the rooting and applause turned into boos and cries of protests, as they handcuffed him. Almost all the patients had come out of their rooms to watch and Doug noticed that most of them were smiling and nodding at him.

As Doug took his walk of shame down the hallway, he asked one of the officers. "Yall gonna take me outta the hospital naked?"

"Shut the fuck up!" The officer ordered. "You'll be lucky if you make it outta the hospital."

The strong looking Jamaican nurse that Doug spoke to earlier approached the officers with a gown in her hand. All the women nurses, along with a few males had gathered around lustfully, watching and whispering as the officer tied the gown around Doug's waist. Doug noticed the muscle-bound orderly looking at him passionately while licking his lips and flexing his pectorals and was suddenly relieved to be taken by the police.

"Shows over!" The officer announced, noticing all of the woman who had gathered in the area.

No sooner than the officer spoke, the crazy Spanish lady with her clipboard still in hand, dashed by Doug and the officers, naked.

"Somebody chase me!... Chase me!"

The crazy man in the wheelchair who also somehow managed to get naked, rolled past them screaming, "Grilled cheese! Grilled cheese!"

*****

"Let's get the fuck out of here!" one of the uniformed officers said.

"Yeah," the other responded. "B'fore all of these nutcases get naked!"

"Let's go asshole!" he said, giving Doug a shove. "Move it!"

*****

World had gotten comfortable, making himself at home, sitting behind Det. Reeves' desk. He was eating a Chubby Burger and looking through the photo's of one of the mugshot albums that Det. Reeves had given him to look through, when Det. Ford and Dooky walked in.

"Oh shit, Dooky, what up my nigga? Yo, look whose picture they have in this book," World said casually.

Dooky was shocked to see World sitting there, but now the puzzle quickly came together.

"Yo, wassup man?" World said, walking over to him with the photo book open. "Look at this nigga, FrankMike."

"You talkin to me?" Dooky said, trying to act like he didn't know World. "Where do I know you from?" He asked, giving World a wink on the sly.

"Dook, stop the bullshit! This ain't no game, son! I almost got killed a little while ago."

"Listen," Dooky said, trying to give World another hint, "I don't know you or how you know my name, but...," He tripled winked at World, then directed the rest of his words to Det. Ford, "...am I under arrest? If not, I would like to go now. I know my rights!"

"You ain't going nowhere you fuckin armpit! Not until you gimmie some answers! You still wanna play games? You still wanna try me? I'm beginning to lose patience with you!" Det. Ford yelled, as he took off his jacket and rolled up his sleeves.

"Yo, Dook," World said, "why you buggin, son? I already told them everything, we straight. They want Lensey and Pat and them dudes, not us. I told you I would take care of it," World explained, almost too proudly.

"Listen," Dooky said, just about fed up with World. "I ain't wit none of this "*cooperating*" shit you doing! Look at you! You sitting up here eating Chubby Burgers with the police! That's you! I don't know shit!"

"You know what, Dooky? You're a stupid ass motherfucker! You think you a gangster? Ha, ha.

Go ahead and get that ass killed then, stupid. Fuck Squirrel! Fuck Lensey! Fuck all of them niggas! Matter of fact, fuck you too! I just told you that them niggas tried to body me earlier! But nooo, you think you know *every fuckin' thing*, don't you? Fuck it then! Go ahead and rob your bank and pass your fake money to the prostitutes! You go right ahead Dooky Dook Booty, you fuckin stupid motherfucker!"

And that was all she wrote. Dooky's punch landed on the bridge of Worlds nose with a loud cracking sound, dropping him to one knee. He followed the punch with a knee-thrust that landed in almost the exact same spot, splitting World's nose open.

Detectives Ford and Reeves both grabbed and restrained Dooky, who was kicking and fighting to get loose.

World was on his hands and knees with his head down, watching his blood run from his nose to the floor. When he finally looked up, he displayed the grotesque disfigurement of his nose that was bleeding like a broken faucet.

"Aagghh, you fucked up now nigga! Yall are my witnesses, yall seen him assault me! I'm pressing charges on this nigga! Lock his ass up! Lock his fuckin' ass up!"

Det. Ford was happy. This was music to his ears. He wanted nothing more than to put the cuffs on this uncooperative nigger.

"You have the right to remain silent..."

*****

After counting and recounting the drugs, Lensey was in a bad mood. He couldn't wait to finish up his business in Raleigh so he could get back to NY and punish Dooky for stealing his shit.

"That little fuckin' dirtbag must've lost his fuckin' mind! I'm gonna kill you, Dooky!" He spat as he wrapped the drugs in a *University of North Carolina* sweat suit.

He placed the sweat suit in the bottom of a book bag, underneath two chemistry textbooks.

After brushing an imaginary speck of lint from his Argyle sweater and putting on a pair of round-framed glasses, Lensey checked his appearance in the mirror. Satisfied with his college campus look, he left the motel and hopped into his rented Ford Explorer. It was over ninety degrees outside and the inside of the vehicle felt like a sauna. He felt his armpits beginning to perspire as he tossed the book bag in the backseat. He rolled down the windows and put his seat belt on before he pulled off for the twenty-minute drive to the projects known as *Warner Terrace.*

This was Lensey's fourth trip to North Carolina since "Randy Tool" gave him the transporter job. The job was a reward for Lensey's assistance from when they were in the joint.

Lensey had unintentionally interrupted an ass whooping that was being served to Randy by four white, racist, correctional officers. They had accused Randy of getting too familiar with one of the female CO's. The bitch was a "dick watcher," but everybody and their mama knew that the male officers didn't play that shit in Great Meadows Correctional Facility.

The only reason why Lensey decided to knuckle up and help him was because he knew of Randy's status in the drug game. They had both been in the same cell block for over a year, and had never said more than two words to each other. But Lensey figured that if he helped him, one hand would wash the other, and he would benefit in the long run. So he jumped in and started swinging, eventually more and more officers arrived and they both got their ass whooped. No new charges were filed against them, and they were lucky to be alive. But, if Lensey would have known at the time that this driving mule job would be his only compensation, Randy Tool would've had to take that ass whooping by himself.

The money he made from the trips didn't outweigh the risk he was taking, but he took the job because he needed the money and he was always extra careful.

At the same time, he made it his business to skim a little from all of the packages and hustle on the side, to make some extra cash. What Lensey skimmed from the packages was unnoticeable, but now, there were over a thousand rocks missing and he knew that somebody was going to notice this.

Fuck it! Lensey thought.

His plan was to just drop the book bag off and keep it moving. And if anybody called him and complained about what was missing, he would act angry or surprised, but he would refuse to be responsible. As far as he was concerned everything was right and exact, when he dropped it off. It would take Lensey about five more trips, without pay, to replace what was missing, and that was not an option. Besides, after this trip, he was done being Randy Tools driving mule. Lensey wanted to get paid and had already scoped the Halifax projects and made plans to open his own drug spot down here.

He cursed Dooky again for putting him in a jam, and made up his mind to shoot Dooky on sight for sneak thieving from him.

Lensey stopped at a red light and was searching for his cigarettes, he cursed loudly, realizing that he must've left them in the hotel room. Nothing was going right and he got a bad feeling.

He was about to pull over into a gas station when he passed a short, red-head chick walking in the same direction. She had on a pair of biker pants that hardly left anything to the imagination. And she had a bubble ass that she was just throwing from side to side. The sight of her ass, when she walked, resembled a drunk tow truck driver towing a Volkswagen beetle.

So far, Lensey's game was tight. No matter what he said, it worked on the ladies in the South.

Shorty red head was all smiles when she saw him get out of his jeep and profile as he waited for her to approach. Lensey was busy trying to hide his excitement once he realized that shorty red head was white. *There's got to be something in the water down here,* he thought. *Even the snowbunnies got fat asses.* Lensey felt like today was his lucky day. He was so caught up in jackin' his slacks and thinking of all the ways that he was going to fuck this white booty, that he didn't even notice the Raleigh sheriff's task force until they swarmed him.

PART TWO

If You Knew Better, You'd Do Better

At the very same moment that Lensey was being escorted into a cell in Raleigh, NC, Dooky was being shoved into a cell in the back of the precinct in Mount Vernon' s police station.

The cell he was put in was cold and dank. The grey graffiti covered paint was peeling, exposing tan graffiti covered paint that gave the cell a gloomy feel. His toilet was stopped up to the brim, full of pieces of tissue paper and chocolate brown water that was dispensing a sickening odor. There were many roaches in his cell, running across the walls and floor. Dooky figured that the way they freely ran around the cell was their way of letting him know that *he* was the visitor. There was a dirty thin mattress resting atop a thick concrete slab that was attached to the wall. The DNA evidence that covered the center of the mattress proved, beyond a reasonable doubt, that there was at least one person who had slept there in the past that was unable to hold their bladder. Three-feet beyond the cell bars was a window. The only thing he was able to see out of the window was the sky. And by the look of it, it was just about evening.

He counted the bricks on the wall until he got tired, then he removed his shirt and covered the urine stain as best he could, before laying on his back. He kicked his feet up on the cell bars and waited.

He laid there for what seemed like hours, thinking and trying to put this shit together. He just couldn't understand, why would Pat shoot Walt and Squirrel? It just didn't make sense. As far as he was concerned, Pat was just some bozo that got used and abused for his car and money. He's harmless. And then World, "*What a silly ass, big mouthed, nigga*!" Dooky thought aloud. He couldn't believe World tried to get him involved in some 'Sammy the Bullshit'. "*He can't be serious!*" But still, Dooky felt bad for what he did to World's nose, especially after he saw it.

World's nose was crooked and smashed; it looked like it had melted on his face. Dooky didn't intend to do that much damage, but he was already fed up and World pushed his button. "*But why? Why would he tell them about the bank? He didn't have to do that.*"

He was tired of wrestling with his thoughts and conscience. He blocked World from his mind and attempted to get some rest.

*****

Darkness set around the Maxima as Pat sat silently outside of Doug's residence. He held the weapon tightly in his lap, with his finger on the trigger, carefully watching and waiting for his childhood friend to arrive.

He made up his mind that before he shot Doug he was going to make him beg for mercy that Doug denied him when he damaged his face. But in the end result, there would be no mercy for Doug; he just wanted to hear him beg.

Pat had been sitting there for more than three hours watching and waiting. Through the front window of the apartment he was able to see that someone was home. But he knew, from the many times he had been inside of Doug's apartment that the window he was looking at was inside of his grandmother's bedroom. He never liked Doug's grandmother. Despite the fact that she was high yellow and probably thought that she was white, she always had something bad to say about him or his mother.

Fuck this! Pat thought. He had gotten restless and was starting to assume that Doug might already be inside. He double checked the *.357,* there were only two bullets left, but that was enough for what he intended to do. He was anxious to put in work, by any means necessary. He stepped out of the car, with the gun at his side, and rang Doug's buzzer. Less than two seconds later, Doug's grandmother's voice boomed through the intercom.

"Who is it!" she barked.

"It's Patrick, buzz me in! Mi came fi see Doug!"

"Doug is dead! You no good, nappy headed, nigger! What you want over here? I knows who you are... and I seent you outside my winda staring at meee! I know'd ya no good mama, and she ain't never turn my curlin' iron back to me! Now get away from my winda b'fore I calls the po-leese and tell em that ya peepin tommin in people windas!"

Pat walked away from the intercom and stood near the window. If she would have looked out of her window, he would've put a bullet in her face. He stood there for a moment longer, waiting for her to show her face and when she didn't appear, he found the biggest rock he could throw and sent it crashing through the glass. He heard her scream then curse loudly before he walked back towards his car. Before he could open the car door, an empty quart bottle of Jack Daniel's flew out her window and shattered into pieces by his feet. He looked to see Doug's grandmother with her head halfway out of the hole in the broken window, screaming profanities at him.

"Yo mama, you dirty nigger! Yo mama was funky and nappy headed! And she drank cheap wine! You did this to my winda, and I'm callin' the po-leese! I'm callin the po-leese, nigger!"

Pat stared at her coldly with his good eye. Without saying a word, he pointed the .357 in her direction.

When Doug' s grandmother saw the weapon that was aimed at her, she gasped. She pulled her head away from the window so fast that Pat thought that she had decapitated herself.

When he realized it was her wig, still in the window, snagged onto a shard of glass, he roared in laughter. "Mi come fi ya later, poosy!" he mumbled as he got into the Maxima. He would have to catch up with Doug later. For now he had to find somewhere to lay low.

*****

Dooky was uncomfortably lying on the bed trying to avoid touching the wall connected to the concrete slab. Along with the graffiti decorated art, there was also several dark colored stains protruding and scattered all over the wall. There was one stain in particular, stuck to the wall right beneath a "gin loves tonic" tag that held his attention. He couldn't decipher if it was food or shit, but it was covered with flies. He curiously watched as a roach crawled towards the unidentified stain, hoping that the flies would battle it out for the lions share. But as the roach got closer, all the flies flew away. "Pussy ass niggas!" Dooky mumbled.

He heard keys jangling then the door that lead to the cell block opened. He listened as the jail keeper gave the new arrival a speech about the "Dos and Don'ts," before he escorted the prisoner into the cell block. Dooky was surprised when he saw the jail keeper escorting a semi-nude Doug past his cell, and into the cell adjacent to his. Dooky didn't draw attention to himself by calling to Doug, and he wasn't surprised that Doug didn't bother to look anywhere but straight ahead, as he walked past.

Their cells were separated by a thick metal wall, so Dooky stood up and stepped close to the bars and waited for the jail keeper to leave before he said anything.

"A yo, money! Yo, you, the brother that just came in!" Dooky yelled out, trying his best to disguise his voice. When Doug didn't answer, Dooky called out to him again. "A yo, son! You! The dude that just came in! I know you hear me calling you!" Dooky said, trying hard not to laugh. "A yo! Why the fuck you ain't answering me?"

Doug cleared his throat before he responded. He tried to make his voice sound as deep as possible.

"I, I didn't know you were talking to me."

Dooky heard how Doug was trying to deepen his voice and almost burst out laughing. He glued himself together and continued.

"Who the fuck you think I was talkin too, nigga? Send me a cigarette!"

"I don't have any cigarettes, uh, um, I don't smoke," Doug answered.

"What the fuck you call me, motherfucker?" Dooky yelled.

"No, no," Doug said. "I said, I don't smoke."

"Oh, you think I'm a joke, huh nigga? Ahiight, when the jail keeper comes back through, I'm gonna tell him to move you in here with me! We gonna get us something to smoke with that pretty ass dress you got on and those sexy ass legs!"

"No, no thank you." Doug said without the extra bass in his voice. "I would like to stay over here by myself."

"Fuck you mean, *No thank you*, you silly ass nigga?" Dooky said, unable to hold his laughter. "You better man-up, Loafer and stop acting all scary-n-shit!"

"Dook?" Doug said excitedly. "What you doin' here?"

"That's the same thing I was about to ask your silly ass. Coming in here with that paper dress wrapped around your waist, lookin' like a crazy ass stripper."

"Ah man, son, the cops ran up on me in the hospital, my grandmoms must've put them on me. I tried to get up outta there, my gown got ripped, niggas punched me in the face... son, it was ugly."

Dook laughed at his story. "You really are a silly ass, nigga, son, f'real, Loafer. The police came to see you 'cause of World! World came down here and told them niggas everything!" Dooky bought Doug up to speed about World, Walt, Squirrel, and Pat. He also told him why he was there.

"F'real?" Doug said, shocked. "Pat? I find that hard to believe, Dook... not Patrick."

"Yep... that's what they saying."

"Wow! And Walt is dead?"

"Yep."

"What about Squirrel?"

"I seen them pushing him in the ER b'fore I left."

"Wow! Why World tell them about the bank?"

"Cause he's a silly ass, big mouth, nigga that don't know when to shut the fuck up!"

What we gonna do now?"

"I got another plan."

What?"

"Are you dumb or Dominican? I know you don't s'pect me to run it down in the back of the precinct!"

"You right," Doug said, apologetically. "When do you think we'll get outta here? I hope they let us go in the morning. I hope they don't try to slay us because of World."

"Kick your feet up, Loafer. I'm pretty sure we here 'til morning."

"What time is it now?" Doug asked.

"Hold on, let me check... it's um, skin dirty, nigga! How the fuck should I know?" Dooky responded sarcastically.

They both laughed. Then there was an awkward silence as each one of them was momentarily lost in their own thoughts.

"Yo," Dooky said, breaking the silence. "You know what, Loafer? No matter what happens... I want you to always remember and know one thing. Seriously Loafer, I mean this from my heart. I know I've told you this before, but I don't think you know how much I really mean this."

"You told me what, Dook? What are you talking about?"

"How can I say this? How can I say it to make you understand?"

"Say what?" Doug said, curious to know what was on his friend's mind. "Just say it."

"Okay," Dooky said subtly. "I really wanna fuck your grandmoms, nigga! She got some long saggy, ass titties, but she still got that firm ass! I'll get up under that ass... I'm tellin' you boy, I'll make her love me! Worms and all! I'm telling you, Loaf..." Dooky said, laughing hard "... I'll make her love me!"

*****

Doug woke up the next morning to the delicious smell of bacon and eggs. He stepped out of his room and almost didn't recognize the woman he saw standing in front of the stove.

"Ma?" he whispered, surprised to see her standing in the kitchen. "When did you get here?"

Doug' s mother turned around with a big smile on her face. She wiped her hands on her apron then opened her arms wide.

"C'mere my baby... come over here and give your mama some love."

Happy tears rolled down his cheeks as he rushed into his mother's open arms. She hugged him tightly, cuddling his head protectively against her bosom. He had so many questions he wanted to ask her, but it felt so good hugging her again that he didn't want to let her go or ruin the moment.

"I've been missing you ma, and I knew you would come back."

"I know Doug, mama is here now, baby."

"I love you, ma."

"I love you more, baby, and I came to get you and take you home with me."

Doug and his mother were still embracing when the sound of his grandmother's voice distracted them.

"Dumpy, are you okay, sugar? You nearly scared the daylights out of me. You had me so worried."

Doug eyed his grandmother suspiciously. She was standing in the doorway of the kitchen with her wig tilted to the side, like a fitted hat. And instead of the stocking cap she usually word under her wig, she had on a doo-rag, he thought that was kind of strange. To make matters worse, his grandmother had on a see-thru nightgown, revealing her nakedness. He noticed that her pubic hairs needed to be trimmed. The hairs were gray and bushy and looked like she had Don King in a scissor headlock.

Doug stood there speechless and confused. It wasn't uncommon for him to see his grandmother baring it all under her nightgown, but this was the first time in a very long time that she called him

"Dumpy," the nickname she gave him when he was a little boy. She was also surprisingly sober, and spoke to him kindly, without cursing. Doug even thought that he detected some traces of affection in her voice... which was something he hadn't felt from her in a long time.

Then he realized that it must all be an act, and she was only being nice because his mother was here.

But everything changed and got strange when Dooky appeared in the kitchen behind his grandmother. He wasn't wearing anything except his boxer shorts as he hugged Doug's grandmother closely from behind.

Dooky then began to fondle her nipples between his thumb and forefinger and Doug's grandmother released a girlish giggle. He ran his tongue down the side of her neck then smiled at Doug.

"What I tell you, Loafer? You thought I was playing, didn't you?" He said, winking at Doug. "And once I'm finished knocking the worms outta your grandmother, I'll come back and get your moms. I can see she has some big ass titties under that apron." Dooky chuckled then blew a kiss at Doug's mother. He slapped Doug's grandmother hard on the ass before pulling her back into the bedroom.

"Save some for me, Dooky." Doug's mother yelled. "Don't wear him out, ma."

Doug jumped out of his sleep dripping sweat. His heart was beating rapidly and the paper gown he had wrapped around his waist was stuck to his body. He was still in jail, but relieved that he was only having a bad dream.

The cell block smelled like bacon, but everything was silent except for the sound of Dooky's snoring. He got up and removed the gown from his waist, being careful not to rip it.

They gotta give me some clothes. He thought. *How can I go in front of the judge looking like this?*

He decided that he would try to convince Dooky to give him his underclothes when he woke up. At least he wouldn't feel as naked as he was now. He draped the gown over his crotch and fell back on the mattress. He laid there silently, staring at the ceiling, blaming his mother and grandmother for all his troubles. He said a silent prayer and hoped that he wouldn't have to go jail. He wanted a better life than this and needed his family's support. If he had the money, he would get his degree from Culinary school then open a Fish & Chips restaurant in the hood.

That was the plan. That was his dream. Doug went back to sleep, hoping that his dream would one day come true.

*****

Doug had just arrived at the grand opening of his restaurant "Dougies" and the hype was that he had the best catfish in New York.

Doug appeared, donning a black Ralph Lauren suit with a pair of red crocodile Penny Loafers that matched his tie. He carried a cane, which was the highlight of his outfit because it was shaped like a catfish.

The crowd of people that attended the grand opening cheered and applauded, and the paparazzi's cameras flashed as Doug cut the red ribbon and opened the doors to the public.

The restaurant was jam packed with celebrities from all screens and arenas, and Doug happily shook hands and took pictures with as many of them as he could.

He had just finished giving an interview to a news reporter from a major network station when his floor manager whispered in his ear. Doug excused himself from the exposition without drawing the attention of his guests, and followed the manager into the kitchen where his head-cook stood waiting for him.

Doug was visibly agitated that he had been summoned away from his guests but as soon as he stepped into the kitchen, he knew that something had gone terribly wrong.

Someone had sabotaged Doug's grand opening by jamming a giant catfish into the deep fryer. They had also rigged the fryer so it couldn't be shut off. Two of his kitchen workers had the giant fish by the tail, vigorously trying to pull it out of the machine. Clouds of grey and black smoke began to fill the kitchen and float into the dining hall. Doug saw Pat Daddy's badly bruised face suddenly appear through a cloud of smoke. He pointed and laughed at Doug, then just as quickly, disappeared. Doug threw his cane in Pat's direction just as the fish burst into flames. The fire spread quickly throughout the kitchen and the paparazzi rushed through the doors with their cameras, snapping photos of the disaster. The sound of a fire alarm filled Doug's ears and he began to panic.

"No! This can't be happening! This is my grand opening! Get it outta there! Please, pull it out! Pull it out! Not my grand opening!"

"Yo, Loafers!" Dooky yelled for the third time, finally waking Doug out of his sleep. "Fuck is wrong with yo silly ass? You having a bad dream or something?"

"Ah man, yo... I was having a nightmare," Doug said.

"I heard your silly ass over there," Dooky mocked. "Pull it out! Pull it out! Not in my grand opening... Pull it out! For a minute I thought that somebody had you in a homo headlock."

"Ah man, nah yo," Doug said. "I was having a dream that Pat put a catfish...."

"Aaah yaaah yaah! I don't want to hear none of that freak shit, Loafer!"

"Man Dook, you stupid... you know that?"

"Pull it out! Pull it out! It's in my grand opening," Dooky mocked him again, this time using a girly voice.

"Man, fuck you, Dook! Yo, what time do you think it is?"

"I don't know, but I know it's morning cause I can see a window from my cell."

Doug realized that he was naked and wrapped the gown around himself. "A yo, Dook."

"What up?" Dooky answered.

"Yo, you have on boxers, right?"

"Fuck type of question you asking, Loafer? Yeah, I got on boxers, nigga... why?"

"Yo, let me get your boxers and your undershirt, I feel mad naked with just this gown on."

Dooky laughed. "I got you, yo. I have on a pair of basketball shorts under my jeans."

"Yo, good looking, Dook."

"Yeah, nigga, that's what they call me."

"Ah man, yo, I hope we see the judge this morning," Doug said.

"Man Loafer, we gonna be home in a little while. As soon as the judge hears our story, he's letting us go. This is a bullshit case... trust me."

"What about all the shit World told the police?" Doug asked.

Dooky sat there for a moment thinking about how World's face looked after he punched and knee'd him.

"Man, Loafer, the police don't give a fuck about what World say, and if they do, the judge won't."

"I don't know about that, Dook. You know I be watching Judge Tyrone Brown on TV and he always believe the informants."

"That's what I'm saying, Loafer, You talking about a silly ass TV show. That shit ain't real, all those people are actors."

"I don't know, Dook."

"Believe me Doug, as soon as the judge hears this shit we locked up for, we going home."

Chapter Thirteen

You Can't Spell Game Without M.E.

"Aahh!" Dooky screamed as he stood up and slammed the last two jokers on the table in the recreational room at Ogdensburg Correctional Facility. "Yall set! Ha, ha, yall stuck! You see this shit? That's a bubble! Matter of fact, this is what you call a Boston! Ha, ha, pay me my money, nigga!"

His opponents, Getty and Blast eyed him suspiciously as he reached to give his partner, Big Rome, a hi-five. Dooky was serving his ninth month of the 1 ½ to 4 ½ sentence that he received from Judge Kenneth Lither, aka "Judge Slither". Even though World had dropped the charges and never showed up in court to testify, the eyewitness testimony from Detectives Ford and Reeves was enough for the state to pick up the charges and convict Dooky of 2nd degree assault.

"What the fuck yall silly niggas still sitting here for? Go get my money! A bubble is double, so that's eight packs of Newports yall owe me... and I hope you got it! I know yall niggas wasn't ass betting?" Dooky yelled.

Blast and Getty looked at each other knowingly. There was no doubt in their minds, they had just been cheated. But Getty kept his cool and gave his hot-headed partner, Blast, a look that said, "*Let me handle this.*" And in return, Blast sucked his teeth and mean-mugged Getty as he gave him a look that said, "*There's only one way to handle this... let's fuck this nigga up*!"

Dooky had just finished his demand for his money when Getty questioned him.

"A yo, Dook, I'm saying, how the fuck you catch a hand with all spades? Explain that! You think I'm stupid or something? You cheated, nigga!"

"Fuck you mean I cheated, G? How I cheat when your partner dealt the cards?" Dooky said.

"What?" Blast cut in obviously angry about the whole situation. "Fuck you trying to say, nigga? Yeah, I dealt the cards, mufucka, but then they called chow and all of us went, except you, nigga! Since when did this mafucka stop eating pizza?"

"So what you saying, Getty?" Dooky said, completely ignoring Blast, "You ain't paying me my money?"

"Yeah, he's gonna pay us what he owes... ain't that right, Getty?" Dooky's partner, Big Rome voiced, speaking up for Dooky.
Big Rome wasn't no fool, he knew Dooky cheated the two youngsters at the table, but he was loyal to his young friend. Never, throughout the eighteen years that he has been in prison, has he ever seen any one player get every single spade in a game of spades. The shit that Dooky just did was not only foolish, it was also dangerous, and he planned to have a sit-down with his handsome young friend about the amateur stunt later. But for now, he would back Dooky and serve as his protector if necessary. Rome's dark eyes, that had seen way too much violence narrowed, and his twenty-one inch biceps bulged through his t-shirt as he spoke.

"I said, ain't... that... right, Getty?"

"Yeah, Rome, I ain't say I wasn't gonna pay him. I'm gonna give him his packs. All I'm saying is I know the nigga cheated," Getty said.

"Fuck you mean you gonna pay this nigga, G?" Blast challenged, "Don't pay that nigga shit! That mafucka cheated, son! He did some funny shit with the cards when we went to chow! Fuck dat! Don't pay 'em shit!"

"Nah, it's cool, Blast. I'm gonna give him his cigarettes. Eight packs ain't nothing," Getty said.

Yeah, I hear that shit, Mr. Trump," Dooky said, humorously, "So what the fuck your silly ass waiting for? Your limousine? Nigga, go get my money!"

Dooky laughed at his own joke as Getty walked out of the rec room. Blast left a few steps behind Getty, staring at Dooky dangerously.

*****

World stayed sober for four months after Dooky went to prison. The result from the reconstructive surgery left a barely visible scar running down the center of his semi-crooked nose.

With the help of his mother's church members, he was able to land a night job washing dishes at Chubby Burgers, while his days were occupied by the trade school his mother paid for him to attend. He hated his job, but it was a job. Plus he was able to take home as many left-over burgers as he wanted.

It was 11:20 pm and World was just about to get off work. He bagged up a few burgers and grabbed a soda to take with him on his seven block walk to his house.

"Ahiight, I'm outta here, yall," he said as he headed for the door. "I'll catch yall tomorrow," he said to his co-workers.

World was only one block away from his job when a black car, blasting reggae music drove past then pulled over a few feet ahead of him. World looked around as he neared the car. There were no other people on the street and all the other establishments were closed. He tried to glance inside of the car to see if someone he knew was driving, but the tinted windows of the Maxima were too dark for him to see through. World only paused for a moment, and when no one acknowledged him, he kept walking.

Seconds later the blunt force of something sharp and heavy hit him in the back of his head, knocking him to the concrete. World clutched his bag of burgers as if it would somehow keep him conscience and take away the flashing pain he felt behind his eyes. When the second blow landed, striking him in the back of his neck, he screamed in pain. He tried to force his body to get up and run, but he couldn't feel anything below his waist. His back felt hot and wet and World didn't know if he was bleeding or sweating. Loud psychotic laughter filled his ears as he painfully twisted his body in an attempt to see his attacker.

“Poosy hole! Gon make mi affi killya dead!” Pat said as he stared down at World remorselessly.

World’s eyes focused on the rusty nails that had been hammered through the bottom of the kitchen table leg Pat was holding, and he nearly passed out. Pat tossed the club inside of the car, then reached in his waistband and pulled out the .357 revolver.

It took all of World’s strength for him to roll over onto his back. He raised his hands, still clutching the bag of burgers and begged Pat to spare his life.

“Please, Pat, don’t do it! Please man!”

Pat released his psychotic laughter again before smacking the bag of Chubby Burgers from World’s hands.

“Suck ya mutha, bumbaclod! Mi affi killya now, batty buoy!”

Pat grabbed World by his collar and jammed his revolver into his mouth, knocking out six of his front teeth. He pushed the weapon deep into World’s throat then cocked the hammer.

"Ya nah gwon feel a ting, batty fish!"

A glob of blood gushed out of World's mouth as he tried to scream and plead for his life.

Pat rammed the gun further into World's mouth until he heard World gag, then pulled the trigger twice.

Click, click was the sound the empty gun made and Pat roared in laughter. He sucked his teeth loudly then pushed World's body to the ground when he realized that World had fainted. He wiped the blood off of the gun with World's shirt before tucking it back in his waistband. Then he drove off in the Maxima, bumping reggae music.

*****

An anonymous tip lead police to the whereabouts of World's unconscious body and he was rushed to Westchester County Medical Center in Valhalla, N.Y. The life-threatening injuries he sustained from the punctures to his head and neck caused him some serious nerve damage. He was subjected to three operations and numerous visits with a physical therapists, but he survived. And in the end, he was very lucky to be walking again. However, doctors couldn't do much to cure what the incident did to him mentally. World had bouts with paranoia, schizophrenia and became a manic-depressive. He was recommended to a psychiatrist that prescribed him medications and weekly one-on-one visits, but World was still a hot mess.

But throughout all his problems, he was able to testify against Pat Daddy, who had been captured in the hallway of Stutter's apartment building, and convicted for the murder of Walt Shaker along with the attempted murder charges that World had filed against him. As a favor of good faith, the Chief District Attorney offered World a new life in the witness protection program. But World refused their offer to relocate to El Paso, Texas, and the DA made no other further attempts to try to convince him. In any event, World felt safe knowing that Pat would be spending the next forty-years of his life behind bars.

But feeling safe was no relief for the damage that had already been done. World could not look at himself in the mirror without being reminded of what he went through. He was becoming impatient, waiting for his new front teeth to arrive, and he felt like a spectacle. So he only left his house during the night time hours and avoided anyone that he knew. He had almost crossed paths with Tammy on several occasions, and each time he ducked, hid, or ran in the opposite direction to avoid being seen. And just recently he bumped into her as she was entering the store that he was exiting, and for the first time since Dooky was sent to prison, he looked at Tammy in the eyes and she acted as if he didn't even exist.

This broke World's heart, along with everything else he had to deal with, it was just too much for him to handle sober, so he started drinking again. He tried to drink all of his pain and depressions away. He drank until he felt encouraged, he drank until he felt handsome, until he felt that he no longer needed his teeth; that he no longer needed to duck Tammy. World felt like *'Fuck the World!'* That was his attitude. He started to seek refuge from more stronger liquors like E & J and Vodka. If his money was low, he would settle for the cheaper wines like Nighttrain or Sisco, it didn't matter, he was chasing a high.

World's luck with the ladies was at an all time low. Even when his inebriated state of mind convinced him that he looked like a young Ralph Tresvant, none of the ladies were interested in his toothless game. So World began to taunt, harass, and verbally... sometimes physically abuse the women who rejected him. And as a last resort for sex, he began to depend on the many crack head prostitutes who worked the streets. To them, his looks didn't matter as long as he had the money for the service. He spent a lot of time fornicating with them in parks and buildings, stealing money from his mother to support his sexual pleasures. Eventually he rebounded back to doing the $20 bill illusions that he learned from Dooky, and he perfected it like a charm.

His mother finally got fed up with his unmanageable behaviors and kicked him out of her home. But World didn't care, he loved the streets. But the streets didn't have any love for him; the streets were slowly eating him alive.

*****

Big Rome eyed the two youngsters until they left the room, before he spoke.

"That was a real foolish stunt you just pulled, Dooky! You don't do shit like that! We beat them three games already, neither one of them youngsters know the game well enough to win."

"Yo, what you talking about, Rome?" Dooky asked.

"Don't fuckin' play like you stupid!" Rome said, raising his voice, causing the veins in his neck to bulge and the other prisoners in the room to look at them.

"Yo, Rome man, later for them two silly ass niggas!"

"Yeah, okay, later for them two, but that ain't my point. Certain things you just don't do. What happens when you try that same shit again and a nigga sneaks up on you and splits your handsome head wide open? Do you know how that would make me feel? You got over this time, because those two youngsters are amateur damagers, but that's a bad habit to practice. You might not be so lucky next time. Now, one more thing, if you planning to be some type of con man or something, you gotta have more finesse than that youngster. You ain't even let them make one book. See what I'm saying? Certain things, you just don't do."

Dooky was only half listening to what Rome was saying. All he heard was bits and pieces and the rest was blah, blah, blah.

Rome was one of the first people Dooky met when he arrived at Ogdensburg Correctional Facility. The very first day Dooky entered the dormitory, he was a little nervous because there were about seventy-five prisoners housed in Dorm I, and there was only one officer. The officer assigned him a cubicle that was in the back of the dorm and all eyes were on him as he dragged his two property bags to his cubicle, which was right next to Rome's. Rome introduced himself and they started talking, which lead to late night conversations with Rome leaning over the five-foot partition that separated their cube. Sometimes, Rome sat in his cube entertaining him with war stories or schooling him on how to move in prison. It went on and on, but Dooky didn't mind because he was amazed at the amount of time Rome had spent behind these walls. If it wasn't for the male patterned baldness, Dooky would've guessed that Rome wasn't a day older than twenty-five.

But Rome was thirty-nine years old, midnight black, and as big if not bigger than the Incredible Hulk. Because of the many years he's been locked up, Dooky had at one point valued his guidance. But lately he had been noticing some very odd behaviors, and feeling a strange vibe coming from Rome. For instance, the manner in which Rome kept trying to persuade him to do squats. After the two times he did squats with him, it was a wrap. Rome had put so much weight on the squat bar that when Dooky squatted down he couldn't get back up without Rome's help.

Rome had been behind him spotting, but the lower part of Rome's body was so close to Dooky's ass, that he felt violated. He felt like he had been dry-humped. When he spoke to Rome about it, Rome told him, "That's the way you're supposed to spot,

you gotta get close." So Dooky brushed it off and made up his mind not to lift anything he couldn't lift by himself. "*Fuck that spot humping shit*!"
Then just recently, Dooky woke up in the middle of the night and found Rome standing over him with his boxers on, watching him sleep. When Dooky questioned him about what the fuck he was doing, Rome gave him some fish story about looking for a cigarette. Meanwhile, the open pack of cigarettes were right there in plain view on top of the locker.

Since then, Dooky had been sleeping with one eye open and paying closer attention to his bulky neighbor. The incident with the squats, Rome watching him sleep, always calling dudes handsome, and most of all, freeballing in the shower, lead Dooky to believe that there was something fruity about Rome. So Dooky asked a few people around the facility, trying to find the inside scoop, and sure enough, he didn't have to go far. Everybody knew except him that Big Rome, aka "Big Romeo the Homeo" was indeed a booty bandit.

But still, even now that he knew that Big Rome was a fag, he didn't flat out disrespect him. Dooky knew enough about the man to be cautious. Under all of his fruitiness, Big Rome was a vicious man. Not only was he convicted of a double homicide that was committed with his bare hands, he was also one of those hardcore prison dudes that took the unwritten rules of prison seriously. So Dooky was careful not to make him his enemy.

"I hear you, Rome. You right," Dooky said, "but at least we ain't smokin none of that "*tough on prisoner Roll-Rich*" shit tonight. Tonight we smokin the green box."

Rome and Dooky were sharing a laugh when Getty and Blast walked into the rec room. Getty tossed the eight packs on top of the table and Dooky grabbed them and slid four packs to Rome.

"Yall niggas wanna keep playing and try to win some of your money back?" Dooky asked, as he opened one of the packs.

"Nah, we good! That's you nigga, enjoy it!" Getty said as Blast stared at Dooky poisonously.

"I will definitely enjoy them Mr. S.A.N." Dooky clowned, ignoring Blast's mean mug. "Ain't no money, like yo money...money!"

Rome shook his head apprehensively as, Dooky laughed at his own joke. He didn't agree with the way Dooky was handling the situation. Honestly, Rome didn't give a fuck about Blast. He thought that Blast was a slimy piece of shit that was fronting like a gangster. All the scars and cuts on Blast face made him look like a razor tester. He had some pretty, black, curly hair, but he had an ashy brown complexion that made him look dirty. Rome got the wire that Blast was sniffing heroin on the low, and also suspected Blast of being a "sneak thief" in the dorm. Rome was just waiting for Blast to get outta line so he could punish him and show him that he's not a gangster. And if the timing was right, he might even get a little booty. But Rome liked Getty. He really liked Getty. There was something charming about the young boy. Rome enjoyed watching the way his cornrows would bounce as he ran up and down the basketball court, with his pants sagging, lifting his ass cheeks up like a push-up bra. Rome's dick got hard thinking about all of the pussy shots that these young handsome boys be giving up. The homo in him was getting aggressive and he needed to satisfy his urges real soon.

"Hey, Dook," Rome said, "C'mon down to my cube, so we can have a talk."

"Yeah, ahiight, I'll be down there in a minute," Dooky answered restlessly. "Let me go check to see if I got any mail first."

Getty and Blast walked out of the rec room first, and Blast turned around and gave Dooky another

poisonous glare. Dooky smiled at him and told him that, "God loves him" before he got up and walked to the officers desk.
"Yo, CO, you got any mail for Douglas?" Dooky asked.

"Which one?" The officer questioned.

"Dookiah Douglas."

The officer frowned at Dooky for disturbing him while he was trying to read his newspaper, and he quickly glanced through the stack of mail he had on his desk.

"No! Ain't no mail for you. Oh, wait, yes, you have one piece."

The officer slid the letter across his desk then went back to reading his paper. Dooky picked up the letter and saw it was from Doug. He ripped it open and read it.

Dear Dooky,

What up, you silly ass nigga? I know it has been a while since you heard from me, but it's been rough out here, son.

Man, me and my grandmoms had another big fight and she kicked me outta the crib. I ain't been back there since. Word, Dook, I was homeless for a while, yo. I was sleeping on trains and in shelters. But now I live with my girl, Linda. I told you about her, remember? I met her the night I had the fight with Patrick. Yo, by the way, do you be seeing that nigga up there? Later for that silly nigga! But yo, I'm staying with my girl now and she's pregnant. I'm about to be a father, son. So I really gotta get my shit together now and I need to get on my feet. I know that if you tell me the other plan, I can get that paper and open my restaurant. Or else, me and my girl's brother, Peanut, is gonna do that first thing we was supposed to do. (You know, R the bank).

Oh yeah, yesterday I saw World and he looked fucked up, yo. I think he's on crack. The nigga is skinny as a toothpick and he walked right past me talking to himself, like a bugout. I went by your house the other day, yo. I went to say what up to your people, but Tammy was home by herself. I stayed for about an hour (Big Smile).

Anyway, I miss you, Dook. It ain't the same out here without you. Write me back. My address is on the envelope. And don't forget to tell me the plan or me and Peanut is gonna do "the other" (R the bank).

I love you, yo.

From your brother Loafer

P.S. Don't drop the soap.

*****

Getty was standing in Blast cubicle eyeing Dooky as he read his mail. The fact that he had just gotten cheated out of eight packs didn't bother him, but he kept shifting his weight anxiously from one foot to the other, and rubbing his palms together, like he was extremely upset.

When they had left to go to chow, Blast had proposed a scheme using code words and hand signals, so the two of them could cheat. But they never got the chance to put their plan to action because Dooky beat them to the punch.

Blast was lying on his bed heated, and he made no attempt to hide his anger. The cigarettes was a small issue. Although he could've used those eight packs to get high, he wasn't paying the tab, Getty was. He just didn't like the fact that Dooky cheated and Getty still paid him. To him, that was some sucker shit. And it was bothering him so much that he was ready to split Dooky's face wide open with his razor blade. But Getty was acting like a straight-up pussy because he didn't want any problems with Big Rome. As far as Blast was concerned, both Dooky and Rome could get sent to the infirmary tonight. He didn't give a fuck about either of them.

Blast stared at his partner, Getty. His eyes were full of contempt. He hated Getty for many reasons, but he hung around him because Getty was his source of survival. No one from Blast's family sent him anything. No money, no packages, not even a letter in the six months that he had been at the facility. But Getty got an abundance of everything that he wanted and needed, so Blast just went with the flow and received many handouts.

Blast was aware of Getty and his affiliation with the 'RAM SQUAD'. Their reputation for robbery and murder was known throughout the entire borough of Brooklyn. But after meeting Getty, Blast was making future plans to put the RAM on him.

They were both from the same projects in the Forte Green section of Brooklyn. But Blast didn't fuck with most of the niggas from the side of the projects that Getty lived on. To him, Getty was pussy! He was nothing like the streets portrayed him to be... at least not in prison. And the only reason why he didn't have his foot pressed on Getty's neck with his hands deep in his pockets was because Getty gave him everything he asked for.

But Blast had it set in his mind that the very first time that Getty denied him of anything, he was going to rob him of all his belongings. And if he tried to act tough, he would run his razor across his face.

Blast had already tested the waters by sneak thieving a bunch of items from Getty, just to see what he would do. But he either didn't miss it or was too soft to say anything. And to Blast, that was conformation that Getty was indeed pussy.

The monkey that was on Blast back grew into a full-grown gorilla. He had a heroin habit that he now needed to feed three times a day. Whatever he had to steal to get high was as good as stolen. It was all about his habit and nothing was getting into his way that wasn't getting knocked down. He nudged Getty with his foot before he spoke.

"A yo, what up, nigga?" Blast said, watching Getty shift from foot to foot. "You cold or you gotta use the bathroom?"

"Nigga, it's always cold in this bitch! We only an hour away from Canada! But that ain't it, I'm tight right now! That nigga, Dooky cheated, son!" Getty responded.

"We already know this shit! That's why I don't understand why you paid them niggas... if you wanna give away free money, nigga, just give it to me!"

"It ain't about that, son... eight packs is nothing. If Big Rome wasn't playing I wouldn't have paid that nigga shit!"

"Nigga! Fuck dat old faggot ass nigga! You shouldn't have paid them niggas nothin'! Fuck you scared of that nigga for? What, cause he been locked up all this time, that make him Superman? Fuck dat homo ass nigga! He washed up!"

Getty looked at Blast and tried to hide the hate that he felt towards his so-called friend. He knew Blast didn't like him, he even knew that Blast had stolen from him to support his habit.

The dopeman had hipped him to Blast from day one. He could have easily put a hit out on his so-called buddy that would've had him internally bleeding from dozens of ice pick holes before the sun went down. But that was just too easy for Getty; he got most of his enjoyment from outthinking his enemies.

After meeting Getty, a person could easily classify him as the *'soft, pretty boy, alternative to violence'* type of dude. And this is one of the reasons he was so successful in tricking all his marks. By the time they figured it out, they were too deep under the brown side of grass to warn anyone else.

Getty's clever thinking is what made him the brain of the RAM SQUAD. In fact, there was no RAM SQUAD. That was just a name that the streets gave his crew, which only consisted of him and the twins, Rachel and Renae from Coney Island. It was how they pulled off their capers that had the streets believing that RAM was a bunch of hired, machine gun, toting gangsters.

Somehow, people from his hood connected him as an associate to the notorious RAM SQUAD, and that made him uncomfortable. This was one of the reasons why he decided that he was done robbing drug dealers. But the real reason that Getty called it quits was because he never ignored the signs...

*****

Getty had just left the Yonkers, NY apartment of a shorty he met in Harlem, and he was on his way to pick up the twins. The job they had set up for tonight took him over a year to plan and he needed to be sure that everybody knew their position. If everything went right, they would each have enough money to live comfortably without ever having to commit another robbery.

Before Getty made it to the highway, Yonkers P.D. pulled his Acura Legend over, claiming that they received reports that he looked suspicious. After a thorough search of his vehicle, he was charged with possession of a firearm and later sent to Westchester county jail in Valhalla, NY.

When Getty never showed up to pick up the twins, the ladies decided to do the job without him and they were both riddled and killed in a slew of bullets. The mark that they had intended to hit was always alone at the time they intended to strike, so Getty took his arrest as a blessing, and never posted bail for himself.

He ended up pleading guilty to gun possession and copping out to 1-3 years in prison. That was ten months ago, and he had just been approved to be released at his first parole appearance.

*****

Getty looked at Blast sympathetically; he was just like all his other enemies.
"My nigga, you must not know who Big Rome is!"

"And you know what, nigga?" Blast responded, "I don't give a fuck who he is! What you sayin'? He can't get it? Fuck that booty bandit ass nigga! He can get fucked up like anybody else!"
Blast was fuming and he started raising his voice. He didn't like the fact that Getty thought that some gay nigga was more dangerous than him. He felt that if Getty feared anybody in the dormitory, it should be him, and he thought he proved that by the way he sliced and diced the dude that accused him of sneak thieving his sneakers.

At that very moment, Blast made the decision to send Rome, Dooky, and Getty to the infirmary to get their faces sewn. But first he had to clean Getty out for all his belongings. Blast looked at Getty distastefully; he felt like bitch-slapping him.

"Man, fuck dat! Like I said before, fuck Rome! He can suck my dick!"

Getty glanced over his shoulder at Rome who was sitting in his cube, only two cubicles away. When he didn't see any sign that Rome had heard what was just said, he directed his attention back to Blast.

"A yo, son, you need to calm down and lower your voice, you buggin out right now!"

"Don't tell me to calm down, nigga!" Blast yelled. "You calm the fuck down! You just paid those two clowns, knowing they cheated! What type of shit is that? That's some straight up bitch shit you did!" Getty paused and stared at Blast without speaking. He had to choose his words carefully because Blast was starting to piss him off. He had never seen Blast get this angry and at one point he thought that Blast was going to try and attack him. Getty took a deep breath to try and calm his temper, then smoothly slipped his hand in his pocket and gripped the scalpel that he had concealed before he spoke.

"Before you take me out the game like Rider, you should really stop and peep game... my games wider," Getty rapped playfully. "You see Blast, the problem is that you get too emotional, and you can't think clearly when you're angry. Look at you, you getting all bent out of shape over eight packs that didn't even come outta your pocket. So what I paid them niggas. That's chump change. I got fifty packs in my locker, fifty in yours and fifty more back there. You should be asking yourself why, why did Getty pay them niggas? You gotta think, champ. You gotta be a thinker Blast... it's the art of war."

Blast sucked his teeth loudly before he sat up on his bed. He stared at Getty like he was the dumbest man in the world.

"Look nigga," Blast said calmly, "first, let me say this. You had fifty packs in my locker. Now that I see how pussy you really are, you dead on those! And I know why you paid them niggas, there's no need to ask. You paid because you pussy and you scared of that nigga Rome!" Blast stared Getty in the eye without blinking. He flashed his razor on Getty so he could see that he was ready for anything before he continued. "I don't know why you think you some politician ass nigga, or like you know something about the art of war... you sound stupid, nigga!" He yelled. "Fuck you know about war, nigga? Yo bitch ass standing here scared to death of some old washed-up gay nigga! Get the fuck outta my cube before I cut yo bitch ass! Punk ass nigga! You, Dooky, and that faggot ass nigga, Rome can all suck my dick!"

As soon as the last word left Blast mouth, Rome appeared like the shadow of death. He snatched Blast out of his bed so quickly and viciously, that he dropped his razor.

Getty followed them as Rome dragged Blast to the back of the dormitory and savagely hit him with power punches to the face and body.

Blast was semi-conscious when he looked to Getty for help. Getty rushed in as if he were trying to break-up the assault, and reached down and slashed Blast from his forehead to his chin.

"It's the art of war, nigga! Now hold that!" Getty whispered as he backed out of the way.

Rome continued to punch and stomp Blast until he was out cold. Then with a look of a lunatic, he pulled Blast's pants down to his ankles and had his way.

The officer in the dorm witnessed the brutal beating and rape that Rome was issuing, but like everyone else, he was too terrified to intervene. He pulled the emergency pin on his radio and waited for back-up.

The officer's back-up, and Big Rome came at the same time. Rome was restrained without incident, and Blast was placed on a stretcher. They both left the dormitory. Getty smiled.

Later on that night, the dorm was unusually quiet, and the tension was thick. Most of the inmates in the dormitory were watching, anticipating more drama to occur.

Dooky was in his cube, lying on his back, reading the new novel, *Stalkers*, by 456, when Getty crept into his cubicle and kicked his foot.

Dooky looked over his book and saw Getty standing over him and got annoyed.
"Fuck you want, nigga? Can't you see I'm reading?"

Getty stared at him unconcerned with what he was doing. "A yo, son. Let me speak to you in the bathroom." Getty said, cuffing his hand behind his back.

"I'm busy," Dooky said. "My office hours are from 10-7, come back later."

Dooky went back to reading his book and Getty kicked his foot again, this time with more force.

"A yo, you fuckin clown, come talk to me in the bathroom! Or do you want me to blow it up right here?" Getty flashed the object in his hand and stared at Dooky.

"Yo, Getty, what the fuck did I just tell you! I'm busy right..." Dooky stopped when he noticed what Getty was holding. "Oh, it's like that son? Say no more!"

"Don't get scared now!" Getty said. "Stop frontin like you know how to read and come to the showers, tough guy. And make sure you bring all that fly shit you was talking earlier wit you!"

Dooky laughed at Getty's remark. "Scared? Man listen, how does it feel to be scared?"
"So why you stallin'? C'mon, let's go."

"I'm coming, nigga, ain't nobody stallin'... I'm saying, you silly ass nigga. If you in a rush, don't meet me there... beat me there!"

Getty left and headed towards the bathroom and Dooky closed his book, put his sneakers on, then he searched through his locker until he found what he was looking for, before leaving his cube.

When he stepped inside of the spacious shower area, three of the six showers were running. The steam from the hot water was so thick that he could barely see Getty posted up in the corner.
There was one inmate who was still showering, that must have sensed that more drama was about to occur, because he still had suds in his hair as he quickly exited the shower room.

"So what up with my eight packs, Dooky?" Getty said as he reached into his pocket.

"Fuck outta here! You dead on that, kid! I don't take nothing and give it back!"

"What? Is you stupid, Dooky? A yo, I'm telling you right now, kid, you better either have mines... or be mines!"

"Hold on," Dooky said, "you said, *have yours or be yours*? Ah man, I see that Big Rome shit is starting to rub off on you!"

"What you trying to say, Dooky? You trying to be funny, nigga? Suppose I just punch you in your..."

"Man, suppose you just light the fuckin' blunt and stop doing all that talkin', you silly ass nigga! The bottoms of my pants is getting wet!"

"You a funny mufucka, Dooky," Getty said as he laughed and lit the blunt he had in his hand. "That's why I fuck wit you, kid."

"I hear you," Dooky responded. "That's why *I* fuck wit you...cause you keep some weed, nigga."

Getty laughed again before taking three long pulls from the blunt and passing it to Dooky. Dooky passed Getty the spray bottle, filled with Muslim oil that he had in his pocket, and he scented the showers with the sweet smell of Blue Nile. He took deep pulls on the blunt and inhaled, holding the smoke in his lungs.

"So what you think," Getty asked.

Dooky blew the smoke in the air then passed the blunt back to Getty.
"I think that this is some homegrown, backyard boogie, bullshit weed I'm smokin'! Where did you cop this shit at, commissary?"

"You always got some slick shit to say, nigga," Getty said, while he snatched the blunt from Dooky's hand. "I'm serious, yo. What do you think about the plan? It came together properly, right?"

"Yeah, it was proper, but, for one. That shit took too long. And two, I thought Blast was gonna knock your silly ass out."

Getty blew out a cloud of smoke then sprayed more Muslim oil before speaking.

"First of all, young grasshopper, the art of war requires patience. I told you what happened to Rachel and Renae. And second, Blast can't do nothing without me! I had the drop on the nigga the whole time. If I wanted to I could've took care of him a long time ago... he was mad easy. But I wanted to build him up first, so he could fall harder... you feel me?" Getty laughed. "It's sort of like what Rome was doing to you."

"Fuck you talking about, nigga? He wasn't doing nothing to me!" Dooky said defensively.

Getty tried not to laugh as he inhaled more smoke. "Stop frontin, kid. What you think he had you doing all of them squats for? He was trying to build you up. And...that homo nigga was checkin on your buns while you were sleeping to see if them shits was perky."

"Man, pass the blunt, yo. Fuck all of that other shit you talking!" Dooky said.

"I thought you said this was some bullshit, commissary weed, son," Getty said, as he passed him the end of the blunt.

"It is, but I need to get my lungs dirty right now. That nigga Rome, man I can't believe he went up in Blast grippers like that, yo. I felt like helping the nigga," Dooky said.

"Helping who?" Getty asked.

"A yo, are you Dominican, son? Fuck you mean, *helping who*? Helping Blast, you silly ass nigga!"

"Helping Blast? Man, fuck Blast!" Getty said.

"I know, I ain't saying it like that. I'm just saying I hate that homo shit, man!" Dooky said.

Dooky puffed the last of the blunt then threw it in the drain.

Nah, I feel you, Dook. I wasn't expecting it to go down like that either. But fuck him!" Getty laughed. "You heard what I just said, Dook? Butt fuck him."

"You're a sick dude, son," Dooky said. "I gotta watch your monkey ass! On some real shit though, I thought the COs was gonna come back and snatch you up. What the fuck you follow them niggas back there for? You could've got yourself caught up in that shit. You about to go home, son. That was the reason why we planned it this way. That was stupid, son. You could've jammed yourself up."

"Yeah, you right, yo," Getty said. "But I had to let that nigga, Blast know that this was a plan, not an accident. You should've seen him. He had the "*why me*" look on his face when I cut him, yo. It was his "*aha*" moment." Getty laughed.

"He gotta get his ass and his face stitched up, damn!" Dooky said. "You should've chopped Rome's gay ass too... word!"

"Nah, yo. I wasn't fuckin wit that maniac! That nigga was in a zone. I don't even think he saw me. But I left the razor right on the floor next to him, so he gonna get charged for that too."

They left the shower area one at a time. Dooky left first and he headed back to his cube. Thirty seconds later, Getty came and sat on Dooky's bed.

"Yo, who wrote you today?" Getty asked.

"My boy, Doug."

"Doug? Who's that?"

"Doug. Remember Loafers? The dude I was telling you about when we was in the county jail."

"Oh," Getty said, "you talkin' about your boy that was in the crazy house?"

"Yeah, that's him."

"What he talkin' about?"

"A yo, this silly ass nigga talking about robbing a bank."

"Get the fuck outta here!" Getty said. "He wrote that shit in the letter?"

"Yep... he made a weak attempt at being cryptic, but basically, he said that's he's broke, his shorty is about to have a seed, and he's ready to hit a bank," Dooky explained.

"You think he'll do it?" Getty asked.

Dooky started laughing. "Yeah, I know he will. We was about to do it before I got locked up."

"Yo Dook, word up. I've been wanting to do that shit for a long time, yo" Getty said, overly excited. "That other shit I was doing is too easy, write your boy back and tell him to chill until I get outta here. You know my plans work, plus I already know what to do. Check it, we gotta get the cars, the mask, the duct tape; dudes don't know about the duct tape. And ooh, I think I know a way we can empty the safe. Yo, we...."

"Are you that high, silly ass nigga?" Dooky said reaching for his book. "Slow the fuck down. You starting to sound just like that nigga. I'll write him and let him know. Now if you don't mind, my office hours are from 10-7... and I'm trying to finish this book."

"Man, fuck you, Dook," Getty said as he playfully punched Dooky in the leg. "It must be a picture book 'cause you can't read, nigga! I'll see you in the mornin', mafucka, I'm out."

Getty got up to leave Dooky's cube, then quickly turned around. "Oh shit, Dook. They let Rome back in the dorm. Be on point, yo, here he comes!" Getty said seriously.

Dooky jumped out of bed and looked. "Word? Where? He coming this way? Where he at?"

Getty laughed. "Nah, I'm just fuckin wit you, my nigga," Getty said. "You should've seen the look on your face, nigga. You was scared to death." He clowned.

"Fuck outta here! Scared of what? I wasn't scared, yo." Dooky lied. "I was just being on point... dat all."

"Yeah, whatever mafucka," Getty said, covering his nose. "Did you just shit yourself or something? Got damn! That shit stink, yo! Spray some of that Blue Nile in this bitch! Got damn! That smell like warm shit, nigga! You better go hop in the shower!"

*****

Tracy frowned at the trick with resentment. She desperately needed to release herself from the crushing grip that the drugs had on her, but she just didn't have the will power to quit.

She had lost so much weight, that it was almost impossible to tell that she was almost 8 months pregnant. Her once beautiful babyface had aged and lost all of its innocence. She now looked hard and angry from experiencing too much indifference.

There had been many lonely nights that she'd spent locked in her apartment getting high and contemplating suicide. She hated Walt Shaker and she cursed his death for causing her the dilemma she was in. If it wasn't for the baby growing in her stomach, she would have probably taken her life a long time ago. Everyday she promised herself that she was going to quit. If she couldn't do it for herself, she had to do it for the baby. But the stress, along with the craving desire she had for crack cocaine, was too overpowering. With every urge she heard the commanding voice of the drugs managing all of her affairs and dismissing her problems.

Although Tracy had lost a substantial amount of weight, the pregnancy along with the HIV medication she had been taking, kept her body slightly curvy in most of the right places. This allowed Tracy to use her body as a tool to get the money she needed to get high... just like she was doing now.

"Nigga, you better hurry up and cum! Stop holding that shit back! If you think I'm gonna be sucking your dick all night for $20, you crazy!"

"I ain't holding nuffin back," The trick said, readjusting his body on the steps. He scooted his ass up another step. "It juss takes me longer too nut wiff a condom on."

"Well then you better figure it out... quick! Cause it ain't coming off! And if you don't cum in five more minutes... I'm done!" Tracy yelled.

"Ahiight, chill out... you fuckin up my concentration, keep suckin it... suck it harder. And let me juss play wiff da pussy a little bit."

"You better hurry up, nigga! You ain't got much time left!" Tracy instructed.

She bent her body awkwardly, allowing the trick to slide his hand in her pants as she continued to suck him off.

"Damn, this pussy is wet! I must be turning you on, huh?" the trick questioned.

"Mmhmph." Tracy encouraged.

"You want me to put dis dick in you, don't you baby?"

"No, nigga! I want you to cum... Now!" Tracy said.

"Let me put it in." The trick insisted.

"I said no!... Listen," Tracy said, "That's it! Your time is up!" She removed his hand from her pants and stood up.

"Whoa, wha choo mean? I ain't even cum yet." The trick complained.

"Oh well!... I've been in this staircase suckin' your dick for the last half-hour! You think I wanna be in here all night with your ugly ass? Hell naw!" Tracy said, "And your fuckin' balls stink!"

She fastened her pants and started to walk down the steps, when the trick grabbed her by her hair and pulled her backwards. She was only able to release a splinter of her scream as he repeatedly punched her in the face.

"Fuck you bitch! What the fuck you just call me?" The trick yelled, punching her in the face a half-dozen more times, until she was dazed.

"You thought that you was juss gonna leave wiff my money, bitch?" He yelled again as he ripped her pants open. "You must be fuckin crazy!"

Tracy felt her pants being pulled down, but her head was throbbing from the beating he just imposed on her.

"Please," she begged in a barely audible whisper, "I'm pregnant."

He punched her hard in the back of her head three more times. "Shut da fuck up, bitch! If you pregnant, den I'm about to get some pregnant pussy!"

The punches he hit her with caused her to see a bright white light, and she thought she was going to pass out, so she submitted to her fate. She laid her face on the dirty, cold floor and stared at the wall. She hugged her baby bump and apologized to her baby, then sobbed as she felt him enter her from behind.

"OOOOH YEEAAA!" He moaned as he pounded her pussy roughly. "Oooh, shit yeah! Dis is that good pregnant shit... dat wet shit, baby!"

He gripped her ass tightly, then spread her ass cheeks open wide, watching his dick going in and out of her.

"I wanna feel all of dis pussy," World said as he removed the condom and re-entered her. "All of dis good wet pussy you got!"

*****

Squirrel avoided prison and accessory to murder charge that he had pending. He changed his life and received a job with the help of his connections, as an assistant soccer coach at the local junior high school.

He fell in love and married Selena Medina, an ex-stripper with basketball sized breast implants from Las Vegas, Nevada. They had two rodent-faced children with long curly hair, and they reside in their home, in a quiet residential area in El Paso, Texas.

ACKNOWLEDGEMENTS

TO MY MOTHER “MAMA LOVE” AKA “CL”, CAROL, MS. CAROL, MY FAVORITE GIRL” L. FOR THE ENCOURAGING ME TO FINISH THIS CRAZY BOOK AND SEEING THE HUMOR IN IT, WITHOUT YOU THIS PROJECT WOULD'VE RUN OUT OF GAS A LONG TIME AGO… F'REAL! THANK YOU MA.

I LOVE YOU TO MY WIFE AND PARTNER NICOLE “LG, “SUGARBOOGA” L. BAY. REMEMBER THAT FIRST DRAFT I ASKED YOU TO TYPE? 35 PAGES IN A RAGGEDY ASS NOTEBOOK. YOU WAS LIKE “WHAT IS THIS?” I WAS LIKE “I WROTE A BOOK”. THE LOOK ON YOUR FACE SAID IT ALL! THANK YOU FOR NOT GIVING UP ON ME.

TO MY THREE SISTERS, MS. MISSY DEE (MY SUPER SECRETARY. ICEMAN THANKS YOU!), JEANNETTE (THANKS BRO!) AND VALERIE ANN (THE ALUMNA). THANK YOU ALL FOR YOUR HELP IN GUIDING THIS PROJECT TO FRUITION.

TO JACQUI SPENCE (AUTHOR OF *AMONGST FRIENDS*). THANK YOU FOR YOUR EXPEDITIOUS SERVICE AND INSIGHT.

I CAN'T FORGET TONY "UN" MARCUS (ONE OF THE FUNNIEST DUDES I KNOW).

LIZZETTE "SWEETPEA" GARVIN (ONE OF AMERICA'S MOST WANTED), I DIDN'T FORGET YOU. YOU GOT MY BACK.

TO MY MAN C-HARLIE, FOR ALWAYS KEEPING IT SOLID GOLD.

TO MY BROTHER KEVIN "TRAXX" SAFFORD (WHISTLE AT ME!), KENNY "SKIP" LEWIS (GIVE THE LORD A HANDCLAP), MY COUSIN MICHEAL TERRY (KEEP TESTING BOUNDARIES), AND MY BOY, MY BRO JERMONE "BLESS" MCCALLUM (ONE OF THE REALEST DUDES I KNOW). TOGETHER, YOUR COMBINING ENERGIES WERE ESSENTIAL TO THE COMPLETION OF THIS STORY. GOOD LOOKIN!!

AND TO THE REST OF MY FRIENDS AND FAMILY, THANK YOU.

- ROCKO BESS

Made in the USA
Las Vegas, NV
20 March 2025

19826607R00207